HAPP

"A delightful p   quirky humor between   familiar and strangers to e   marriage as historical accident."
—*The Times* (London)

These two unique companion novels tell the stories of Jack and Brenda Bowman during a rare weekend apart in their many years of marriage. Jack is at home coping with domestic crises and two uncouth adolescents while immobilized by self-doubt and questioning his worth as an historian. Brenda, traveling alone for the first time, is in a strange city grappling with an array of emotions and toying with the idea of an affair. Intimate, insightful and never sentimental, *Happenstance* is a profound portrait of a marriage and of those differences between the sexes that brings life—and a sense of isolation—into the most loving relationships.

"Carol Shields is a wonderful writer—wry, witty and fiercely intelligent." —Janette Turner Hospital

"With brilliant formal skill each story is made to act as figure and ground to the other . . . the exuberance of the book comes from the way trivial scraps of experience are used to make and change the pattern of lives . . . explores the complexity of choice."
— *The Times Literary Supplement*

VINTAGE CANADA

HAPPENSTANCE

Carol Shields' most recent novel, *The Stone Diaries*, was short-listed for the Booker Prize and was the winner of the 1993 Governor General's Award for Fiction. Her other books include *The Republic of Love*, *The Orange Fish*, *Small Ceremonies*, *Swann*, *Various Miracles*, and *Box Garden*.

HAPPENSTANCE

The Wife's Story

Carol Shields

Vintage Books
A Division of Random House of Canada
Toronto

For Catherine Mary Shields

All rights reserved under International and Pan-American Copyright
Conventions. Published in 1994 by Vintage Books, a division of Random
House of Canada Limited, Toronto.

Canadian Cataloguing in Publication Data

Shields, Carol, 1935–
Happenstance

ISBN 0-394-22359-4

I. Title.

PS8587.H66H36   1993   C813'.54   C93-093838-0
PR9199.3.85H36   1993

Happenstance, The Husband's Story was first published as *Happenstance* in
Canada by McGraw-Hill Ryerson in 1980. *Happenstance, The Wife's Story* was
first published as *A Fairly Conventional Woman* in Canada by Macmillan
of Canada 1982. This volume first published in Great Britain by
Fourth Estate Limited 1991.

Printed in the United States of America

3   5   7   9   10   8   6   4   2

Chapter One

EVERY MORNING BRENDA WAKES UP, SLIPS INTO HER BELTED robe, and glides – *glides* – down the wide oak stairs to make breakfast for her husband and children. The descent down the broad, uncarpeted stairs has something of ceremony about it, it has gone on so long. She and Jack have lived in the Elm Park house for thirteen years now; Rob was a baby when they moved in; Laurie, twelve last October, has never lived anywhere else.

In the kitchen she reaches for the wall switch. It's seven-thirty, a January morning, and the overhead fixture blinks once, twice, then pours steady, lurid light down onto the blue countertops, causing her to reel slightly. Her hands set out plates, reach into the refrigerator for frozen orange juice and milk, into the cupboards for Raisin Bran and coffee beans. Her husband, Jack, has given her a new coffee-grinder for Christmas, a small Swedish toy of a machine which is still a little unfamiliar to the touch. A button on its smooth side sets a tiny motor whirring, a brief zzzz which releases a pleasing instantaneous cloud of coffee smells. 'Philadelphia,' Brenda murmurs into the coffee-softened air of the kitchen.

She boils water, pours it carefully. 'Philadelphia.' Her voice is low and so secretive she might be addressing a priest or a lover.

For a month now, ever since she decided to go to Philadelphia, she has had her flight schedule thumbtacked in the lower right-hand corner of the kitchen bulletin board. Departure time, arrival time, flight number – all printed in her own hand on one of Jack's three-by-five index cards.

Above where the card is pinned there are a number of other items. It seems to Brenda, yawning and retying the belt of her robe, that some of them have been there for weeks. Months. She tells herself she could get busy and weed out a few, but the confusion of notices and messages mainly pleases her. She likes to think of herself as a busy person. *Brenda Bowman – what a busy person!*

1

The clutter on the brown corkboard speaks to her, a font of possibility, firmly securing her, for the moment at least, against inactivity. On the other hand, she sometimes feels when she glances at it a stab of impatience; is there no end to the nagging of details? Appointments. Bills. Lists. Announcements. Furthermore, these small reminders of events past and present carry with them a suggestion of disappointment or risk. That old theatre programme, for instance, the one from the Little Theatre production they'd gone to – when was that? last November? *The Duchess of Malfi.* She had hated *The Duchess of Malfi.* So, surprisingly, had Jack.

Someone – Jack, of course, who else? – had pinned up a newspaper cartoon about the School Board scandal, two pear-shaped men balancing on penny-farthing bicycles and grappling over a sack labelled $$$. The point of the bicycles, though Brenda has been following the scandal with some interest, escapes her.

And there, snugged cleanly in the corner – she has cleared a small area around it – is her flight schedule. It looks purposeful and bright, winning from the welter of other items its small claim to priority. Brenda glances at it every morning when she comes downstairs to make breakfast. It is the first thing to catch her eye, and even before she plugs in the coffee-grinder and starts the eggs, she examines and is reassured by her own meticulous printing, Flight 452, United Airlines, departing Chicago at 8:35. Tomorrow morning, Saturday. Arrival at Philadelphia at 1:33.

There are two short stops, Fort Wayne and Cleveland. The round-trip ticket – she will be gone only five days and so cannot qualify for the one-week excursion rate – comes to $218. Her tickets lie in an envelope on the hall table under a piece of pink quartz someone once brought them from Greece. The thought of the tickets touches her with a wingbeat of happiness which is both absurd and childish and which makes her for a moment the object of her own pity. Ridiculous. As though her life at forty was so impoverished that the thought of spending five days in Philadelphia could stir her to exaltation. Pathetic!

Not only pathetic, but unrealistic. She and Jack have been to New York a number of times. Once, when she was a child, she went for a trip to the Smoky Mountains with her mother. Later there was her honeymoon in Williamsburg; to Denver and to

San Francisco with Jack for a meeting of the National Historical Society; twice to Bermuda; and four years ago to France. Philadelphia wasn't even supposed to be a particularly attractive city. Someone – she's forgotten who, someone at a party recently – referred to Philadelphia as the anus of the east coast, one of those cities that suffers from being too close to New York, nothing but highways and hotels and factories and an inferiority complex. Nevertheless, when she murmurs the word 'Philadelphia' into the rising coffee fumes, she feels engorged with anticipation, a rich, pink strangeness jiggling round her heart that interferes with her concentration.

In recent days she has felt impelled to disguise her excitement, to affect calm. A hand on her shoulder seems to warn her to be careful, to practise sanity and steadiness. (A false steadiness that has nevertheless yielded a real calm, for she *has* succeeded in making lists, she *has* been orderly.) She even managed a shrug of nonchalance when the printed programme from the Philadelphia Exhibition arrived in the mail a week ago with her name listed on the back: Brenda Bowman, Quilter, Chicago Craft Guild.

Admittedly she was one of hundreds listed; the print was the size of telephone-book type, all the quilters crowded together with the spinners, the weavers, even the tapestry-makers and macramé people. Yes, Brenda has told Hap Lewis, herself a macramé person, yes, she's glad she decided to go. Why not? It would be interesting (and here she had shrugged, lightly, dismissively) to see what quilters from other parts of the country were doing. It might even be (another shrug) inspiring. She had held herself in check, even with Hap, whom she regarded as one of her closest friends, projecting a half-grimace over the cost of domestic flights, passing off the trip to Philadelphia as a mere whim – though a whim which required a certain amount of preparation. Jack and the children weren't used to having her gone. There were the meals. There was the laundry. 'Fuck the meals, fuck the damn laundry,' Hap had encouraged her.

Leaving 8:35, arriving 1:33. Brenda has taken this information over the phone asking the United reservation clerk to repeat the times and the flight number. She loves the busyness of facts, but distrusts them, and today, after breakfast, after everyone has left for the day, she plans to phone United again for a confirmation.

In the frying pan she melts a minute quantity of butter and cracks in four eggs, two for Jack, one for each of the children, none for herself. She is watching her weight, not dieting, just watching. Maintaining. And keeping a restive eye on her daughter Laurie, who in the last year has gone from a child's size twelve to a fourteen Chubette. Laurie's brand-new Big Sister jeans hardly fit as it is, but when she finishes her egg this morning she will be sure to reach for a second piece of toast. Only the stuffing of carbohydrates keeps her civil these days. Puberty is the worst of diseases, worse in its way than diseases of withering appetites and painful restrictions. Brenda stares at the shiny side of the percolator and sees beyond it the tender beginnings of Laurie's breasts, melting and disappearing under new layers of fat. She imagines returning home in a week's time and finding her daughter obscenely bloated with food and maddened by sugary cravings. Poor Laurie. 'It looks like we're going to have a baby elephant on our hands,' Jack had remarked to Brenda only a week earlier. Brenda had reacted with fury. 'It's only baby fat. All girls go through a period of baby fat.'

She should, though, sit down with Laurie today; have a little talk, just the two of them.

But there is so much still to do, and she hasn't started packing. Two of her blouses need pressing: the green one, the one that goes with her suit and with the pants outfit as well, and the printed one, which she plans to wear to the final banquet. At 3:15 she is having her hair cut, tinted, and blown dry at a new place over on Lake Street which has wicker baskets and geraniums in the window and scarlet and silver wallpaper inside. And if there's time, she wants to make a casserole or two to leave for Jack and the children – lasagna maybe, they love lasagna. Not that they aren't capable of looking after themselves; even Rob can cook easy things – scrambled eggs, hamburgers – and Laurie's learned to make a fairly good Caesar salad. They're not babies any more, Brenda says to herself, either of them.

Tomorrow morning. Saturday. Jack will drive her to the airport. They should plan to leave the house by seven; no, earlier, the car's been acting up lately, the rear brakes. She'll have to take it in herself when she gets back from Philadelphia and have it checked over. Jack tends to be vague and overly trusting (or overly distrusting) about mechanical things. What if

4

they get a flat tyre on the way to the airport? Unlikely, but still
. . . She should set the alarm for six, have her shower, get
dressed, and then wake Jack. She will say goodbye to the
children tonight. No point hauling them out of their beds on a
weekend morning.

Besides, there's always the danger that Laurie might cling to
her. She should be past clinging, but she's not. Even going off to
school in the morning she sometimes stands in the open
doorway, letting the heat escape, clinging to Brenda. These
embraces are wordless and pressing, and Laurie's breath seems
imprisoned inside her heaving chest. Brenda can feel, or
imagines she feels, the desperate, irregular thud of her
daughter's heart through the material of her ski jacket.

And Rob has been so bad-tempered in the morning lately.
Loutish, Jack calls it, though Brenda rises to his defence; Rob, or
Robbie as she still sometimes thinks of him, is, after all, her first-
born child, and his lowered eyes (sulkiness) and dark, curling
hair still make her heart seize with love. 'It's only adolescence,'
she tells Jack. 'It's hormones. Fourteen's the worst age. We
should be thankful he isn't on drugs. Or skipping school. Look
at Benny Wallberg. Even Billy Lewis . . . '

She puts forks and knives on the table, checks the eggs. She
will have to stock up on eggs today. They could always fall back
on eggs. Eggs, the compleat food; where had she read that?
And she should buy some canned soup. Jack likes chicken and
rice, but Rob only likes tomato, and Laurie . . . and what else?

From upstairs come noises, the familiar early-morning noises
coming from different corners, but weaving together into a kind
of coarsely made filament of sound from which the house at this
hour seems suspended. A radio (Rob's) playing behind a closed
door, and the uneven clumping of Laurie's Swedish clogs
across the bedroom floor. And the endless running of the
shower; don't they realize – even Jack – what hot water costs
per month!

In another two minutes they will all be down, hungry,
frowning, slouching in their chairs, demanding, accepting,
preoccupied, still bound up in sleep and resistant to smiles or
greetings. Rob will have sprouted a colony of new pimples on
his chin, and last week's batch, the old ones, will be tipped with
scabs – 'never scratch, never squeeze' the doctor has advised.
Poor Rob. Laurie's blouse will be pulling out of her skirt already,

5

and there will be a dribble of egg, round as a tear, next to her mouth. Jack will come down smelling of talcum, smelling of a male sort of privacy, as though his body has already completed half its daily rituals. He will reach out blindly for the *Trib*.

Should she perhaps resent the fact that he always helps himself to the front section of the *Trib* and, like a potentate, hands round to the others the lesser sections, the fashion page, the sports, the business pages. Brenda herself tends to get stuck most mornings with the business section, which she has found over the years to be surprisingly interesting. Not that she studies the graphs or reads the articles about Gross National Products or falling cocoa prices in west Africa; what she likes is to look at the photographs, the column-wide pictures of men – an occasional woman too, of course, times are changing – who have achieved some sort of recent executive splendour, who are freshly appointed to some distinguished board of directors, or who have been transformed into vice-presidents of silverware companies or management-consulting firms or fire-and-casualty companies. Or else they are rising through the hierarchies of curious firms which manufacture mysterious products like vacufiles or turfspinners or gyrograters. Their success seems to Brenda to be dazzling but contained; they are poised for action, about to leap off the page, but something restrains them. There's a withheld muscularity in the pleasant, truncated necks and knotted ties, a darkness at the hairline which gives an air of brisk loyalty and purpose and probably good health. No perilous sodium nitrates or cholesterol-loaded eggs for these chosen stars. So-and-So, a graduate of Northwestern (A.B.), master's degree in Business Administration from Harvard, long record of service with firm since joining as trainee in 1960. (1960? – that was the year Jack had been taken on part-time at the Institute.)

This public recognition, Brenda supposes, is deserved, richly deserved. And where do these rising executives live, she cannot help asking herself. Wilmette? Clarendon Hills? The Near North Side? Here in Elm Park perhaps? – of course; she has several times seen people she and Jack know featured in the business pages. But for the most part these men are strangers, mere names attached to faces. Are they married? Divorced? Are there children? Children grown difficult and morose? Never

6

mind, they are the climbers of ladders. Their faces are fleshed out, made smooth and calm and American by success.

It is amazing, Brenda thinks, that every day there can be a new batch of these success stories; it is a wonder that there is room in the world for so much success and money. These photographs and announcements aren't cheap, she's been told. Space in the *Trib* costs money. The Great Lakes Institute where Jack works considers these announcements an unnecessary extravagance.

Otherwise he might have had *his* picture in the paper when he was made Acting Curator of Explorations. And though he's never expressed any disappointment about this lack of public recognition, Brenda knows that he would probably like to have had his picture in the paper. He is surprisingly photogenic. That picture of him at the lake last summer in his gold-striped golf shirt – he could pass for thirty-eight, not forty-three. He has a useful, temperate face, and he's been lucky with his teeth, which are both straight and white. In the summer he tans more easily than many men, and his sandy-coloured hair doesn't show up baldness the way dark hair does. Poor Jack. He would have liked his picture in the paper. He would have bought extra copies: one for his parents, one for his Aunt Ruth in the retirement village near Indianapolis. When he went to Elm Park wine-and-cheese parties or barbecues at the weekend he would have been happy thinking that his friends knew of his promotion, that they had seen his picture alongside those of stockbrokers and equipment salesmen. 'Well, yes,' he would have said, 'there will be a little more responsibility, maybe a little more travelling, but more headaches, too.'

But the Institute where he works is funded by trust money and has a board which examines finances and which has recently suggested that air conditioning be cut back except during July and August. The library budget is under review too, and the decision to upgrade the office equipment has been postponed. Furthermore, Dr. Middleton, who heads the Institute, is attached to the scholarly ideal of anonymity, and so staff promotions are soft-pedalled rather than celebrated and announced in the newspapers for the entertainment of women in the suburbs who sit idling over their black coffee and dry toast.

But tomorrow, Brenda thinks, tomorrow at this time she will

be gone. The newspaper, the coffee-grinder, the window over the sink with its red curtain, the morning skin of frost on the backyard grass – all this will remain, but she will be gone. Like the reassembled atoms in Rob's science-fiction stories, her bones will rise from this room and soar brightly over the city of Chicago. She will give a small salute to the coloured roofs below, to the plumes of smoke, neat as a painting. Around the tip of the lake, then Gary with its evil fumes dissolving in blueness, then Fort Wayne – she has never been to Fort Wayne, nor to Cleveland either for that matter. Lunch on the plane, followed by coffee, and then Philadelphia. (She and Jack had talked once about taking the children to visit Independence Hall and to see the Liberty Bell, but they had wanted to go to Washington too, and at that time Jack had only two weeks' vacation.)

So much to do: the packing, her hair, then the groceries. The backs of her legs ache too; she's expecting her period. What timing! She will be running furiously all day, a thought that floods her with happiness so that she wants to weep. And tomorrow someone else will be jiggling the coffee-maker; someone else will be slapping the side of the toaster to make it pop. Her eyes won't be here to seek out the specks of dust on the dining-room rug or light upon the breadcrumbs around the toaster. Tomorrow she will not be standing here in this room chanting into the mild early-morning silence this irrational and unasked-for prayer, her ritual lament of pity and helplessness: *poor Laurie, poor Rob, poor Jack.*

It is an incantation which she knows is addressed to no one in particular, but which returns often to scrape along the edge of her vision like a piece of pumice. *Poor Laurie, poor Rob, poor Jack.* She supposes it is a blessing of sorts, but one from which caring has lately been subtracted.

Ah well, she brightens, turning over the eggs and pouring herself some coffee. Ah well. And then she begins to hum, as she often does in the morning: *Amazing grace! how sweet the sound that saved a wretch like me.*

Chapter Two

ELEVEN O'CLOCK IN THE MORNING, AND HAP LEWIS STOOD at Brenda's back door, her arms clutched in a fit of shivering and a smile breaking across her long face.

'Come on in,' Brenda cried through the storm door.

It was cold outside, less than twenty degrees according to the radio, and getting colder. Snow was forecast. Brenda, wearing an old brown sweater and a new pair of jeans, could feel the damp outside air reaching her ankles.

Hap's voice came buzzing through the glass. 'You sure you've got a sec, Brenda? Jesus, you must be up to your neck.'

'Sure I've got a sec. Come on in. It's freezing out there and you don't even have a coat.'

'But, God, you must have a million and a half things – '

'I'm getting there,' Brenda said, waving one hand over her shoulder and shutting the door with the other. Already she'd made the beds, done a load of laundry, and put together a casserole of Spanish rice with cheese topping which she'd covered with foil and placed in the refrigerator ready to be heated up. Her suitcase – a good thing she owned one decent suitcase – lay open on the bed; her blouses, carefully pressed, were on hangers waiting to be folded; she could put them in at the last minute.

'Look Bren, the reason I dashed over – I wanted to pop in to see if I could give you a hand or anything.'

'I don't think there's a thing, Hap. But thanks anyway. I appreciate it. For once, everything's more or less organized.'

'Honest? You sure?'

'I think so. Really. Unless you're going out to the A & P – '

'The A & P? Oh, Jesus, of all days. The trouble is the car isn't here. Bud took it downtown, he had a special meeting or something. A sales meeting. I hate those lousy sales meetings. Otherwise – '

'It doesn't matter – '

'Look, just tell me what it is you need. Maybe I've got – '

'No, really, Hap. I've got to go out anyway. My hair. I'll just stop at Vogel's and pick up a few things when I'm out.'

'Look, you know how I've always got the goddamned freezer full of food, if it's food you need. Corn, zucchini, gobs of hamburgers, just let me know – '

'No, really – '

'If there's anything else. Christ, what are neighbours for? Anything at all – '

She was a good-hearted woman; even Jack admitted she was good-hearted. At times she seemed to Brenda to be almost lopsided with good will, as though an excess of kindness had somehow deformed her. And her energy was prodigious. It made Brenda feel weak looking out the back window at the Lewes' house and seeing Hap scramble up ladders, scraping off chipped paint with a wire brush, getting ready to paint the house in the spring. She and Bud and the boys were going to tackle it themselves. Last year they'd put on a new roof; Hap had seemed right at home perched over the gables, her hammer flying. She also made lemon layer-cakes to present to new neighbours on the block, a gesture which Brenda could only think sprang from Hap's Danville, Illinois, upbringing. (Brenda had never been to Danville, Illinois; she had rarely been downstate at all, in fact, and imagined it as a simple oblong, pleasantly populated by neighbourly-minded souls waving to one another from porches of trim wooden houses.) She and Jack, thirteen years ago, moving into the house in Elm Park, had been recipients of one of Hap Lewis's lemon layer-cakes. It had come on a pale blue Fostoria plate, accompanied by a breezy note: 'Hi folks. Welcome to the ol' neighbourhood.'

Brenda had been amazed, she who had grown up in Cicero in a three-room apartment over a dry cleaner's; such a gesture had seemed a leftover from another age. It made her think of Broadway musicals like *Oklahoma!* or *The Music Man*. Returning the plate a day or two later, she had brimmed with gratitude. This stranger, this Hap Lewis, was happy to have her as a neighbour; this wonderful warm-hearted woman wanted to be her friend.

Hap Lewis did other things besides bake cakes. She played tournament bridge, good, consistent tournament bridge; she and a woman called Ruby Bellamy twice won the West Suburban Champion Playoff. Hap was chairperson of a book group

10

that was presently tackling Solzhenitsyn and thinking about Flaubert for spring. She ran a Girl Scout troop, old Troop Twelve, the oldest troop in Elm Park, and still found time to knit sweaters for her husband Bud and for her two teen-aged sons – beautiful sweaters, with raglan sleeves and intricate animal patterns worked into the backs. She froze vegetables from her own yard – string beans artfully concealed behind the peonies, a border of cauliflower running inside the petunias – and made pickled zucchini from a secret family recipe, a recipe which she had nevertheless passed on to Brenda – and to Leah Wallberg and Ruby Bellamy and one or two others in the neighbourhood.

And in the last few years she had started to make, and occasionally sell, large wall-hangings composed of unbleached wool and tree bark and other natural materials. These wall-hangings, with their swags and knots, reminded Jack of certain dark portions of the human digestive tract which had been flayed open with a knife and left to rot. 'They're considered very good,' Brenda told him. 'Would you want one on your wall?' Jack demanded. 'You have to think of them as a form of sculpture,' Brenda told him. 'I'd rather not think of them at all,' Jack said.

She was Brenda's age, but taller and heavier. Her hips swelled downward in a savage double roll, and to conceal these haunches she wore over her jeans long, loose-fitting tunics which she designed and made herself. Her face, poking through the tops of these tunics, was surprisingly angular, and seemed to contain more than the usual amount of bone. It was a long, nervous, mobile face; behind her glasses her eyes shone bright, inquiring, naive, and hopeful. A large, homely woman with a lumbering body. She had been, Brenda imagined, an even homelier girl; a long history of homeliness could be read in all those wild, random acts of kindness.

'Will you look at you, Brenda,' she raved, grinning. 'You're all organized, for crissake. If it were me going away tomorrow, there'd be bedlam, pure unadulterated bedlam.'

'Believe me, it has been – '

'And will you look at this goddamned kitchen. Floor wax! My God, I haven't had a whiff of floor wax for years – '

'It isn't really – '

'Listen Brenda, I promise you, on my word of honour, my Girl Scout honour – ha – that I'm not staying. I know you've got a million and one things to do, but I just thought, I got to thinking – have you packed the quilts yet? Or not?'

'Jack said he'd give me a hand tonight when – '

'I just had to come over and say bon voyage to *The Second Coming*. Did you get it finished?'

'Just about. All but a little handwork on one corner. And the quilting part's done.'

'That's terrific. I never thought you'd – '

'I took it off the frame yesterday. At, let's see, four- thirty-five, I think it was.'

'Bren, you're fabulous. You should have called me up. We could have celebrated. I don't know how you do it.'

'Come on upstairs. I was just getting started on it. You can give it your good-luck pat.'

Brenda's quilt room – sometimes she called it her workroom – was in the southeast corner of the house. Only four years ago it had been the guest room, containing not much more than a chintz-covered studio couch, which they opened up for the occasional overnight guest. The studio couch was still there, but Brenda had moved it into a corner and upholstered it with one of her early quilts, a staggered-circle design in several shades of blue; the three back cushions were covered with a reduced version of the same pattern. She liked to sit here late in the afternoon, sipping coffee and running her fingers over the raised squares, testing the springiness between the rows of stitching, thinking: I made this.

Her quilting frame filled all of one wall. It was so large that it had to be angled slightly at one end to make it fit, an arrangement which made the room look cheerful and slightly off-balance, reminding Brenda of the matted print they once had of Van Gogh's bedroom, a golden cube of a room which tilted and swayed under the weight of thick, straw-coloured fairytale furniture. It may have been with this particular print in mind that Brenda decided on the colours for the quilt room. She had painted the walls herself – three of them white, the fourth a brilliant yellow.

With its paint, with its hooked rug on the polished floorboards, it was the brightest room in the house. It seemed to have sprung of its own accord out of the cluster of duller rooms: the living room with its pale-green walls and toneless carpet (stick with neutral, the decorating magazines had advised); the dining room with the gold Bigelow (not bad) and the Italian provincial table and chairs and buffet (a mistake, all of it); and their bedroom – beige walls, a scatter rug that was too small, a chest of drawers that had seen better days. The quilt room, on the other hand, though it was the most recently decorated room in the house, seemed to Brenda to be the room of a much younger family, belonging to more cheerful, more energetic people, people who knew the kind of thing they liked. There was a white cutting-table of shiny plastic, picked up at Sears sale, but looking smartly Scandinavian. Across from it was a pine dresser, where Brenda stored her patterns and sewing things. Above it, Rob, newly competent after a single semester of woodworking, had installed a shelf that held wicker baskets in which Brenda stored her material. (She had started with blues, then gone into greens. Now she was working into the yellow family.) 'Brenda Bowman, local quiltmaker, is not afraid to confront the simplicities of primary colour,' said a September article in the *Elm Leaves Weekly*. In a corner of the room stood a low table made of bricks and boards, rather like the brick-and-board table of their long-ago student apartment, only somehow more stylish, where Brenda kept a small electric coffee-maker and a tray of earthenware mugs. Lately she had taken to bringing her friends up here when they dropped in.

There was only one window, but it was large and square and on good days filled with sun. She had decided, finally, against curtains. Instead there were hanging plants: a spider plant, an asparagus fern, and a new one in a plastic pot called string-of-pearls. There were elm trees outside in the backyard, and Japanese cherries, and a small scrub oak which was gnarled and scabrous but healthy – when the children were younger they used to spend hours perched in its branches. There was, in addition, a view of the new cedar deck next door, which Larry and Janey Carpenter had put in. Across the alley was Bud and Hap Lewis's house, a large Victorian three-storey clapboard which, now that it was winter, could be seen through the bare branches. In summer it was almost completely obscured by foliage.

Brenda loved her house, a two-storey red brick dating from the twenties; she had loved it on sight. Most of all she loved the oak hall and stairs, which for some reason had been built on a grander scale than the rest of the house. The broad stairs had a kind of power over her; to descend them each morning was to launch her day with calmness. It was the stairs that commanded her to *glide*. The wall panelling was solid and heavy; the banister had a satiny coolness that imparted serenity.

After the hall, Brenda like the backyard best, especially the trees. Some of the elms had died, of course, and the three that remained were undergoing a radical new treatment which involved injections of serum. Expensive, but worth it in the long run, Jack had decided. And she loved the Japanese cherry trees that they had planted in front of the garage the summer they moved in.

Jack had been nervous; he had never planted a tree in his life, and the occasion had seemed to him, and to Brenda too, to be serious, almost a test that they were forced to undergo. They had both grown up in city apartments and feared they might harbour certain city-bred deficiencies. They had bought – recklessly, Jack's father maintained – a house in one of the oldest, most established suburbs. Perhaps they overreached themselves, acquiring, along with this solid brick structure, a garage, a toolshed, soil and grass, flower beds and shrubbery. Mysteries.

They bought the two young Japanese cherries at the nearby Westgate Nursery, where the manager was happy to dispense advice. Jack, listening politely, wrote the instructions down on a small pad of paper: the depth of the holes to be dug, the distance the trees should be planted from the garage; tree roots can interfere with foundations, they were told. And they were also told that late fall was the best time for planting trees. It was only July; it might be risky putting in trees in the middle of the summer. 'Well . . . ' Jack said, rubbing his chin with the back of his hand.

Together he and Brenda regarded the tree roots, bundled blindly in sacking; how would a tree know which month it was, they seemed to ask each other. They decided to take a chance. 'Don't say I didn't warn you,' the man from Westgate Nursery threatened.

At first one of the trees showed signs of withering, and Jack went back to the nursery and bought a recommended brand of insect spray. Every evening, arriving home from the Institute and setting his briefcase down on the grass, he checked the undersides of the leaves for mites. Brenda, often carrying Rob

14

in her arms, came out of the house to watch. 'It looks okay to me,' she always told him.

'I should have bought a hardier strain,' Jack grieved. They both recalled that Bud and Hap Lewis across the alley had suggested a certain kind of flowering plum, which was just as decorative but stood up better to the cold winds. They dreaded the first frost.

But the fall had been unexpectedly moderate that year, and that winter one of the mildest on record. By mid-March the two fledgling trees were in bud. The second summer they grew a spectacular two feet, and the stucco garage behind the rosy branches seemed softened by their presence. Jack talked about planting asparagus. He still mentioned it, twelve years later, from time to time, how it might be a good idea to try asparagus.

'I'm sure this view from your studio is an inspiration in your work,' the reporter from the *Elm Leaves Weekly* said. She was a young girl wearing an embroidered blouse, a journalism student hired for the summer, and she had come to the house one afternoon to interview Brenda.

'Well, yes,' Brenda replied in a voice weighted with doubt. 'I suppose you could say that.'

Perhaps it was even true. Certainly her first real quilt – the first one she actually sold – had contained the natural green harmonies of shadow and light. She had called it *Spruce Forest*. 'Why *Spruce Forest*?' Jack had asked. 'Why not oak or something?'

'Because I had to call it something,' she said. 'I was filling out the entry form, and *Spruce Forest* just popped into my head.'

'You'd have to go up to Wisconsin to see a spruce forest,' Jack said in a nagging tone, unusual for him.

In fact, the quilt had looked more like an expanse of grass cooling off late in the day, a suburban lawn overlaid with the darkened, simplified shapes of spirea and mock orange and grape leaf. She had cut long spears of dark linen (grass? spruce boughs? waves perhaps? knives?) and had arranged them so that they swept and curved the length of the quilt. The forms advanced and overlapped, and the green, drenching effect of colour was carried right to the borders, and even beyond, for Brenda, in a sudden awakening of inspiration, decided to make the border of the quilt irregular. (Later the use of the irregular border became something of a trademark for her.)

Spruce Forest: it won first prize in the Chicago Craft Show four years ago. There was a ceremony; the mayor was in attendance; there was a medal and a bouquet of roses. 'How did you feel at that moment, Mrs Bowman?' the girl reporter from the *Elm Leaves Weekly* asked. 'Did you feel you were standing at the gateway to a new career?'

She hadn't. She'd felt only that she had had an extraordinary piece of beginner's luck. Someone had paid money for something she had dreamed into existence. It was days before she could bring herself to deposit the cheque in the bank.

The quilt had been bought by a flamboyant-looking middle-aged couple, Sy Adelman and his wife, Slim Morgan. They came to the craft-show reception, saw *Spruce Forest*, and on the spot wrote Brenda a cheque for six hundred dollars. 'It'll be incredible in our living room,' Sy Adelman said. 'We live down in Oldtown, a little gem of a house, high ceilings, skylight, you know the type.'

'Your living room?'

'He means on the wall,' Slim Morgan said in a red-plum voice. 'Over the piano. It's just what we've been looking high and low for.'

'High and low,' Sy Adelman said.

'Who's Sy Adelman?' Brenda asked Jack later. 'Who's Slim Morgan?'

'You remember Sy Adelman. That nightclub act? The old Chicago Review group. And Slim Morgan's practically a classic now. Someone was telling me the other day that her early records are almost priceless.'

'Imagine that,' Brenda said.

When she was working on a quilt, she seldom looked out of the window, or anywhere else for that matter. Occasionally she made a small sketch, very rough, just a few lines on a sheet of paper, but the patterns seemed to come from some more simplified root of memory; sometimes they arrived as a pulsating rush when she was pulling weeds in the yard or shovelling snow off the front walk, but more often they appeared to her early in the morning before she opened her eyes, an entire design projected on the interior screen of her eyelids. She could see the smallest details, the individual stitches. All the pieces were there, the colours and shapes and proportions selected and arranged. When she opened her eyes to the light, she always expected the image to dissolve, but it remained intact, printed on an imaginary wall or beating slowly at the back of her head. She had no idea where the ideas came from.

There must be, she assumed, some interior reservoir, and she wondered what this might be. She imagined a vibrating organ, half-heart, half-placenta. She thought of patterns stacked up like china plates on a neat shelf, and it puzzled her to think that she could extract these complicated images from the same section of her head where she stored simple recipes and kept track of the birthdays of friends. She had never considered herself introspective or original. ('Brenda is such an open person,' Hap Lewis has said several times in Brenda's hearing.)

'I think there's a Byzantine or Turkish influence in Brenda's work,' said Leah Wallberg, who had studied art history. Brenda, who had been a secretary-typist before she married Jack, knew little – nothing really – about art history. Nevertheless, despite this, it seemed that she did indeed possess an inner pool of colour and pattern which was oddly accessible and easily drawn upon. It pumped naturally and steadily and in a form which she was able to translate without serious difficulty. It seemed at times almost ridiculously easy, in fact, and Brenda guarded a belief that this was something anyone could do, anyone at all.

At the same time she recognized the fact that her quilts were changing. The birds and flowers and boats and houses of her early designs – what Leah Wallberg called her folky thing – were giving way to something more abstract. The shapes interlocked in different, more complex, ways. A year ago she wouldn't have risked her new feather-shadowed borders. She was thankful no one asked her anymore what such-and-such a quilt was 'about'. She wouldn't have known. And she was thankful, too, that she was seldom pressed about the reasons behind the naming of her quilts. Even Jack no longer cocked an eyebrow and asked: Why *Spruce Forest*? Why *Buddha's Chant*? Why *Rock Splinter*? It was assumed that she must have her reasons, that along with her gift for stitchery went a body of belief, an artist's right to interpret and name.

She might, of course, have called them after colours or numbers – *Study in Green, Burnt Yellow #2* – but she preferred real names, which tied the design to her, even though she knew the quilts themselves would pass into other hands. She remembered that Rob and Laurie, when they were younger, gave names to the tiny islands near the summer cottage they rented each August. Naming was a form of possession. It was a privilege; there were lots of people who never had a chance to bestow names.

The name of *The Second Coming* had come to her less than a month ago. She and Jack were driving downtown one night for a reception at the Institute and happened to pass a small, blackened Baptist church on a weedy corner off Madison. The lit-up message on its roof proclaimed: 'The Second Coming Is at Hand.' The Second Coming. She said it aloud.

'What?' Jack said, braking at a red light.

'Nothing.'

She said it again, this time to herself. The Second Coming. It sounded important. It sounded lucky.

'It's a great name,' Hap Lewis was saying, following Brenda upstairs and into the quilt room. 'I mean, it's got all kinds of overtones. If you know what I mean.'

Brenda unfolded the quilt briskly, spread it on the cutting-table, and announced with a shaky flourish, 'Well, here she is.'

'Jesus!' Hap's gravel voice dropped.

'Well?' Brenda held her breath. 'What's your honest-to-goodness opinion?'

'My honest opinion, my gut reaction' – Hap paused – 'is that this is the best thing you've done. Terrific, in fact, *A* plus. Better than the Buddha thing. Je – suss! Here, let's hold it up.'

'You don't think that purple is too purple – ?'

'God, no, it's fucking sensational, that purple. Sort of unexpected, but just right at the same time.'

They lifted the quilt, each taking two corners, and together carried it toward the window. The grey January light fell inward onto a blocked bed of colour – greens and yellows mostly – with a kind of frenetic heat rising from one end. And, like a footnote or an inscription, dark-purple stains printed the edges with shapes that resembled mouths.

'If you don't come back from Philly with a ribbon or two, I'll eat my chicken feathers.'

'I'm not counting on – '

'Now you're doing your modesty thing, Bren. Wait'll the judges see this. You've seen the junk some of these gals churn out. I mean, Brenda, you've done it. You know what I mean. There's something so contained about this, not quiet exactly, but you know, slow-moving, like someone trying to say something, but they can't get the words out. Know what I mean?

'Well – '

'I mean, it's got the sensual thing all sewn up – pardon the lousy pun – but it's also got, you know, sex.'

'Sex?' Brenda was laughing.

'Like you want to reach out and touch it. Or hop out of your clothes and roll around in it. I don't mean just plain old intercourse sex, ugh, not that there's anything wrong with intercourse. I mean, well, energy. But the kind of energy you keep the lid on. Energy contained – you know what I mean? About to jump out at you if you let it.'

Over the slanting expanse of the quilt, Brenda regarded Hap fondly, gratefully. She felt her throat grow warm with tears.

Hap Lewis is a babbler, Jack always said. And it was true. She did have a tendency to go on and on. Verbal overdrive, Jack called it. She got on his nerves, and he wondered, sometimes aloud, how Brenda could stand her. His heart bled, he said, for Bud Lewis, the poor sap; what kind of sex life could you have with a woman who never shuts up for ten seconds!

'But she means it,' Brenda always said. 'That's the thing about Hap. She means every word.'

They stood for a minute longer, holding the quilt up to the window. Brenda had the dizzying sensation of something biblical happening: two women at the well, gathering light in a net. Neither of them spoke, and the silence seemed to Brenda to be unbreakable and dipped into earlier memories of happiness. 'I wish you were coming, Hap,' she said impulsively. 'I wish you had decided to come after all.'

Hap, still gripping the quilt, shrugged. 'How could I? Bud, the boys – '

'Aha! Remember what you told me when I said I didn't think I could get away?'

'What did I say?'

'You said, and I quote, fuck them all.'

'Hey,' Hap shrieked. 'Hey Brenda. You did it. You said it. The big F. You finally said it. Do you know what I think that means?'

'What?' Moving together they began refolding the quilt, first in halves, then in quarters.

'I think,' Hap said, 'that it's some kind of omen. That something good is going to happen to you.'

Chapter Three

'JACK?'

No answer.

She tried again, a little louder. 'Jack.'

'Yes.' The voice, husky and toneless, cracked from a deep sleep.

'It's six-fifteen.'

He turned over, buried his face in the pillow.

'It's time to get up, Jack.'

'Ten more minutes. It's still night-time.'

'I've brought you some coffee. Here on the table.'

'Bribing me,' he groaned into the feathers.

She sat on the edge of the bed. 'How'd you sleep?'

'Fine. While it lasted.'

'Ask me how I slept.'

'How'd you sleep?'

'Terrible.' She began rubbing his back through the striped pyjamas. 'Terrible.'

'Don't stop. That feels good. Ahhhh.'

'I kept thinking of all the things I'd forgotten. Like the man coming to fix the valve on the furnace. I think he said it was Monday he was going to come.'

'Hmmmmm.'

'I just lay there, it seemed like hours. I could hear the clock ticking downstairs, that was how quiet it was. Then I got to worrying how I was going to get the quilts out of air-freight when I get to Philadelphia. Do they bring the package to the luggage place or do you have to pick it up at the air-freight place?'

'I think – '

'I decided I could get my suitcase first, and if the quilt box wasn't there, I'd get a cab and then get the cab-driver to stop at the air-freight place.'

'Hmmmm.'

'What did you say?'

'I said that sounds like a very solid and well-thought-out plan.'

'You're falling back to sleep again.'

'I was having the best dream.'

'Your coffee's getting cold.'

'Oh, that feels good. A little lower.'

'Here?'

'We ought to get a new mattress. How about it? A waterbed.'

'What's wrong with this mattress? It isn't even worn out.'

'After twenty years we deserve a new mattress. They say it does wonders for – '

'What was the dream about?'

'I don't know. I think it was about bouncing on a waterbed. It all disappeared when someone with a loud voice bellowed six-fifteen in my ear.'

'I don't want to be late.'

'Take my word for it, you'll be early.'

'Jack?'

'What?'

'I forgot to buy the material for Laurie.'

'What material?'

'For school, her Home Ec class. They're making skirts or something, and she was supposed to have her material last week.'

Silence.

'Do you think,' Brenda said, 'you could take her out to get it? This afternoon maybe? Zimmermans or Mary Ann's or some place like that?'

'Okay.'

'And she needs a pattern too. She knows which one. I asked her yesterday.'

'Okay.'

'You won't forget, will you?'

'On my honour.'

'And another thing, I was thinking about Rob.'

'What about him?'

'I was just thinking about him. Last night when I couldn't sleep. I mean, maybe you should have a talk with him.'

'I think he's fairly well informed – '

'I think you, or maybe both of us, should have a talk with him about his attitude.'

21

'Brenda.'

'What?'

'Why don't you just crawl under the covers for a minute and we could discuss it.'

'You're stalling. You just don't want to get up.'

'Not true.'

'Anyway, I'm all dressed. I've been up for an hour. Didn't you hear the shower running?'

'No. I was having this beautiful dream – '

'Was it raunchy?'

'Raunchy?' He turned over, smiled at her lazily. 'Now that's a word I haven't heard in – what? – twenty years.'

'Horny then. Was it one of your horny dreams?'

'You sure you wouldn't like to crawl under the covers for just two minutes?'

'I'm sure. It's six-thirty, almost – '

'One minute then. I promise to be quick.'

'Jack – '

'You smell like toothpaste. I love a woman who reeks of toothpaste. Eau de Crest.'

'It's Infini. It's that perfume your aunt sent. Smell my wrist.'

'Hmmmm.'

'Nice?'

'I won't ask what I smell like,' Jack said.

'It would be better if you didn't.' He smelled of sheets, unbrushed teeth, and something vaguely fecal. His body was warm and relaxed under the electric blanket – bonded with the heat of the blanket, in fact – and for an instant she considered slipping off her skirt and getting in beside him. No, there wasn't time. And she would have to shower again, maybe press her blouse . . .

'Spurned,' Jack said. 'Spurned and abandoned. That would make a good title for a movie.

She touched his cheek. 'Your coffee – '

'You career women are all alike.'

'You don't say.'

'Always rushing off to catch planes.'

'How cruel.'

'You could bring a little joy.'

'And why didn't you think of this last night, bringing a little joy?'

22

'Because you made me watch that Barbra Streisand thing on TV, you and your children.'

'I thought you liked Barbra Streisand. You used to love – '

'Fatigue is what Barbra Streisand gives me. A wracking case of fatigue.'

'Anyway, you never answered my question, Jack.'

'What question?'

'About the man coming to adjust the furnace valve.'

'He'll come, Brenda. He'll ring the bell. No one will answer. So he'll go away, quietly.'

'They might charge for making the call.'

'I doubt it.'

'But it seems to me I said I'd be here. They phoned last week and asked if the lady of the house would be home on – '

'The lady of the house?'

'And I said – '

He squinted at her and said again in a tone of wonderment, 'The Lady of the House.'

'What's so funny about that?'

'Like the Lady of the Lake. Are you really,' he paused, 'the Lady of the House?'

'If you aren't going to drink this coffee, I am.'

'No, you don't.' He propped himself on one elbow and reached for the cup.

'Maybe you should drink it while you're getting dressed.'

He took a swallow. 'Strong.'

'On purpose. To get you awake.'

'I always did love cold coffee. It goes with cold toothpaste.'

'You won't forget about the material. It's supposed to be part polyester, she said.'

'What?'

'The material for Laurie. I just told you. She – '

'Oh, *that* material.'

'And, Jack, maybe you could let the furnace people know I won't be here. The number's in that little book of mine. Under O for oil. Or else it's under – '

'Brenda, lovey.'

'Yes.'

'Let me ask you a question. If it's not too early in the morning that is.'

'What question?'

'What is the population of Chicago?'

'The population of Chicago? How on earth would I know the population of Chicago?'

'You've lived here all your life. You must have some vague idea of – '

'Three million. It just came to me.'

'When you were in school it was three million. Or thereabouts. Now it's more like six.'

'And?'

'Well, if you figure four to a household, that makes, let's see, one and a half million – *million* – households that manage to get along on a day-to-day basis without that famous lady of the house, Brenda Bowman, steering the ship.'

'Up!' she ordered, standing abruptly and with one move stripping the covers down.

'My God, it's freezing.' He made a grab for the blanket and missed.

'It's cold because of the valve on the furnace. It cuts the heat back. When the man came to clean the filter he explained – '

'What a job! I wouldn't mind having a job like that. Going around all day talking to women about how valves work.'

'He was really nice. Young and – '

'Do you know, you look really beautiful this morning.'

'Do you know what time it is, Jack?'

'Sort of Olivia de Havillandish.' He caught her hand. 'Thank you, Brenda.'

'For what?' She sat down on the edge of the bed.

'For not looking like Barbra Streisand.'

'If only I did.'

'And for not sounding like Barbra Streisand. And for not opening your mouth wide wide wide like Barbra Streisand – '

She put her arms around him. The hair at the back of his head stood up in tufts, and she smoothed it with her hand. Soon there would be a completely bare patch; the thought of this vulnerable spot made her throat contract, and she bent over and kissed him on the forehead, where she detected the faint taste of salt.

'Ah, lovey,' he murmured and closed his eyes.

'We really should be getting going,' she said after a minute. He opened his eyes. 'Is this new?'

'What?'

'That blouse.'

'This? I got it last week. At Field's. I showed it to you, remember?'

'Oh, yes.'

'Don't you like it?'

'I love it.'

He was undoing the buttons. She, half-protesting, uttered a girlish meow, and he reached around and unhooked her bra.

It was an old game of theirs: he the pursuer, the flatterer, the one with all the lines, some of which were both true and untrue. And she: silent, sly, pretending reluctance, pretending to be preoccupied, and then, finally, allowing herself to be won. There were other games, other scenes, some sharper and more savage, but this was the one they returned to again and again. It was a way of invoking youth, it seemed to Brenda, a kind of play they put on for the entertainment of their younger selves. He murmured into the long cavity between her breasts the words *beautiful beautiful*, and she felt herself grow opaque and speechless, making small gasping sounds as his tongue circled her nipples. Slowly.

Her blouse lay under them, and her skirt – wool tweed, black and emerald – was hiked up in a roll around her waist. Far away at a green and more level distance she found herself thinking that the wrinkles would probably fall out. And that the blouse would be under her jacket anyway; who would see it? She might even have minute to touch up the collar while Jack shaved.

Philadelphia, Philadelphia, she chanted to herself, pushing up against him, and like a mantra the word opened the door into a space wider and warmer than usual. She was assailed by familiarity, cotton, skin, the pressure of Jack's legs, and her eyes sealed shut to a large, dark corridor lit by small sconces of light, reddish in colour and vaguely Victorian in design.

'I love you,' she said, as she always did when the lights flared, and then – this morning, because she was going away – she added, 'I really do.'

'My lovey,' he said into her collapsing hair. 'My Brenda-Bear, my only only.'

25

Chapter Four

IT WAS BRENDA'S MOTHER, ELSA PULASKI, WHO TAUGHT HER to sew in the first place. All the time Brenda was growing up in Cicero, Illinois, her mother's black sewing machine had stood in a corner of the crowded living room, squeezed in between the radiator and the saggy couch. The machine was a Singer Standard, made of shiny black metal, always a little dusty, with gold scrollwork about its base and a lever which was operated by pressure from the knee. A busy, oily fragrance rose from the region of the motor. Its sound was sweet and rhythmic, almost human. Elsa like to boast about how little she had paid for it; with only a little bit of finagling she had got it for thirty dollars wholesale, which was almost half-price. It was a cabinet-style machine and could be folded away into a little walnut-veneer table – though, in fact, it seldom was.

For what was the use of putting it away, she used to say, with a rising intonation she had; what was the sense of it when she was always working away on something – in the evenings, at weekends, whenever she had a minute. Elsa's knee resting on the pedal, so delicate for a heavy woman, had constituted for Brenda an education in lightheartedness. She made all her own clothes, the size twenty-two dresses – long sleeves for winter, short for summer – that she needed for work. (For thirty years, until she died, she sold men's socks and underpants at Wards – five days a week, nine to five, and on alternate Saturday mornings until the unions came in and a put a stop to that.) She made her skirts and blouses and even her own winter coats: 'Just try and find decent ready-to-wear for a gal my size.' She made herself nightgowns out of remnants – some of them were of strange non-nightgown materials, moire or taffeta, that were more suitable for evening wear – and she would have made her own underwear, too, if Wards hadn't allowed their saleswomen fifteen per cent off. She sewed nylon curtains for the front windows of the apartment on 26th Street and the stretch slip-covers for the two armchairs and for the couch which she opened up at night for her bed. She hemmed her own dish towels and sheets. 'Better goods,' she explained to Brenda. 'One hundred per cent better, and they don't ravel out their first time in the wash.'

Brenda can remember the tone of her mother's voice when she said this, but can't recall whether she spoke in English or Polish. Elsa alternated easily between the two, and Brenda, in childhood, was accustomed to the rapid movement between the two languages; not just the shifting vocabularies but the towering structures of consciousness and mood. When Elsa was happiest she spouted a loud, comic, Cicero-flavoured English.

Brenda grew up wearing beautiful clothes. At Wilmot Public Grammar School in Cicero, when other girls wore dresses of faded rayon passed on to them by their older sisters, Brenda Pulaski wore fresh cotton dresses – Egyptian cotton; 'Irons like a hanky,' Elsa said – made from the latest back-to-school Butterick and Simplicity patterns. There was hand-embroidery or white piqué trim on the sleeves and the collars. In fourth grade Brenda was the first in school to have a New Look ballerina skirt, the first to have a blouse with a Barrymore collar. Never once in all the years she was growing up did she reach into her closet in the jumbled back bedroom and find she had nothing to wear; never once did she wear a dress or a jumper or a blouse that had not been finished with French seams and bound buttonholes; never was she embarrassed to find her hem coming down or a button missing or a blouse opening up under the arm when she raised her hand in class. At the age of nine or ten she went to neighbourhood birthday parties wearing royal blue or wine-coloured velvet dresses with bows at the back and lace at the yoke; when she twirled around, the skirts of these dresses spread out in a full circle. At Morton High School, where she was Senior Class Secretary, she had a wardrobe of coordinated corduroy skirts and weskits and wool dresses with the plaids matching at the back and the sides as well, and white, handmade Peter Pan collars to pin to the necks of her sweaters. For her first school dance when she was fifteen, Elsa made her a 'formal' of nylon net, boned and strapless, with a matching circle of tulle for her ponytail. There is a picture of her wearing this dress in one of her old yearbooks. She is standing beneath a basketball hoop which is draped with paper streamers, looking popeyed and happy on the arm of a slim boy, Randy Saroka, with short, curly hair and a striped necktie, and at the waist of her full-skirted dress is a corsage of two gardenias.

When it came to Brenda's clothes, Elsa had done most of the actual sewing, and she had done all the cutting. 'Cutting tells,' she liked to say, emphatically and mysteriously. She had insisted, too, on putting in the zippers and setting the sleeves. 'When you're older you can set a sleeve,' she promised Brenda. 'Plenty of time for that later on.' (Brenda at age thirteen or fourteen ran up side seams, basted, and did hems.) In the evenings while Brenda did her homework, or later, when she was in bed, Elsa sat under the lamp with the radio playing and worked on inverted pleats or handmade eyelets. 'Sewing's damn hard work,' she used to say with just a hint of Slavic inflection, 'so it's just plain stupid to use cheap yard goods.' Thus, for her daughter, Brenda, there were no bargain blends and no remnants; even during the war, Elsa managed to find one hundred per cent virgin wool for Brenda's school clothes. For a yard of real English jersey she once paid six-fifty. 'Just look at the way it hangs,' she exclaimed, holding the material up to the light, stretching it between her fingers and giving it a sharp sideways tug. 'I always say, don't skimp when you sew. Quality shows; it shows every time.' (The wool jersey, Brenda still remembered years later, had been made into something called a tube dress. She had been one of the first to have a tube dress.)

She felt certain that, had her mother been alive, she would have admired the new red raincoat she'd bought for the trip to Philadelphia. Elsa would have turned it inside out and laid it flat on a table; she would have examined the seams and the lining and pronounced it, at last, a well-made garment, a quality garment. She would have read the label, nodding, approving, blowing through her teeth: 'Cheap at the price.'

The thought of her mother's posthumous approval – Elsa died four years ago at age fifty-six from complications following a routine gall-bladder operation – comforted Brenda, sitting in the car, wearing her new coat over her suit. Jack was silent now, driving to the airport, his teeth set in an attitude of grim dutifulness.

'Damn window-washers.' He leaned forward, peering through the smeared windshield. 'Cheap window-washers they put in these cars.'

His earlier good humour had evaporated, dispelled by the small mechanical failings of the car, and possibly by the cold wind blowing across the highway and the early-morning darkness, purplish with arc lights. A truck-driver passed them, swerving suddenly, causing Jack to curse violently. 'Fuck.' All these things seemed to Brenda to be inexplicably her fault, tied up in some way with her decision to go to Philadelphia.

No, that was absurd. Ridiculous. She recalled that it had been Jack's idea in the first place that she go. He had been the one to suggest it, and it was he who finally persuaded her that it would be a valuable experience. He had used those very words: 'A valuable experience.' She was about to mention this to him when he braked suddenly, pitching the two of them forward. 'Did you see that? Christ! He didn't even signal. We could have ploughed right into him.'

Brenda said nothing, concentrating instead on her hands, which rested on the smooth fabric of her new raincoat. She had bought it a week ago at Carsons for $250.

Peering at the price tag under the subdued store lights, she had felt panic. It was unbelievable. Two hundred and fifty dollars! And tax on top of that! She had been aghast. ('I was aghast,' she imagined herself saying to someone – anyone – later.) She had no idea coats had gone up so much. When did it happen? Inflation? It seemed not all that long ago that she had paid eighty dollars for a warm winter coat with a chamois lining and a real fur collar on it – no, that had been ages ago, the year Jack got his first promotion at the Institute – her blue tweed coat; she had worn it for eight years.

The red raincoat at Carsons had been reduced from $315. What a laugh, Brenda heard herself saying in some future conversation, her voice rising. A mere raincoat, and they had the nerve to ask $315.

On the other hand, it was a good make, she could say. She had seen those ads in the *New Yorker*: that long-haired girl standing out there on the rock; that grey-haired man, strongly muscular, finely featured, a few steps behind her, turned to half-profile, his gaze sternly directed at the surf. And it did have a zip-in lining, which meant she would be able to wear it almost year round. She would get all kinds of wear from it. If it faded – reds sometimes did – she could return it. She would put the sales slip away carefully in her dresser drawer. . . .

The tag said size twelve. Perfect. It wasn't that easy finding size twelves, you had to look and look. (Already she was going to buy it; of course she was; it would be idiotic not to.)

She slipped it off the hanger and tried it on. It fit smoothly across the shoulders – it *better* fit for that price, she muttered to herself, making a face. She was feeling cheerful now. It made her hips look almost slim – something ingenious about the way it was cut. ('Cutting tells . . .') There was a gathered yoke at the back, and top-stitching on the collar and pockets, the kind of detailing that costs money, that has to be done by hand. ('You can tell quality by the detailing.') Still, $250 was an incredible amount of money. Two and a half weeks' groceries at least. You could buy a man's suit for $250, a three-piece suit. She could get a new glass-topped coffee table for the living room for $250. They needed a new coffee table; the old one, that scratched, phony Duncan Phyfe, was looking tackier by the day. Two hundred and fifty dollars was a sizeable chunk of money.

On the other hand, she had been shopping all morning – Field's, Stevens, Saks – and was beginning to feel discouraged and hot. She pictured herself putting on this coat and walking down a street in Philadelphia, a neutral sky overhead – a narrow street, medieval-looking and chilly, with small shops; a bakeshop flashed into view, fresh buns lined up in a window. She would be warm and courageous, marching past it, swinging her leather shoulder-bag as she went.

She wrote a cheque for the coat instead of putting it on her charge account. When she got home she carried it upstairs to the bedroom, lifted it from its box, and removed the tags. She tried it on again, examining herself in the full-length mirror on the back of the closet door. The material felt silky to the touch. Even the hem was perfect, just meeting the top of her boots – at least she wouldn't need new boots this year. It was worth every penny of two hundred and fifty dollars; her mother's lightly accented voice reached her through the silvery bevelled edge of the mirror – 'Cheap at the price.' 'Quality shows.' Brenda curled her hands under the lapels and smiled.

She and Jack no longer had to watch every penny, she reminded herself. Jack earned a comfortable salary at the Institute; eventually he would move up to Senior Administrator. Dr. Middleton was due to retire in five years. Anything could happen. And there was her quilt money. She was close to being a regular earner now. For the last two years she had even filed her own tax form. ('Now that's a milestone and a half, you lucky duck,' Hap Lewis had raved, 'when you get your own tax form. You've made it, kiddo.')

She had been lucky. Her first quilt selling for six hundred dollars. A fluke, she'd thought at the time; it was only because it had won the prize and been written up in *Chicago Today*. 'Elm Park Housewife Turns Hobby to Profit.' At the time she'd thought it could never happen again. But it had. People seemed willing to spend exorbitant sums for original handworked articles. The last quilt she'd sold, *Michigan Blue*, had gone for $800. Some people from Evanston had bought it, a dentist and his wife. They'd paid the price cheerfully, no dickering, no suggestion that she knock off fifty dollars or forgo the sales tax. They had heard about her work from an acquaintance; they had driven down from Evanston one evening, phoning ahead for an appointment. Her signature was embroidered in the right-hand corner, and they had fingered it with satisfaction. ('I love it,' the wife had whispered. 'We'll take it,' her husband said.)

She now had printed business cards of her own, Jack's idea.

Brenda Bowman

HANDMADE QUILTS
ORIGINAL AND ADAPTED

576 North Franklin Blvd. Elm Park, Ill.

She had a receipt book and a ledger where she kept track of expenses and sales. And this week – today – she was going to the National Handicraft Exhibition, where the top quilters in the country would be showing. Eleanor Parkins, *the* Eleanor Parkins. Sandra French. Dorothea Thomas. W.B. Marx. Verna of Virginia. These quilters asked a thousand dollars, even fifteen hundred dollars, for a commissioned piece. Verna of Virginia had recently sold a quilt to the Metropolitan Museum of Modern Art; there had been a write-up in *Quilting and Stitchery* and a suggestion that the price had been in excess of $4000.

And *she* was stewing about paying $250 for a coat! A few days' work – that was all; the thought gave her a glimpse of a dazzling new kind of power.

And Jack had liked the coat too. She modelled it for him when he got home, parading the length of the living room, showing how it looked with her boots and shoulder-bag, pointing out the zip-in lining and the buttonholes which had been worked by hand so that each one looked like a perfect, satiny tear. 'Nice,' he had told her. 'Really nice.'

He appreciated good clothes. And was not above impulsive extravagance himself. Just weeks before he'd bought himself a suede vest, he who had never worn a suede vest before in his life and probably, Brenda suspected, never would. (He had not told her how much it cost; she had resisted asking; meanwhile it hung in their closet, smelling expensive and new.)

'You really do like it?' She turned so that the hem of the coat swirled out girlishly. Her hands smoothed the material over her hips and, impulsively, she gave a short, sharp, forward kick – a cancan kick, neatly executed.

'You'll be the smash hit of Philly,' he told her, smiling.

She gave him a long, level look. He was sitting back, relaxed on the brown sofa, sipping a gin and tonic from his favourite frosted glass. One leg was crossed over the other; a year ago he had started wearing executive-length socks at Brenda's suggestion. In his eyes stood approval. And he was nodding, *beautiful, beautiful* – but he was reaching sideways for the newspaper; the smile was slipping already from his face. She longed suddenly to restore it, to hold it there an instant longer, and so she announced with a final swirl: 'And guess what, Jack? It was on sale.'

His eyebrows went up. The smile seemed on the point of resurrection.

'A special sale. Marked down to a hundred and fifty dollars.'

She had said this, freezing in front of the coffee table, her hands caught voguishly in the side pockets of the red coat.

There was an instant's pause; then Jack made a gesture of celebration, lifting his glass in her direction. 'A steal,' he said.

'A steal?' She smiled icily. 'You call a hundred and fifty dollars a steal?' Her voice, she knew, sounded shrill. And she felt a shameful expression of foxiness resting on the bones of her face.

'Well, these days . . . ' Jack swirled his drink in his glass. 'Inflation . . . '

He was a man too easily deceived; there was no resistance in him; she had felt obscurely cheated. And furious with self-loathing. Why, why, why? Later she had torn up the sales slip. What if it did fade? What did it matter? She would never return it now.

This small deception was coupled with another – though in a way that owned nothing to logic; the $218 air fare to Philadelphia.

When she first decided to go to Philadelphia, the air fare had seemed the least of her worries. The real worry was how she could get away for a week.

'It's not a week, it's five days,' Jack had reminded her. 'Still . . . '

It would be different if her mother were still alive and could come and look after things. Jack's parents, though they lived close by, were too old, too nervous, away from home, even overnight; the children got on their nerves after a few hours.

Jack assured her he could manage. The children were old enough now anyway. They didn't need looking after. All they needed was food in their stomachs and someone to boot them off to bed at night. He was certainly capable of doing that.

Two days later she got around to phoning United Airlines. The fare was $218. 'What about an excursion rate?' she'd asked. Jack had suggested that she inquire about special fares.

'There's our night flight,' the sweet-voiced United girl told her. 'That's only $176.'

'What time does that get into Philadelphia?' she asked.

'Three-fifteen. A.M.'

'Three-fifteen?'

'It's very popular with businessmen.'

Brenda hesitated. Three-fifteen in the morning. In the dark. Gary, Fort Wayne, Cleveland would all be traversed in darkness. And in January, when the year seemed at its weakest point. She imagined the plane burrowing through black Appalachian air, eastern air. And over Philadelphia there would be the steepness of descent, and then stepping off into blindness and confusion and the garish lights of an unknown airport. There would be gateways and ramps leading off in unfamiliar directions. The thought made her feel uneasy and faintly sick.

Where could she possibly go at that hour? How? She would require sleep, a bed, a pillow.

$218 take away $176. That was $42 difference; Brenda had always been good at arithmetic, better than Jack at tabulating prices and figuring percentages. It was she who handled their bills and worked over their tax forms in the spring.

$42. It wasn't even worth considering. She gave her head a violent shake. What was $42 these days? A small price to pay for safety; she had the children to think of, and Jack too. Flying at night was riskier, everyone knew that, although Jack, who flew often, professed that it was safer than driving down the expressway at five o'clock.

Furthermore, in the few days since Jack had suggested she go, she had had time to envision the trip to Philadelphia, and part of the vision had included a morning departure – drinking coffee out of a Styrofoam cup at the airport while the sun struggled up through the streaky Chicago dawn, and finally, minutes before the actual takeoff, a burst of broad daylight.

'I think I'll just stick with the morning flight,' she said into the phone.

'Fine. I'll put you down for Flight 452 then. Bowman, you said. Is that Miss or Mrs.?'

'Mrs.' She was brisk now, all business.

'Thank you, Mrs. Bowman. And thank you for phoning United.'

A few days later the tickets arrived in the mail. She showed them to Jack.

'Seems reasonable,' he said. Then, 'I guess they didn't have a special fare?'

'No,' Brenda said. 'Not for five days.'

'Oh well . . . ' He was preoccupied, busy at the Institute and frustrated because he never seemed to find time to work on his book.

Brenda put the tickets on the hall table under the chunk of pink quartz.

Chapter Five

'Excuse me,' a very young man in a bright-brown suit was saying. He stood in the aisle, addressing Brenda, his head ducked down like a diver about to plunge. 'Excuse me, ma'am?'

Brenda looked up from her magazine. 'Yes?'

'I'm afraid you're in my seat.'

'Your seat?'

'14 A.' He opened his mouth – a pink cushion of a mouth in an eager face – revealing a surprising amount of lower gum. 'I'm supposed to be in 14 A.'

'I think it said on my boarding pass – '

'There's gotta be some mistake,' he said firmly.

Brenda, rattled, reached for her bag. 'I'm sure I've got my boarding pass here somewhere.'

'You're probably supposed to be in 14 B. The middle seat here. There isn't anyone in 14 B. Or in 14 C either. And practically everyone's on. They're shutting the doors.'

'I don't know what I did with it, my boarding pass. I had it in my hand just a minute ago.'

'Isn't that it there? That pink card. Under your coat there?'

'Oh, yes, here it is.'

'Well?'

'It says 14 A. At least it looks like an A to me. Isn't that funny. And you said you had 14 A too.'

'Here.' He thrust it at her. 'You can see for yourself.'

'Isn't that strange.'

He shook his head, knocked it back fiercely, showing his lower gums again. They were as pink as a child's. 'It never fails. Every single time I get on an airplane, something gets botched up. Last time – '

'Look, why don't we just ask the stewardess if – '

'Last time,' he perched on the edge of 14 B and spoke confidentially, 'last time they put me in the smoking section. All the way from Chicago to Cleveland in the smoking section. Not that I object to smokers per se, but it triggers off my allergies. And that triggers off my motion-sickness.'

'Oh,' Brenda said, unable to think of anything else.

'When I was a kid, even, I used to get sick in the car. Car sickness. We had only to go around the block and I'd be upchucking. That's why I always ask for the window seat. If you got problems with motion-sickness, they say you're better off if you sit by the window. Something psychological about – '

'I'll be happy to move over – '

'Somebody at the desk must have made a mistake or why would they give us both 14 A.'

'The computers,' Brenda suggested frailly.

'Computers. I'd like to tell them what they can do with their computers.'

'You sit here,' Brenda said, suddenly resolute, gathering her things together – her magazine, her bag, her red coat – 'and I'll sit in the middle seat.'

'You sure you don't mind?'

'Not at all.'

'You don't get motion-sickness?'

'Never,' she said, stirred by the affirmative ring in her voice, the plump, healthy strength of it.

'Someone ought to write a letter to the airline,' he said, rising, 'and tell them what they think of their service. Their so-called service, I should have said. Maybe when I get back to Chicago I'll – '

'Actually, I'd just as soon – ' Brenda stood up and squeezed past him into the aisle.

'Hey, at least let me put your coat up there for you.'

'Thank you.' Brenda handed him her raincoat and, with sorrow, watched as he wadded it into a tight ball and stuffed it into an overhead compartment.

'Whew, that's better.' He sank into the window seat and reached up to adjust the oxygen vent, a bony wrist shooting out past the shiny edge of brown sleeve. 'That too draughty on you ?'

'No, it's fine.' She sighed, feeling suddenly elderly and sexless and accommodating; a kind of gummy pleasantness adhered to her like plaque; she could feel it coating her teeth and tongue. Her awful niceness.

'I always like to grab a good lungful of oxygen before takeoff. They say it helps fight down that queasiness you sometimes get . . . '

Brenda opened her magazine. *The Quilter's Quarterly.* Jack had given her a subscription for her birthday. The latest issue contained, among other things, diagrams for three-dimensional animal quilts for children. At one time these kinds of quilts would have interested her; now they struck her as gimmicky, especially a bright-hued elephant quilt which had large button eyes and a three-foot-long stuffed trunk. Only four years ago, she would have looked at that and thought –

'Hey, that's really something!' The young man was peering over her shoulder. She could feel his breath on her neck.

'Pardon?'

'That elephant thing there. Cute idea. For a little kid, I mean.'

'Hmmmm.' A strand of hair fell over her eyes and she brushed it aside. She had never worn her hair in quite this way before, blown loose like this, rising from a centre parting. Hairspray was a thing of the past, she'd been told by the hairdresser the day before. Nowadays the look was strong and healthy. Perms – forget them. Everyone wanted the natural glossy look. Let it flow, let it find its own shape.

When she emerged from the He/She Salon on Lake Street yesterday, her body had seemed exceptionally buoyant; the air around her head had felt tender, and, looking about, she had experienced an acute longing for – what? – spring. Almost a belief that it was spring.

But today sections of her hair kept falling over her eyes. ('You should try one of the new ornamental combs,' the hairdresser had urged her. 'Or a flower.' The thought of herself with a flower pinned in her hair made her want to laugh out loud. She had meant to tell Jack about that – couldn't he just see her, cooking dinner with a flower over one ear.)

'Hey, it looks like we're taking off,' the young man shrilled. He glanced excitedly at his watch. Bony wrist, Brenda noticed, an absence of calcium. And freckles, hundreds of freckles; the kind of skin that was hopelessly vulnerable. 'Five minutes late. We'll make up for it once we're up there.'

'Probably,' Brenda said pleasantly. Pleasant, pleasant, always pleasant. Aside from quiltmaking, pleasantness was her one talent. (She said this to herself with sour pleasure, not for a minute believing it.)

'Oh, boy. This is the part I don't like. Going up. Once you're up there it's not so bad, you can relax.'

'Yes,' Brenda agreed,

'And coming down. That's bad news too.'

'Uh-huh.' She watched him grope for his seatbelt, his hands flapping pinkly at his sides.

'Here,' she said, coming to his rescue. 'Here's the buckle.'

'Thanks. Tricky things these belts.'

'Yes.' She turned the page to an article on intaglio quilting. It was a European technique; she'd heard about it at the Craft Guild; it was difficult to do well, but offered some interesting effects. She would have to try it some time, she decided.

'You off to Cleveland too?' came the voice at her side.

'No. Philadelphia.'

A short silence. Then, 'I've never been to Philadelphia.'

This time the silence was longer. Brenda decided to give up on her article.

'We don't have a branch in Philly,' he confided. 'Only Cleveland. And Syracuse, New York.'

'Oh.'

'And Chicago, of course. As a matter of fact, Chicago happens to be our head office.'

'Hmmmm.'

'As a matter of fact, I just might be in line for a transfer to the Cleveland office next year. Permanent. Not that I'm all that hot about Cleveland as a city. It's a dying city. Practically dead. That's what they say, anyhow.

'Is it?'

'I don't really want to get transferred all that much, but the thing is, the supervisor in the office, he and I don't always see eye to eye.'

'That's too bad.'

'It's not policy. On policy we see eye to eye. It's more what you might call a kind of personality conflict.'

'Uh-huh.'

'Most of the time it's not so bad, him and me. But then, for no reason at all that I can put my finger on, some little thing will trigger him off. This guy gets just violent. A real temper like you've never seen. Irish, but they say that doesn't hold any

more. Still, he's Irish by descent, for what it's worth. We were
having this discussion one day and all of a sudden he called me
a dumb bastard.'

'Oh?'

'Excuse my French. But that's what he called me. Just came
right out and called me a bastard. Right in the office there, with
everyone standing around listening. Oh, boy.'

'Terrible.'

'You can imagine how that made me feel.'

'Yes, I certainly can.'

'Imagine how you'd feel if someone called you a . . . ' he
paused.

'Someone did once.'

'Did what?'

'Someone called me a bastard once,' Brenda said.

'You? Really?'

'Yes.'

'I . . . I didn't think that word was, well, was ever used with
ladies. Only men.'

'This was when I was very young. A little girl in school.'

'So what did you do?'

'Well, not much. I mean, I'd never heard the word before. I
must have been only about six.'

'Six! But you still remember, huh?' His mouth fell open.
Yellow teeth, plump pink gums, a soft, nursery look. 'That must
have been really awful.'

'The funny thing is, I found out later that I really was a
bastard.'

'Huh?'

'In the real sense of the word, yes, I was a bastard.'

'You – '

'Meaning,' Brenda said, 'I didn't have a father.'

'Everyone has a father.' He giggled slightly at this and
reached up to readjust the oxygen vent.

'What I mean is, my mother never got married. So that makes
me, technically speaking anyway, a bastard.'

'And this kid at your school, I guess he knew it, huh? About
your mother.'

'He must have.'

'Kids can be cruel, you know that.'

'The funny thing is, I didn't mind. At least not very much.

Not when I found out what it meant, that it was a real word. I remember I looked it up in the dictionary at school. I must have been older than six, maybe about eight or nine. Anyway, it was right there in the big school dictionary we had at the back of the room. So it seemed all right.'

'It must have been tough, not having a father.'

'Oh, I don't know . . . '

'I mean, no dad coming home at night.'

'The only thing was that my mother had to work. And this was in the days when most of the mothers stayed home and just kept house. But that was the only thing. Otherwise I don't think I missed much.'

'My old man was a pretty good guy. I'll say that much for him.'

'That's nice.'

'But, gee, I'll bet it was sort of rough at times. I mean the stigma, carrying the stigma. Like, nowadays it isn't anything. Look at Vanessa Redgrave. But back then – '

'Actually,' Brenda cleared her throat, making her voice clear and firm – several of her friends had commented over the years on the clarity of her voice – 'actually I don't remember being particularly conscious of any stigma. Maybe it was the neighbourhood I lived in. Or maybe it was just my mother, the kind of person she was.'

'You must have had a lot of self-confidence then. They say if you're born with a lot of self-confidence you can rise above just about anything.'

'You may be right.' She smoothed the cover of her magazine with the palm of her hand, regarded the ring on her finger, a small sapphire; Jack had given it to her two years ago. A sentimental occasion.

'Me, I never had much self-confidence. I'm taking this course now at the Y. Wednesday nights. How to be more assertive, push yourself forward. I figure it will help me in business.'

'How's it going?'

'I don't know. I just don't know. Either you've got it or you don't, that's what some experts think. That's another reason I'm thinking seriously of transferring to the Cleveland area next year. It would be kind of a new start, if you see what I mean.'

'I think I do.'

'You can't run away from your problems though, I know that.'

'No, that's true.'

'Of course, I'm young.' He shot her a glance which seemed to Brenda to be partly apologetic, partly sly. 'I've got lots of time to develop my, you know, my potential.'

'Oh, yes,' Brenda said. 'That's true.'

'Hey, look out there.'

'Clouds.'

'Pretty, huh?'

'Yes.'

The clouds rolled by the window, white as steam. Brenda brightened, feeling suddenly at peace. The relief of not being young! The pleasure of being bored, of deserving that pleasure, of being able to admit to it. This poor, freckled creature beside her, working his jaw, struggling against airsickness, gasping for oxygen and courage. She should feel pity for him; he had all his life to cope with, all of it. She should reach out and give his knee a consoling pat. Consolation – that was what he most needed, though he didn't know it. She smiled past his lap, sending her soft look of pity out across the clouds. Poor boy, poor young man.

Nevertheless, when he opened his mouth a minute later to inquire again where it was she was going, she replied with uncharacteristic sharpness, 'Philadelphia.'

She said it curtly, a sting of vinegar on her tongue, not at all the way she had pronounced it at home, not the way she had whispered it over the morning coffee: Philadelphia.

Stupid. Foolish. What had she expected? What on earth had she expected?

Not this. She glanced at her travelling companion, who with his little finger was attempting to dislodge something from a back tooth. He had already forgotten what she had told him – or rather he had disregarded it. What had she expected? Not this, not this.

Chapter Six

THE WORLD WAS NOT FILLED WITH BEAUTIFUL PEOPLE, NO,
certainly it was not; and Brenda was not such a fool as to
believe it was.

Fashion models, TV stars – they had nothing to do with the
way people really were. Real people, even the strongest of
them, were sadly perforated by weakness and inconsistency.
Failure was everywhere, also selfishness, cowardice, dishar-
mony, and physical imperfection – gross physical imperfection.
People did not live for great ideals or for noble visions; they
lived for their divorces, their promotions, the instant gratifica-
tions of sex and food. They told lies, they smiled slyly at
themselves in mirrors as they passed. Brenda knew this only
too well. 'Brenda is a realist,' Jack used to say, back in the days
when he made such statements. 'Brenda sees things the way
they are.'

Did she? In their early married days, when her husband Jack
made these claims for her sense of reality, he was, she suspected, stating something else as well: that *he* was *not* a realist.
That his vision of things was romantic, withheld, speculative.
There was such a thing as allegory, there was such a thing as
metaphor, there were the rewarding riches of symbol and myth.
There were layers and layers – infinite layers – of meaning.

Perspective altered events, Jack liked to say; he was working
then on his thesis, a new view of the explorer LaSalle and his
voyages of discovery. Brenda, who was doing the typing in the
evening and helping him with the index, thought at the time
that he would never get it finished. The research and writing
took all of one year and part of a second summer. That second
summer was the worst. Their student apartment near Lincoln
Park was hot and airless, especially at night when the heat had
been piling up all day – ninety degrees, ninety-five.

Brenda remembered how the two of them, hot and irritable,
had gone for a walk late one night in the park, and had come
unexpectedly, upon a genuine sixties phenomenon, a love-in.

42

She had been reading about flower children in *Time* magazine and had heard the slogan, 'Make Love Not War.' And now, here was a demonstration right in the middle of Lincoln Park, not six blocks away from where she and Jack lived.

Bodies were everywhere, stretched on the cool grass; guitars, long hair, some singing, low voices calling, strewn flowers, a smell of sweet smoke rising in the air – she knew what *that* was. There were swaying shadows from large trees, and overhead, a blown nursery-rhyme globe of a moon. A TV camera, WGTV, whirred away, making its own circle of light.

Brenda had been amazed and excited by the spectacle, but Jack had watched from a distance, standing back under a tree, observing, commenting, and composing, it seemed to Brenda, instant documentation. This bizarre scene might be viewed as a morsel of history. Already, a fraction of hindsight could be attached to it. Events, said Jack, even while they were unfolding, could be softened and explained by context, suspended on thin strands of reason and analogy. And – most difficult of all for Brenda to grasp – they could be undercut by a disturbing existential edge: is this real? is this really happening?

Brenda's view of the world was simpler, Jack seemed to believe. Things were a certain way, and that was all there was to it. It was what he loved about her. He had fallen in love with her level glance, with her quick way of nodding and absorbing and calling a spade a spade, and especially, oh especially, with the way she held up her hands and, with a gesture of ripe female acceptance – lucky, lucky Brenda – shrugged.

The simple act of shrugging. It was so exotic, so European, but at the same time so primitive; he saw it romantically as a chunk of ancestral heritage which had luckily come his way.

Shrugging, in truth, was almost the only visible characteristic Brenda had inherited from her Polish mother: an atavistic raising of the shoulders, elbows levitated, hands opened up to the sky, a gesture which proclaimed with wonderful helpless Slavic silence – let it be, so be it, God's will be done. Jack always maintained, fondly, that Brenda had given one of her famous shrugs the first day they had met, eating lunch at Roberto's. She had been halfway through her bowl of vegetable soup when it happened. Up went her hands. Up went her eyebrows. Something about it, the simplicity, the grace; it had done him in, he liked to say, done him in on the spot.

He was not a shrugger himself. (It was a joke of theirs, in the early days, that he was equipped instead with all the good lower-middle-class gestures: chin-stroking, lip-biting, finger-drumming, foot-tapping.) Nor were their children, Rob and Laurie, given to shrugging; they were nail-biters, shin-scratchers; Rob sometimes wrinkled his forehead in a peculiarly lopsided way; Laurie kicked at table legs and ground her teeth at night. Only Brenda shrugged. She was, she supposed, the last of the line.

But even she seemed to be shrugging less frequently these days – though Jack liked to claim she had a way of shrugging with her voice. Something had happened, she wasn't sure what, but nothing seemed as simple as it once had. She had children who were growing up. Her mother was dead. She herself was forty years old. There was a reluctance, now, to say: well, that's the way it is. When she looked at something these days – a face, a house, an expanse of scenery – she was more likely to think, is this all there is?

At times she found herself longing for that other self, the Brenda of old, smiling and matter-of-fact. (Her organization of the LaSalle index had been a model of logic; Dr. Middleton at the Institute said he had never seen anything to equal it.) Whatever it was that had come into her life during the last year or so had brought frustration with it. A restless anger and a sense of undelivered messages. Early in the fall, soon after they got back from the lake, she had begun work on a new quilt. It was still unfinished, lying there on a chair in a corner of her workroom. She had set it aside temporarily in order to work on *The Second Coming*, which, while experimental in workmanship, was more traditional in design, less risky for an exhibition (judges could be quirky; it was better to strike a balance in these things.) The unfinished quilt – that was how she thought of it, *The Unfinished Quilt* – had no real pattern to it, only a cauldron of colour, yellow mostly. There was a bounty and a vigour to it which magnetized her. Yet it represented a worrying departure, almost a violation of the order and equanimity of her early quilt. 'There is a satisfying orderliness in Brenda Bowman's work,' the article in the *Elm Leaves Weekly* had declared.

Sometimes at night she dreamed about it. Only three-quarters finished, it already contained hundreds of pieces. There were particles of colour as small as the tips of her fingers, a

44

pulse of life travelling atop a torrent of private energy. She had felt a wish to trap this torrent in stitches, but had put off the moment of completion. The quilting frame seemed altogether too rigid to contain what she wanted. Instead, she had begun the process of quilting on a lap frame – and before the actual piecing was finished. She was, in fact, uncertain about how to finish it, and feared that the weight of her hand might be overly heavy. She wanted a pattern that was severe but lyrical; she would have to be careful or she might rush it toward something finite and explanatory, when all the while she wanted more. Perhaps, she admitted to herself, staring out the window late one afternoon at the weak sunlight striping the garage roof, perhaps she wanted more than mere cloth and stitching could accomplish. Nevertheless, more was suddenly what she wanted. What she spent her time thinking about. *More.*

'You've got terrific cheekbones,' Leah Wallberg once told Brenda.

When Leah Wallberg was younger, before she and Irv were married, she had worked as a stage-designer for the Goodman Theatre. She still dabbled in this and that, working in what she liked to call a semiprofessional capacity. It had been Leah Wallberg who designed the set for the recent Elm Park Little Theatre production of *Hamlet*. (White and yellow drapery and an arrangement of stairs, all very stark and pure, it was reported to Brenda, who had missed the play.) It was said that Leah had a good eye for line; cheekbones were the kind of thing she took note of. 'It's not like Hepburn bones. What you've got, Brenda, is wide bones. Which is really more interesting-looking in the long run.'

Where had these cheekbones of hers come from? From her mother? Elsa had been a heavy woman all her life – or at least as far back as Brenda could remember. At one point, shortly before she died, she had weighed over two hundred and thirty pounds. She was a big-boned woman, she said, big all over. Large breasts under print-jersey dresses – she favoured blues and whites – spoke of bulk, and also of a perfumed looseness. Girdles and brassieres gave her cramps, and so she dispensed with them after work and at week-ends, allowing her flesh to flow as it wished. 'Wait'll I get this girdle off and have a cup of coffee.' For years that had been her greeting to her daughter,

Brenda, when she came in from work at night. Her hips, almost sighing with release, spread wide; her escaped thighs were baggy and blotched where the elastic had cut in. (Brenda, growing up and sharing with her the dimly lit bathroom, had observed these lacerations calmly – clearly this was to be her future too.) Elsa's upper arms were round and as thick as the waist of a smaller woman. After a big meal she slapped her hips in a friendly conspiratorial way. Fat, if not prized, was at least accommodated. Elsa's face had melted into something wide and florid, and imbedded in that face had been a pair of small, lively eyes and a mouth that went into a crimped, lipsticked H when she laughed. If Elsa Maria Pulaski had even been known for her wide cheekbones, Brenda had not heard of it; her face was a circle of smiling fat. Where in that circle was there a need for cheekbones?

Brenda's cheekbones, on the other hand, had a sleek, pulled-back look of cleanliness. Her eyes were slightly creased, faintly Oriental – what Jack called Magyar eyes. In her high-school graduation picture she had looked healthy and winsome; some of her friends had seen a strong resemblance to June Allyson. She had been voted 'Miss Friendly Personality' of her class, and that title was printed in shaded script beneath her picture. In those days her hair had been lighter – dishwater blonde – though in her daydreams she liked to think of herself as a honey blonde. ('I absolutely adore your honey-coloured hair,' he whispered softly.) The light hair, the Magyar eyes, and the sleek, flat bones of her cheeks had given her a look of amiability.

The image was a true one. She had a certain natural ease, which, as she grew older, earned her the reputation for great reasonableness. 'How come you don't have any hang-ups like the rest of us slobs?' Hap Lewis had once asked her. She didn't know. Her own reflection stared back at her, pleasant, serene, a little sly. Behind that face lay acceptance and good nature. Perhaps Jack was right. She was a realist. She took things as they came.

Why was it then that during the last few years certain things had begun to annoy her. Enrage her. She found it hard to account for the contempt she sometimes felt, this new secret fastidiousness. Who was she anyway to make judgments? Brenda Pulaski Bowman (fatherless) of Cicero, Illinois, now a resident of Elm Park – though not the best end of Elm Park.

Graduate of Katherine Gibbs School of Secretarial Science. She had taken the two-year course instead of the twelve-month one, but even so, that wasn't the same as going to college, not even teachers' college. Who did she think she was, she asked herself roughly, who the hell did she think she was? Why should it suddenly start to bother her that Jack stuck business cards and Chargex receipts in the frame of their bedroom mirror? He had been doing this ever since she'd known him. Sometimes he left them there for weeks. He also had a habit of putting old rubber bands around doorknobs. Why did he do this? Frugality? Tidiness? She didn't know. But suddenly she minded. She broke them off with a snap and threw then away. She yanked the cards out of the mirror, tossing them into Jack's dresser drawer on top of his rolled socks.

Other annoyances: the name Farrah Fawcett-Majors made her go numb. 'You should see her on *Charlie's Angels*,' her son Rob said in one of their pally moments. She watched one night. Disbelievingly. She felt herself twitch with boredom and contempt. 'It's only supposed to be entertainment,' Rob had said stiffly. 'Hmmmm,' she said in a condemning way – she who had grown up on *Fibber McGee and Molly* and *Duffy's Tavern*. Who was she to harp about Farrah Fawcett-Majors?

When she went to a party not long ago at Larry and Janey Carpenter's she noticed, with inexplicable fury, that there was a copy of the *New Yorker* in their bathroom. The bathroom itself was the showpiece of the Carpenter house, with its tinted skylight, its suspended sculpture carved from the backbone of a whale, its antique bathtub painted purple. Aubergine, Larry called it. Aubergine! Most of the things in the bathroom she admired; only the presence of the *New Yorker* seemed intolerable, positioned as it was on a neat white shelf over the toilet. *New Yorker* whimsy combined with private gruntings and strainings; it seemed to her to be obscene. She sneered at herself for this new delicacy. Who was she anyway to look down on the Carpenters? Larry Carpenter had gone to Princeton. Or one of those places.

She had had a note from Laurie's teacher which began with the words: 'As you know, we feel that Laurie is one of the most unique kids in the seventh grade.' 'Unique is unique,' Brenda had stormed to Jack. 'You can't be one of the most unique anything.' ('You're overreacting,' Jack replied with a puzzled look.)

She cringed when Rob left the house on the way to school in the morning and called out a loud, hoarse 'Ciao.' Ciao yourself, she wanted to yell at him. Anything would be better than ciao; nothing at all would be better than ciao.

She had been irked with Jack's best friend, Bernie Koltz, for sending her a floral arrangement for Christmas. 'Does he think I'm ready for the geriatric ward?' she complained to Jack. 'Look at these. Gladiolas!' ('Gladioli,' Jack had corrected her absently. 'Go to hell,' she told him, which immediately cheered her up.)

She went one day to buy a new blouse in a store called The Cockeyed Cat. It was on Michigan Boulevard. There was a deep café-au-lait carpet, a mirrored ceiling, and soft, Lucite lighting fixtures. The blouses were encased in transparent bags and cost between eighty and a hundred and eighty dollars. Tweed skirts cost two hundred dollars. There were matching tweed blazers, and she was inspecting the label on one of these when she heard in the background the soft sounds of Simon and Garfunkel singing 'Scarborough Fair'.

> Are you going to Scarborough Fair
> Parsley, Sage, Rosemary and Thyme.
> Remember me to one who lives there.
> She once was a true love of mine.

It was a song she had loved once. It reminded her of lying on the pier at the lake or cutting the grass in the backyard. But in this store, issuing from louvered openings in the wall, it sounded sweet and sappy. The lyrics were shallow, meaningless. Why hadn't she ever noticed that before?

Just before Christmas she and Jack had been invited to dinner at Milton and Shirley McInnis's in Evanston. Milt was the new head of restoration at the Institute, and Shirley, tall, brisk, brunette, was a social-worker in the Evanston school system; the family had spent two years in Zurich, and the children, when they came into the dining room one by one to be introduced, had shaken hands gravely. 'She's quite bright,' Shirley McInnis had murmured of Daphne. 'He's awfully bright,' she said of Roger. 'We think she's going to be bright,' she had confided about little Stephanie, four years old. Brenda, with a forkful of risotto halfway to her mouth, had felt indignant, then put upon, finally angry.

Last week they had gone, as usual, to have Sunday breakfast at Jack's parents'. Ma and Dad Bowman lived in a dark, old six-room apartment in Austin. Breakfast was always the same. Sara Lee coffee cake, cinnamon or cherry. Perked coffee. Plates set out at the kitchen table. Jack's mother humming, wearing bedroom slippers, pouring coffee into striped mugs. Brenda loved them both; they loved her and thought of her as a daughter. But last Sunday, sitting at the table, they had handed her an envelope. It was a bon voyage card with sparkles on it and a picture of bluebirds winging through a blue sky. Inside the card was a ten-dollar bill folded in half. 'For your vacation trip,' Ma Bowman had smiled, suddenly shy. 'To have yourself a real good meal on us,' Dad Bowman had winked.

Brenda had felt wounded, indignant. She was going to a national exhibit; she was one of the exhibitors; she had been *invited* to participate. Ma and Dad Bowman didn't present Jack with ten-dollar bills when he went off to Milwaukee or Detroit to present papers at the other branches of the Institute. Further-more, the card seemed a reminder that she was, perhaps, abandoning her family, that the trip she was taking was not one of necessity, but merely an indulgence. She thanked them profusely – they meant well, they meant only to be kind – but she had barely managed to restrain her tears.

What did this mean, this new impatience, this seething reaction to petty irritations? It could get worse, she saw. You could become crippled by this kind of rage. It was all so wasteful in the long run. And what, she wondered, was the name of this new anger, this seismic sensitivity to the cheap-ness of things?

Part of it, she sensed, was regret, for lately she had been assailed by a sense of opportunities missed. Events from the past reached out and inspired fruitless feelings of resentment. She recalled that long-ago summer night in Lincoln Park – the love-in, the long-haired flower children lying on the grass. She had watched, excitedly at first, but then, too soon, had suc-cumbed to Jack's watchful detachment. Now she wanted the scene replayed. She wanted to set down her handbag by the shadowy roots of a tree and take off her shoes. She would step forward, a little hesitantly. She imagined the moon touching her smooth cheeks; she imagined how the ground would feel, cool, a little gritty where the grass was worn down. In no time at all she would be submerged in the sweetness of music and the proximity of those other bodies. Brothers and sisters, all so young. Someone would call out her name in a low voice . . .

Two problems faced her, it seemed, and both involved an inability to make distinctions. *The Unfinished Quilt* lying on a chair in her workroom; it was either the best thing she had ever done or it was the worst. She did not know which. And this new anger she felt; it might mean no more than that she needed a few days away from home. A vacation. A change of pace.

Or it might mean – and a new wave of anger overtook her at the thought – it might mean that all her life had been a mistake.

Chapter Seven

'Name?'

'Brenda Bowman.'

'Spelled like it sounds?'

'Yes.'

'You're one of the last ones to register.'

'Am I?' Brenda set down her suitcase.

The woman at the desk ran a ballpoint pen down a list of names. Her greying hair, the colour of roofing paper, was caught in a careless roll and anchored with a slice of tortoise comb. She had a look of intelligence and frenzy, and an extreme accuracy about her make-up. 'And you're from?' she asked.

'Chicago.'

'Chicago?' She looked up and gave Brenda a smile which was wide and bright and which seemed to take in all of the hotel lobby. Then, 'I'm afraid I can't find you listed here. Did you go through our preregistration procedure?'

'I sent in a form – '

'Hmmmm, funny, you're not listed here under Chicago.'

'Elm Park, maybe?' Brenda had to speak forcefully because of an ornamental fountain bubbling noisily behind her. 'I'm a member of the Chicago Craft Guild, but I live in Elm Park, Illinois. That's a suburb of Chicago.'

'Oh!' A look of lively interest. 'I've heard of Elm Park. Isn't that the place where Hemingway – ?'

'That's Oak Park. It's right next – '

'Here we go. I knew I'd find it. Brenda Bowman, Mrs. From 576 North Franklin Boulevard?'

'That's it.'

'All the way from Franklin Boulevard to the Franklin Court Arms.' She gave a dry little laugh and threw back her head in an animated way.

'I hadn't thought of that,' Brenda said.

'I'll tell you what I'll do. I'm going to make a little note here that you're really part of the Chicago delegation.'

'Fine,' Brenda said, feeling happier and liking the sound of the word delegation. 'Thank you.'

'Everything looks A-OK, Mrs. Bowman. You're all registered now. And we received your cheque for the fee. Just a min and I'll type you out a receipt on the spot.'

'Oh, you don't need to bother with – '

'You'll need it when tax time rolls round.' Her bright eyes rolled upwards. 'You can deduct it on your form. It's a valid deduction.'

'I keep forgetting about things like that,' Brenda said. 'I've only been paying taxes for the last two years.' She gave a laugh, more girlish than she'd intended.

'Every penny counts these days.'

'That's right,' Brenda said with enthusiasm.

'And your exhibit? It's quilts, right?'

'I've got them with me,' Brenda pointed to the large carton beside her suitcase. 'Right here.'

'If you want to leave it with me, I'll make sure it gets looked after.'

'Oh, that would be wonderful. I'd really appreciate it. It's so bulky – '

'And here's your name tag. We've got this new kind with adhesive backing this year. You just peel off the strip and stick it on your coat. They won't poke holes in your clothes like last year. We had I don't know how many complaints. So we switched to these – '

'I didn't come last year. In fact, this is my first time – '

'And here's your kit, all ready for you. As you can see, it's got your name on it already.'

'That's beautiful. The kit, I mean.'

'Isn't it gorgeous? It was designed for us in New York. Sort of captures the craft theme, we all thought – '

'With that textured look – '

'And the earth tones. We asked for earth tones.'

'I like earth tones,' Brenda heard herself saying.

'Now here, inside, you have your map of Philadelphia. Courtesy of the Tourist Board, bless their hearts. You been to Philly before? It doesn't matter, it's easy to get around here. And here's your bumper-sticker.'

'Bumper-sticker?'

'It says "I'm a Quilter." We've got versions for the weavers too, and the spinners. That's the one I like – "I'm a Spinner."'

'Are you a spinner?'

'Oh no, not me. I'm the PR person for the Association. Betty Vetter. I should have introduced myself before now. I got the idea for the bumper-stickers last year, and they were a real hit.'

'Oh,' Brenda said, smiling across the welcome desk at Betty Vetter.

'Besides the map and the bumper-sticker you'll find a card listing the inner-city churches and synagogues, the service of your choice, courtesy of the Interfaith Council of Phil – '

'I don't think I'll need – '

'And, in case you've got some time on your hands, which I very much doubt – we've got a great programme this year – but, just in case, there's some touristy info. They've got one of those Ye Olde Walking Tours. Which is supposed to be excellent. All run by volunteers. Women who really know their stuff.'

'That sounds – '

'And a little sewing kit, thread, needles. And here's one of those disposable raincoats. Donated by one of the yarn companies. You never know, it might come in handy. Although I see you brought a raincoat.'

'Yes. At least it's supposed to be showerproof – '

'And here's a make-up kit, sample lipstick, sample blush, what have you. Donated by New Women Industries of Houston – '

'Thank you,' Brenda said, hearing her thank-you drowned by the hotel fountain, which seemed to be pumping and splashing more furiously now. For an instant she imagined she felt a fine spray reaching the back of her neck.

'And here's the brochure on theatres in town. *Mame* is playing; that's always good entertainment. And some new thing about a man dying. If you want tickets to anything, just talk to them at the desk. And here's your directory. You've got the name of everyone taking part in the Exhibition, plus their spouses or whatever. You don't have any accompanying person with you, do you?'

'No,' Brenda said, resting her eyes on Betty Vetter's tiny brown earrings. 'No,' she said more loudly. 'I'm here on my own.'

'Wonderful, wonderful,' Betty Vetter said. Besides the earrings she wore a man's antique pocket-watch on a chain around her neck, and when she leaned forward to write, it bumped softly against the desk. Her hands were reddish, thin, without rings, and under her eyes there were small, scaly pouches, which were oddly attractive. 'Since you're alone,' she said to Brenda, leaning forward on her elbows, 'could I ask you one great big favour?'

'Of course,' Brenda said, wanting to be helpful.

'Well, it seems we've got a' – Betty Vetter paused and pursed her lips – 'a leetle bit of a problem on our cotton-pickin' hands.'

'Oh?'

'What happened is, we're the victims of our own crazy success. Everyone had such a great time last year that, well, all of a sudden we've got more people registering than we thought we'd get in a million years. I mean, they're literally coming out of the woodwork. And with the spouses and accompanying persons, well, it looks like everyone wanted to come to Philadelphia, Pennsylvania all of a sudden. Anyway, to make a long story short, the Franklin is seriously over-booked.'

'Oh?' Brenda said again.

'We had to get some extra rooms at the Holiday Inn and even at the Travelodge. The problem is really because of the metallurgists.'

'The metallurgists?'

'Metallurgists. International Society of. They're overlapping with us, wouldn't you know it. Hundreds of them. What I'd like to ask you, Mrs. Bowman – or is it okay if I just call you Brenda?'

'Brenda's fine,' Brenda said quickly.

'And you call me Betty. Everyone does. Crazy Betty, the wild woman. I know it's sort of inconvenient, Brenda, and I hate like hell to even suggest it, but, well, would you mind very much if you had to share a room?'

'Share a room? Well, I . . . ' Brenda's voice stopped working. She could feel the dryness of her lips.

'Like, we've got quite a few women here on their own who're doubling up. And it isn't as if they're really strangers. I mean, we're all part of the craft movement, right? So it's not like they're, you know, untrustworthy. We feel sure that – '

'It's not that.'

'And,' Betty Vetter's voice hurried on, 'it's not for long. Only five nights. And you know how much time you spend in a hotel room when you're at a conference. Hardly any at all – just to sleep, really, and take your shower. Furthermore,' she took a breath and tugged at her watch,' it goes without saying that the room rate would be way down. Let's see, you were originally booked at $41 per day. If you share a room it would be $32. I've had the absolute assurance of the management here that we could get it for $32. That's a net saving of, let's see, $41 take away –'

'Nine dollars.'

'Nine dollars.'

'It's not the money, ' Brenda said.

'Well, then? The ballpoint pen paused, hooked in air.

'It's just –'

Damn it, damn it. Brenda felt tired. She *was* tired. She was expecting her period; that always made the backs of her legs ache. And the Philadelphia airport had been enormous and oddly organized, so different from O'Hare, and the air-freight man had been abrupt, almost, in fact, impolite. Her red raincoat was wrinkled down the front, and there was a tiny spot on the collar which just might be grease. Yes, she was tired. She wanted to lie down on a bed and close her eyes. And she had visualized – for a month she had visualized – a small room of her own, a single bed, severely made up with hotel linen, almost a nun's bed. A chair in one corner, and a table where she might, if she liked, have coffee and muffins in the morning. Bran muffins. There would be a long, narrow window which overlooked a street; this street would be faintly historical and there would be a wall of pinkish brick opposite; and a street lamp probably, one of those ornate old iron –

It was not to be. A wave of disappointment struck her. She looked at Betty Vetter, who sat waiting. She tried to smile at her, and did. Betty Vetter smiled back. Suddenly all that was left of her disappointment was a mild pang of regret – and even that began almost immediately to recede. The plate of muffins spun off into space. The fountain behind her bubbled cheerfully.

'I can't tell you, Brenda, how much we do appreciate this. I mean – the fact is, I don't know what else we can do at this moment in time.'

'It really isn't that important –'

'That's great. That's terrific. Frankly, that's the spirit we were hoping for. But you'd be surprised how many people don't adjust to the idea of – '

'It's only for five nights after all.'

'And we all of us believe in the same thing.'

'Uh-huh,' Brenda said inadequately.

'They'll give you your key at the desk. It's room 2424.' She gave Brenda a twinkly look and said, 'Hope you're not scared of heights.'

'Oh, no. Heights never – '

'And your roommate will be, let's see, Verna Glanville. Another quilter.'

'Did you say Verna Glanville?'

'She's a great girl. You're going to get along like a house – '

'From Norfolk, Virginia?'

'I think so.'

'Verna of Virginia. That's the name she goes by. Professionally.'

'Is that right? She checked in a couple of hours ago, and she was a really good sport. About the balls-up with the rooms. "The more the merrier," she said. That was when I asked her if she'd mind sharing a room –'

'It's really funny,' Brenda said, 'but you know I was just reading an article about her the other day. Verna of Virginia. About a quilt she's just sold to the Metropolitan Museum in New York – '

'She's pretty well known in her field – '

'Oh, she's one of the best, the very best – '

' – and a smile for everyone, that's how she struck me.'

'I was hoping I'd get a chance to meet her. And now, here I'm going to be – '

'One more thing, Mrs. Bowman. Brenda. They asked us to have everyone meet in the Constitution Room at four sharp for the rundown on the programme. That's just one floor up. The Mezzanine. It's just going on four now, so if you want to go there directly, I'll send your baggage up to your room.'

'Thank you so much' – Brenda paused – 'Betty.'

'It's nothing.'

'I really appreciate – '

'No trouble at all. Glad to help out. That's what we're here for.

Chapter Eight

THE LOBBY OF THE FRANKLIN COURT ARMS, WITH ITS BITTER-
green carpeting and its natural-wood walls, reminds Brenda
of the out-of-doors, in particular of a corner of Columbus Park
in Chicago where she and Jack and the children used to go for
walks on summer evenings. There are large potted plants –
trees really – and near the Welcome desk, the big noisy fountain
made of stainless steel sheets and glass tubes. Everywhere
the lighting falls with a soft-tinted focus that seems to emit,
along with its invisibility, a kind of purring sound. The stairs
that rise to the mezzanine level – the convention floor – are
made of light-coloured wood. Oak perhaps, Brenda thinks. The
steps are exceptionally thick, with open risers; she almost
floats on her way up. Baskets of greenery hang overhead, most
of them of a variety Brenda doesn't recognize, pale-green,
feathery, threaded with light. Some kind of fern almost
certainly.

The Constitution Room is rapidly filling up with people; most
of them, Brenda notices, are women. Well, that was to be
expected. There are two or three men sitting together on one
side, and there is a handsome man with a grey beard standing
at the front, gesticulating largely. At the far end of the room is a
platform draped with beige-and-brown burlap panels – the
same burlap used on the kitbag which she carries in her hand.
Folding chairs have been lined up in curved rows, hundreds of
them, most of them occupied, and hotel attendants are struggling to fit one more row in at the back. The room echoes with
voices, a friendly-sounding hubbub bouncing off the smooth
walls and rising to the wood-arched ceiling, where three chandeliers twinkle and glitter. Brenda touches her name card with
the tip of her finger and looks for a place to sit down.

'Shhhh,' a woman is saying. 'Shhh.'

'They're trying to get started up there.'

'Ladies and gentleman – '

'What man?' A raucous laugh.

'Excuse me,' Brenda whispers. 'Is this seat taken?'

'I'm saving it for someone. She's coming in a minute or two.'

'Sorry.'

'Shhh.'

'Ladies and gentlemen, can we please come to order.'

'Excuse me, is anyone sitting here?'

''Fraid so.'

'Can you hear me in the back of the room? If you can't hear, would you mind putting up your hand. Testing, one, two, three.'

'Sounds okay,' a hoarse voice calls out, 'but what about some more chairs back here.'

'They're coming,' a man's voice says. 'They should be here in a few minutes.'

'If I could have your attention – '

'Excuse me, Madam Chairman, Madam Chair*person*, rather.' It is the same hoarse voice, booming from a back corner of the room.

Brenda feels a tug on her sleeve and hears a sweet voice saying, 'There's an empty place over here.'

'Oh, thank you.'

'I'm Lenora Knox. From Sante Fe.' She wears glasses with pale blue frames, and her hair is brown and slightly wavy.

'Oh, you've come a long way.' Brenda says this in a social way.

'And you're . . . ?' Lenora smiles pressingly. Her features are tiny.

'Brenda Bowman. From Chicago. Well, the Chicago area – '

'I've never been to Chicago. But someday we hope – I mean with the Art Institute and everything – '

'Will the Fourth Annual National Handicrafts Exhibition please come to order. '

'What are you in?' Lenora Knox whispers in her girlish voice.

'Quilts.'

'Me too!'

'Really?'

'Isn't that a coincidence. We'll have to get together and have coffee and really talk quilts.'

'Madam Chairperson, may I pose a question?' It is the voice again.

'Out of order.'

'Not on the agenda.'

'It so happens,' the voice persists, 'that this is a matter of the greatest urgency. Which I am sure the Chair will recognize if she will just give me a chance to speak.'

'I'm afraid – ' The chairperson is a stout blonde woman of about forty. She has a soft, pretty face and an air of calm.

'May I assure the Chair that this is a question that concerns each and every one of us here.'

'Who's that?' Brenda whispers.

'I don't know.' Lenora Knox has a way of speaking that is sweet and small and clean. 'This is my first time at one of these things.'

'Mine too.'

'I had no idea there'd be this many people.'

Brenda looks around. One of these women must be Verna Glanville, Verna of Virginia. If only she knew what she looked like. Too bad there hadn't been a picture –

'Order, order.'

'I humbly request – '

'The Chair recognizes Charlotte Dance.'

'Madam Chairperson. I thank you for your cooperation, and I think that when you hear – '

'But can you make it brief, Char. And non-political. This is supposed to be an orientation session.'

For some reason, which Brenda doesn't understand, there is loud laughter at this. Even Charlotte Dance laughs in a deep New England-sounding way. 'All I ask is for a mere two minutes.'

'Go ahead. You've got the floor.'

'Whew! The problem I want to raise is not exactly political but it does concern us because it concerns the violation of our rights as women – '

Cheering. One or two groans.

'It seems that the hotel, the hotel which we have *favoured* with our exhibition – I speak of the Franklin Court Arms – it seems this hotel has proven itself no different from any other male-dominated commercial institution – '

'Do you think you could get to the point, Charlotte.' The chairperson is smiling broadly. 'We've only got this room for one hour and it's already – '

'Perhaps some of you here are aware that there is a serious problem with accommodation.'

A scattering of applause at this.

'It seems we are being told by the management of this hotel that there are not enough hotel rooms for all of us. And this in spite of the fact that our organization has had bookings, *confirmed bookings*,' she pauses, 'for several months.'

'What room are you in?' Lenora whispers.

'2424,' Brenda whispers back.

'Were you asked to share with someone?'

'Yes, I – '

'Me too.'

'I wish to direct the Chair's attention to the fact that quite a number of us have been asked to double up, and let me say that this in itself is fine. I have no objection to doubling up. But quite a lot of our membership is also being asked to stay at the Ramada Inn, which just happens to be two miles from here. Two miles! Naturally, I inquired the reason for this. And it appears we have been – I believe the word is bumped – by the International Society of Metallurgists. Does the Chair agree that this is what has, in fact, occurred?'

'There does seem to be a problem with overbooking. I was told an hour or so ago that some of our members will be bussed free of charge – '

'In spite of the fact that we had the prior bookings, we are now being asked to give way to another body – '

'I think it was only those with accompanying persons – '

'Excuse me, Madam Chairperson, but what I wish to point out, loudly and clearly, is the fact that we are an organization which is made up almost entirely of women – '

'Not entirely, Charlotte my duck,' came a good-natured male voice – the grey beard – from the front row.

'Pardon me. An organization, *mainly* made up of women, is being asked to give way to an organization which just happens – just happens – to be almost entirely made up of men.'

There is loud cheering. Foot-stamping. Applause. Brenda and Lenora exchange looks. Lenora looks frightened. The Chair raps for order.

'I know I've been asked to be as brief as possible,' Charlotte Dance continues, 'and I think, having said what I've just said, that there's no need to say any more. The very fact that this has been allowed to happen says it all. The circumstances themselves are enough to point to a blatant lack of moral responsibility on the part of the management of this hotel, and I would like to propose setting up a committee to look into the matter at once – this evening if possible.'

'Count me in.'

'We're with you, Charlotte.'

'And to those of you from the press – I presume that the press is in attendance – I would be happy to get together with you after this meeting and discuss further manifestations – '

'Thank you, Char, for bringing this to our attention. I think we'd better get to the programme now. We have a number of items to deal with – '

'Question.'

'I'm, afraid we just can't allow any further – '

'One question. That's all, I promise.' The speaker is a woman in front of Brenda who has risen and is holding up her arms. She is young – at least she looks young from the back – and has long, black hair falling to her waist. She is wearing a knitted shawl in tones of purple and mauve. Could this possibly be Verna of Virginia?

'Let her talk. Give her a minute.'

'All right.' A sigh comes whistling through the microphone. 'One question only, and one minute only, too. Then, I'm afraid – '

'I want to protest, on behalf of every woman in this room – '

'Will you kindly state your name, please, for the record.'

'Margaret Malone, Atlanta Craft Guild.'

'The Chair recognizes Margaret Malone.'

'She's gorgeous,' Lenora Knox breathes.

Brenda nods. 'Yes.'

'I wish to protest the so-called gift we have all received today from a group calling itself New Women Industries. I speak' – and she holds up the make-up kit – 'of this, this gratuitous tribute to traditional female vanity.'

'You tell 'em.' Charlotte Dance is on her feet again.

'I wish to inquire,' Margaret Malone continues, 'whether the International Society of Metallurgists has also been given little bundles of . . . of goodies like this. Like aftershave lotion, for instance. Or some good, manly, seductive cologne.'

'You know, she's got a point,' Lenora Knox says quietly.

'You've raised a valid point,' the chairperson says, 'but we really have to – '

'I just happen to have here in my hand a large green garbage bag, which I propose, with the permission of the Chair, to put in the back of the room. If anyone would like to part with this unasked-for gift from' – she pauses – 'New Women Industries, perhaps you will join me in – '

'Thank you very much. I'm sure we all appreciate what it is you're saying – '

Suddenly everyone in the room is talking. Some of them are getting up and walking to the back of the room where the garbage bag has been placed. Brenda thinks of joining them but worries about losing her seat. The chairperson's gavel is going up and down, but the microphone system appears to have broken down. On one side of the room a woman is climbing up on a chair. Someone else is helping her up; and now she has started talking. Brenda strains to hear what she is saying, but with all the noise she can scarcely make it out. Something about abortion legislation. Something about basic rights in the states of Mississippi and Alabama. Someone else in the room seems to be crying; or perhaps she is only shouting to be heard. There is an electronic squawk from the sound system; the room seems to Brenda to be tilting. Two or three women are singing in the back of the room. 'The Battle Hymn of the Republic'? *Glory, glory, Hallelujah.* Someone is laughing hysterically. The man with the grey beard is whispering into Charlotte Dance's ear. Charlotte Dance has placed her hands on her hips. Her mouth has gone slack; her head is rocking back and forth.

'Heavens,' Lenora Knox says in her sweet voice.

Chapter Nine

THE MAN IN THE ELEVATOR WITH BRENDA, RIDING UP TO the twenty-fourth floor, was wearing a pinstriped suit. She regarded it appraisingly out of the corner of her eye; she had recently talked Jack into buying a pinstriped suit, and this one was really quite similar in cut, only a dark blue instead of brown.

As it happened, the man in the suit was getting off at the twenty-fourth floor too, and as though this coincidence were some sort of joke they shared, he sent Brenda a fleeting, absentminded smile. On his breast pocket she saw a small plasticized card: International Metallurgical Society. One of those, she thought, and eyed him more sharply. His name in smaller print was on the card as well, but Brenda, stepping out of the elevator, didn't catch it, and felt it would be impossible to stare too closely. And what did it matter anyway? He moved off down the hall in one direction, and she, more hesitantly, in the other. The twenty-fourth floor; she thought of Betty Vetter asking if she were afraid of heights, and then, with a shade of triumph, she remembered the young man on the plane, the one with the pink gums. How would he, with his whining fears, like being put on the twenty-fourth floor?

Once, when the Historical Society met in New York, she and Jack had stayed on the thirty-third floor of a downtown hotel, and lying in bed they had imagined they could feel the building sway slightly in the wind. She had not felt at all afraid; she had liked the idea of the slim steel tower bending a lean quarter-inch in the gale, of feeling herself part of that minute technical surrender. Heights could actually make you feel safe – everything was left behind, the lobby and coffee shops and bars were all miles away. Up here the rooms were unmoored and loosened into their own sweep of darkness. It was utterly quiet in the corridor.

Brenda pulled the heavy key out of her raincoat pocket to check the number. Room 2424 must be at the end of the hall;

yes, there it was, the room next to the ice machine. She was anxious to open the door, to get her shoes off – the right shoe especially, which was too tight across the toes; she should remember never to buy Italian shoes, even when they were on sale. It wasn't worth it.

Would Verna of Virginia have arrived? Brenda hoped not. She was looking forward to meeting her, but at the same time she wanted, needed, a few minutes to herself. She would take off her shoes, and perhaps her skirt as well. There was an hour and a half before the reception. Time to slide between the sheets, enough time, if she wanted, to shut her eyes and allow herself the luxury of a few minutes' sleep. A short nap could be amazingly revitalizing; ten minutes of what Jack's father always referred to as 'shut-eye' could do wonders. (Occasionally, if they were going out in the evening, Jack would stretch out for a few minutes first.) It was a good thing she had brought along her little travel clock; if she set the alarm for six she would still have time for a shower before the reception. That is, if Verna wasn't in the room.

But Verna *was* in the room. She was lying on her back on one of the twin beds.

At least Brenda assumed it must be Verna. There was a woman, at any rate, without any clothes on, lying on the bed next to the window. The lights were turned on – a lamp on the dresser, a floor lamp in one corner – but it was altogether impossible for Brenda to see Verna's face – or much of her body, for that matter – since there was a man lying on top of her. He was unclothed as well. He had smooth, muscled shoulders, Brenda noted, and a broad, oval back. She perceived moderate hairiness and white skin beneath. And a pair of buttocks which were reddish in colour and rather small. It always came as a surprise to her to realize how small male buttocks were.

From the bed came the sound of music. No, it wasn't music, it was moaning – his or hers Brenda was unable to tell for sure. The curtains were partly open. It was five o'clock in the afternoon, dark outside, wintery. The man's buttocks rose and fell in a strenuous, fitful way. Verna's (Verna's?) long legs kicked outward, then closed over the hairy back, the feet locking together. Brenda thought of statuary, something mounted on a heavy pedestal in the middle of a park, a Henry Moore, all angles and openings. There was another low moan, almost a whisper, then the drier sound of panting and thrashing, and a woman's muffled cry: 'Almost, almost.'

Brenda regarded them for perhaps two or three seconds. The word *humping*, a word she had never used, struck her with a wallop; nevertheless, she felt extraordinarily calm. Her suitcase had been brought up, she noticed. There it was, standing primly between the two beds. Over the beds was a framed picture, a still life, fruit, what looked like apricots, and –

An instant later she was in the corridor again. She had managed to close the door behind her without making a sound. Nearby, just around the corner, someone was rattling the ice machine. She glanced down the length of the hall, which seemed endlessly and unnaturally serene. Every door was closed – a series of smooth slabs, proclaiming privacy, decency. And behind those false doors: she had a dazzling multiple vision of fierce couplings, strange wet limbs coming together, muffled cries, inhuman late-afternoon murmurings. Peaks of ecstasy. Randomness. Accident. Risk. She had a glimpse down a deep historical hole containing millions of couplings – it was bottomless. She dropped the room key back into her pocket and leaned, swaying slightly, against the wall; her teeth for some reason were chattering.

'Locked out?' someone was asking her. It was the man in the pinstriped suit, carrying a plastic ice-bucket in his hand. He spoke in a merry voice, a neighbourly voice. 'No, ' she told him.

He came to a halt in front of her and peered at her rather closely. 'Well, then, can I . . . Is there something the matter?'

He was looking into her eyes. Intently. Perhaps he thought she was drunk. Or sick. The size of her pupils? And there was the matter of her teeth chattering. She was, in fact, shaking all over.

'Perhaps you should sit down,' he advised kindly. The pin-stripes danced before her, hurting her eyes. She observed that the knot of his blue-and-maroon tie was luxurious and silky.

'Yes,' she nodded, and waved a vague hand. Where?

'Or maybe you'd like me to call someone for you?'

'Call someone?'

'They must have a hotel doctor. Or a nurse. Or someone like that on call.'

'I don't need a doctor,' Brenda said, dazed by this suggestion.

'I just thought, well, that perhaps you weren't feeling well
. . .'

'I'm just . . . a little dizzy, I think.'

'Look, why don't you let me see you to your room. Make sure
you're all right.'

'This is my room. Right here.' As proof, Brenda patted the
smooth wood of the door.

'I see.' He waited.

'I'm really feeling better now.' Why didn't he go away, just
take his ice-bucket and go away? 'I mean, I'm not feeling dizzy
at all now.'

'Good, that's good.' He was a slightly built man, not much
taller than she was. His brown eyes were alert, lively, worried,
and his hair – Brenda always noticed hair, just as Leah Wallberg
noticed cheekbones – was a mixture of brown and grey, exceptionally thick, the hair of a healthy man. A man in his late
forties, Brenda imagined.

'I'll be just fine.' She did feel better, and for some reason was
now on the verge of laughter. Nerves probably. Don't laugh,
she instructed herself.

'Look,' he said after a pause. 'I was just going to make myself
a drink. Would you like to come along – I'm just down the hall a
little way – and join me?'

'Oh, thank you but – '

'You could sit down for a few minutes, pull yourself together – '

'Really, I'm fine.' She shook her head hard to prove it.

'If you're concerned about me, I promise I'm not a rapist or a
murderer or anything.' As though to confirm this, he touched
the card which announced him a member of the metallurgical
profession. 'If you sit down a minute or two, maybe have a
drink, you'll be fine.'

'But I am fine – '

'To tell the truth, if you don't mind my saying so, you still
look a bit on the shaky side.'

'Really.'

'Sometimes these damn elevators bother people, these
heights . . . ' He smiled in his merry way, and Brenda thought,
what a kind man, what a thoughtful man, to have thought of
the elevators.

'Actually,' she started to explain – she owed him some sort of

66

explanation – 'it's such a funny thing. The thing that just happened.'

'Funny peculiar or – '

'Both.'

'Well . . . ' He waited, smiling quizzically. The way in which his front teeth overlapped made Brenda feel friendly toward him.

'Not exactly funny.' She stopped; smiled. 'Sort of – '

'Bizarre?'

'Bizarre, yes, that's the word for it. Surreal too. And,' now she was starting to laugh, she couldn't help herself, 'and I guess just plain, well, funny.'

She recalled the red buttocks, firm as apples, cheerful, though oddly menacing. She began to laugh even harder. She leaned against the wall, her head rolling back and forth, her mouth open. She must sound crazy; this man in the striped suit, hanging on to his bucket of ice cubes, must think she was insane.

But he didn't appear to. He began to laugh along with her, in a manner which was easy and companionable. Brenda couldn't imagine why. She could hear his ice cubes rattle, a nice social sound, restorative and normal. She took a breath.

'It *would* be nice,' she said. 'Having a drink, I mean.'

'Good. Great. I'm just down this way. Next to the elevator.'

'This is very nice of you. I mean, when I don't even know – '

'It's my pleasure.' He took her elbow, a gesture she felt she should find alarming, but for some reason didn't. His voice sounded faintly English, the way he pronounced elevator – elevatah.

He had a double room. Over the beds were more pictures of fruit, wobbly-looking and bruised and lost in the bottoms of deep pottery bowls. There was a suitcase on a rack, the lid up, a necktie dragging out, rumpled underwear. In one corner a swag lamp hung over a smooth brown armchair of padded vinyl. 'Why don't you sit there,' he suggested, helping her off with her coat and folding it neatly across one of the beds. He did not say, what a lovely coat, or, did you know you have beautiful cheekbones. He said, 'Please. Make yourself at home.'

'Isn't it strange!' Brenda sat down and immediately felt sharp pains piercing the back of her knees. It had been a long day. She leaned forward and with one hand rubbed the instep of her right foot. Would it be impolite to take off her shoe? Probably.

'Strange?' He was standing by a table, slipping glasses out of their paper wrappers.

'Being here, I mean. Having a drink. When I don't even know your – '

'Barry Ollershaw. I should have said earlier. Sorry.'

Barry. It was a name she had never particularly liked. As a name it lacked seriousness; something about it that was fetching and coy. 'And you're from – ' she asked politely.

'From Vancouver, B.C. That's Canada.'

'That's supposed to be beautiful,' Brenda said, not entirely sure where Vancouver, B.C., was. Mountains . . . ? She wondered suddenly what she was doing in this man's room, and involuntarily her eyes went to the door.

'Would you like me to leave the door open?' Barry Ollershaw asked her.

'It's not that – '

'We used to have to do that back at university. In the fraternity house. When we entertained girls in our rooms – that was the word we used, entertain – we were supposed to leave the door ajar.' (He pronounced it ajah.) 'House rules. Of course, that was back in the fifties. Almost the dark ages.'

'Really?' Her nervous laugh again.

'I wouldn't blame you for being uneasy. Good God, when you read the newspapers – so if you'd rather have the door open . . . '

'It's fine the way it is.' Rapists and murderers didn't look like this: relaxed, intelligent, wearing name tags. What did they look like? She felt sure she could tell.

'Is gin okay? I'm afraid it's all I've got. And tonic water and a little bitter lemon, that's about it.'

'Tonic is fine. I like tonic.' She was babbling, as bad as Hap Lewis. 'With not too much gin.'

'How's this?'

'Perfect. I'm glad you came along when you did. I really was feeling dizzy.'

'Cheers.' He lifted his glass.

'Pardon? Oh, cheers.'

'And you are,' he peered down at her name card, 'Brenda Bowman. Of the Chicago Craft Guild.'

'Yes.' She was beginning to relax. 'How do you do.'

He perched on the side of the bed and faced her, his drink cradled in his hands. 'And now I hope to hear about this strange and bizarre and surreal thing that made you dizzy.'

'It's going to be an awful letdown, I'm afraid. To tell the truth, it seems sort of silly now.'

'I could use some light entertainment. I've been in meetings all afternoon.'

'You're not' – she looked him in the eye, brown eyes, reddish eyebrows – 'you're not prudish by any chance?'

'Prudish? I've never been accused of it. Do I look as though I might be prudish?'

'Well I've never met any Canadians.'

Why had she said a ridiculous thing like that? What was the matter with her? And it wasn't even true – there was Bill Lawless at the Institute. He came from Winnipeg, and he certainly wasn't prudish. In fact –

'Well?' Barry Ollershaw said, and gave his glass an encouraging swirl.

'Well,' Brenda began, 'I should explain first that I'm here with the National Handicrafts Exhibition.'

'So I gathered. Your name tag.'

'And I was supposed to have a room of my own. But for some reason there weren't enough rooms to go around. As a matter of fact, there's a rumour going around that we've been bumped by the International Society of – '

'Say no more. I know all about it. I've just come from a committee meeting, and it seems we're really in the shit.'

'So they asked me at the Welcome Desk if I'd mind sharing a room. With another quiltmaker. That's what I do. Quilts.'

'I'm nuts about quilts. My mother used to make quilts. And my aunt. Patchwork. Of course they wouldn't be in the same class. Anyway, go on.'

'I didn't know this other quilter, except by reputation. I mean, we'd never met. But when I went up to the room, well, there she was.'

'Yes?'

'When I walked in the door just now, there she was – but she wasn't . . . alone.' Brenda was having trouble with her mouth, which felt oddly loose and moist. And she wasn't sure where to look.

'She wasn't alone.' Barry Ollershaw repeated this as though it were a mere statement.

'As a matter of fact, she didn't even see me come in. She was . . . well . . . with a man. Making . . . you know . . . love.'

'Aha!' Barry's head went back. 'Yes, I do see.'

'You do?'

'Even we Canadians – '

'It was just, I don't know how to explain it, just sort of surprising. But only for a minute or two. I guess I was a little overwhelmed. I mean, it was the last thing I expected. When I opened that door. The lights were all on. Only now – ' Brenda had started laughing again. A drop of gin spilled on her suit skirt and she brushed at it with her hand.

'Only now?'

'Now, well, it just seems funny. Absurd. Crazy when you stop to think about it.'

Barry smiled broadly and shook his head appreciatively.

'Position one?' he asked abruptly.

'Pardon?'

'Missionary position? Is that how they were – missionary position?'

'Actually,' Brenda paused and took a gulp of gin, 'yes.' She drained her glass quickly and stared past Barry Ollershaw's head at the fruit on the wall.

'I can imagine it must have been something of a surprise.'

'And when you think about it in the abstract – '

'Think about what?'

'Sex. In the abstract it really is a little bit, I don't know, ludicrous.'

'The beast with two backs.' Another statement.

'What? Oh yes, that's right. So you know what I mean then?'

'I do. It's a sort of joke on the human race. To keep us humble. But who knows, maybe in ten million years, if we last that long, we'll evolve toward something a little more . . . graceful.'

'Like fish,' Brenda heard herself saying. 'I was just reading an article about fish – I think it was in *Newsweek*, maybe you saw it. About fish eggs just sort of . . . expelled . . . and spreading out like fans in the water.'

'Would you like another drink?'

'Maybe some tonic water, if you've got enough. I don't know why I'm so thirsty. Nerves probably. But I don't want to keep you. You've probably got something – ' She held her breath. The last thing she wanted to do was to get up out of this chair.

'Nothing until eight. So please have another. To keep me company. Here, let me get it for you.'

Perhaps she could take her shoes off. At least the right one. On second thought –

'Are you married?' she said to Barry Ollershaw's back. He was busily shaking more ice into her glass, somewhat awkwardly trying to avoid using his fingers.

'Yes,' he told her.

'So am I. And it's funny. I've been married for twenty years, a long time. But I've never seen, never actually seen, anyone – anyone else that is – making love. Isn't that odd when you think about it.'

'A little, I suppose, considering what a common activity it is. But probably not all that strange.'

'I'm glad to hear you say that. Because it suddenly seems very strange to me.'

'Well,' he said, turning around, 'of course some people go in for mirrors on the ceiling and that sort of thing.' He said this in a slow, speculative way which made Brenda wonder if he might be one of those people.

'I suppose.'

'And there are always movies. Blue movies, I mean. Sometimes at stag parties – but I don't imagine you go to stag parties.'

'But that's not quite the same thing as . . . as actually being in the room where two people – '

'I suppose not. But then, most kids, growing up, come across their parents once or twice, by accident – '

'Did you ever?' She thought of the mother who made quilts.

'Once, as a matter of fact. My brother and I. Of course it was dark, so we didn't see much. Just bedclothes moving around, that sort of thing. I can remember how it affected my brother and me. I think we were half hysterical, laughing like crazy, but at the same time deeply shocked.

'I think that's how I felt today.'

'And *your* parents? Didn't you ever – ?'

'The thing was, I never really had a father.'

'Oh?' His face showed interest. Halfway through his second gin and tonic, his look of merriment sparkled even more brightly, and Brenda wondered if this might be some social trick of his, professional and perfected – always respond, always radiate energy. What was it a metallurgist did, anyway? Something with metal – testing it probably.

'That is,' she said carefully, 'my mother never really got married.'

'I see.' An emphatic nod, brown eyes held still.

'Of course, there must have been someone once. Not that my mother ever talked about it. But there was never anyone else – not that I know of anyway.'

'Hmmm.'

Why lately, was she making such a point of telling people, especially strangers, about this, her lack of a father? This was the second time today; she would have to watch that. Was this the only interesting thing she had to confide, the only thing about her that set her apart: her fatherless state? She couldn't, having read a number of magazine articles on psychology, entirely dismiss the idea of exhibitionism, and what lay just beneath it. The desire to shock? Or maybe she just wanted to impress people with how easily she had absorbed this supposed psychic trauma. People went into therapy over things like this. Endless years with shrinks, nightmares, neuroses. People placed ads in the newspapers, hoping to find their lost fathers, hoping to complete themselves somehow. They hired detectives. And they tormented their mothers with questions and accusations. But not she, no, not she. She preened herself on the robustness of her mental health – just as she flaunted her lack of fear of heights.

Barry Ollershaw gave a little cough. 'So there was no one – no man anyway – in the picture?'

'Never. So, needless to say, I never came across – and, of course, now at home – '

'Yes?'

'Well, we have a lock on our bedroom door.'

'Oh?' His bright look. 'A good idea.'

'Well,' she felt she had to explain, 'the lock was there when we moved into our house, just one of those little hooks. We thought it was funny at first, my husband and I, but later, when the children got older – '

'Of course.'

'Well, anyway, nothing like this has happened to me before, walking into a room like that. I'm just glad they didn't see me.

72

At least, I'm fairly sure they didn't notice me coming in. I mean, what do you say in a situation like that?'

'Maybe, "Please don't let me disturb you."'

'Carry on folks.'

'Even if they had seen you,' Barry said, 'it would hardly have been your fault. They could have double-bolted the door if they really wanted privacy. That's what people usually do.'

Did they? Brenda supposed they did. 'Maybe it was just, you know, unpremeditated.'

'Maybe. Human nature being what it is.'

'That's an expression my husband Jack uses – human nature being what it is.'

'Are you hungry by any chance? I could have some food sent up, sandwiches, some coffee.'

Brenda almost leapt out of her chair. The reception. It was almost six-thirty. 'I've got to go,' she told Barry. Her feet, oh, her feet! 'Would you mind, would it be all right, if I used your bathroom, just to clean up a bit?' She touched her hair, pushed it back, reached for her coat on the bed.

'Of course not.' He stepped aside and indicated the way. His face seemed to Brenda to be innocent, to be scoured with trustworthiness. She felt she should say something, anything. 'I really appreciate your not raping or murdering me.'

In response he gave her a mock bow, and she noticed again the thickness of his hair. It was remarkable hair. Coarse as grass, with its own energy. She would like to have placed her hand on it for a minute to test its resilience. Then she remembered her desire, earlier, to reach out and touch the knee of the man on the plane. But she would never have done either of these things, she realized. Never.

Chapter Ten

AT THE RECEPTION THERE IS A FREE BAR, TABLES OF FOOD, and hundreds of people standing about eating and drinking, and talking. The blended sound of human voices is brain-numbing but pleasurable, and Brenda, arriving late and helping herself to a small, square sandwich, feels a surge of anticipation. Anything could happen.

There is something rubbery in the sandwich, herring probably. (She loves herring; at home she keeps a jar of it in the refrigerator and sometimes in the middle of the afternoon she dips her fingers in and helps herself to a slice.) There are pastries the size of her thumbnail, which ooze with orangey cheese. And something hot on toothpicks – what is it? – some kind of meatball thing with a slice of mushroom on top. Delicious. A waiter in a white uniform offers her a drink from a tray. 'Punch, madam?'

Brenda looks around the Republic Room for someone she knows, anyone at all. Lottie Hart should be here from the Chicago Craft Guild. At least she said she was coming, but that was two weeks ago. And Susan Hammerman – Susan Hammerman was on the national executive – she would be here for sure. Of course Brenda hardly knows Susan Hammerman; she has only met her once, and that was last spring at a reception in Chicago which had been large and noisy, rather like this reception in fact. Still it would be nice if – then Brenda catches sight of Betty Vetter standing only a few feet away. A familiar face; she tries to catch her eye, but Betty is talking to a waiter with a tray of punch cups. She is waving her arms – not exactly waving them, but taking little chops at the air in front of her – and Brenda hears the fervent rising end of a sentence which is: 'keeping in mind the contingency plan and allowing for possible cancellations.' It sounds like a serious and urgent conversation.

Behind Brenda two women are talking. One of them is saying: 'At least the programme looks better than last year. Meatier, if you know what I mean.' The other woman replies, half peevish, half nostalgic, 'Yes, but when these meetings first started, we knew everyone. Remember? Remember that first year in St. Louis? I'll just never forget it, the spirit there was . . . We knew absolutely everyone. And now – '

There was Susan Hammerman now, standing on the other side of the room. Beautiful – she looks beautiful, Brenda thinks. The swing of grey hair, expensively cut. That yellow silk dress. Not everyone can wear yellow, not after a certain age, it does something to the skin, but not Susan Hammerman's skin. Brenda sees that Susan Hammerman is deep in conversation with a group of women, and for a moment she considers joining them. She could interrupt with, 'I don't know if you remember me, but we met at the Craft Fair last spring.'

It is not very likely that Susan Hammerman *will* remember her, but she was from the same city and –

'Another drink? More punch, madam?'

'Not just yet, thanks.'

Brenda wonders if Verna of Virginia has come down to the reception. She might be here now, glowing, freshly showered, drinking a cool cup of punch; and *he* might be here too, standing at her side, looking ruddy and pleased with himself.

'Hi there, Brenda.' It's Lenora Knox from Santa Fe, appearing out of nowhere, smiling sweetly and wearing a long pink cotton skirt which is faintly wrinkled. The scent of musty flowers rises from her combed hair. Brenda comes close to embracing her. 'I don't know a soul here,' she tells Lenora, and the words settle on her own ears like a confession of inadequacy.

'Did you find your room all right, Brenda?' Lenora inquires.

'Yes,' Brenda pauses. 'How about you?'

'Well,' Lenora begins – and already Brenda knows it will be a long story – 'well, my roomie is from Texas, Fort Worth, real sweet, she designs needlepoint patterns. I guess they thought with both of us coming from the Southwest . . . but she's the shyest thing. I don't know what to do. She hardly says two words, just seems lost, you know. When I said, are you coming on down to the reception, she said, no, she didn't know anyone, so what was the use. I said, well that's how you meet people, that's the purpose behind these receptions, just to mix us all up and get us acquainted.'

'Brenda Bowman!' a powerful voice cries. It's Susan Hammerman's voice; and there she is, striding like an opera-singer across the room, dodging the waiter, dodging Betty Vetter, the yellow dress shining over her hips. 'I didn't know you were coming, Brenda. You should have let me know. I must say, the Chicago contingent isn't exactly out in force this year, is it? Lottie Hart had to cancel. Isn't this fabulous though, people from all over the country. I've just been talking to this marvellous woman from St. Paul, Minnesota, who started weaving at the age of sixty-five. Can you picture it, sixty-five? My God, if I can just keep going that long without the old fingers seizing up. It's really an inspiration, isn't it?'

'Yes,' Brenda says, 'it is.'

'It certainly is,' says Lenora Knox in her small, straight, oboe of a voice.

'It was my grandmother who got me started,' someone is telling Brenda. 'My grandmother on the maternal side. I used to think, poor old Nana and those poor old cronies of hers with their Tuesday sewing circle. I'd rather curl up and die than spend my life doing that kind of thing. I majored in biology, Missouri State. But my grandmother got me going on this. I was married at that time and had the kids. I just started with little things, time-filler sort of thing. I can honestly say that I had no idea in the beginning of the kind of satisfaction that comes from making something with your own hands, just making something out of nothing. Well, practically nothing. What's in this punch anyway? Rum? Sort of sneaks up on you, doesn't it? But now I think I really understand those women better, the sewing-circle women. All those afghans and aprons and potholders. Who's to say those women weren't artists? Folk artists, anyway. You're from Chicago, I see.'

'Yes,' Brenda says.

'I've got a brother in Chicago. Well, Riverside to be precise . . .'

'What I don't understand is how he got asked to be the Keynote Speaker. I mean, what does he know about anything?'

'I think he's going to talk about the new international trends in the craft market –'

'But what does he *know* about it. Sure, he may know about marketing, but there's selling and there's making.'

'Someone told me he was very amusing – '

'Amusing! Who needs amusing!'

Brenda helps herself to a small pickled artichoke heart and bites down into something hard at the centre. An almond. Who would have thought of that! She will have to remember to tell Bev Coulson about that. Bev will write it down on one of her cards and file it away with her other appetizer ideas. The last time she and Jack were at the Coulsons', Bev served curried soya balls, a vegetarian recipe she had adapted herself from something she and Roger had been served in Japan.

Is cooking an art? Brenda and Jack had discussed this afterwards, driving home. Jack said no, because it lacked permanence, even the pretence of permanence. Brenda said yes, cooking was an art because it appealed directly to the aesthetic sense and it involved aesthetic deliberations. (Lately she has grown more skilled at this kind of discussion.) Jack was doubtful, but agreed she might have a point. Brenda reminded him of origami, how impermanent origami was. She mentioned the string sculptures made by Eskimos. She reminded Jack how far Bev Coulson was from the days when she used to invite them to post-football suppers and serve them something called Crowd-pleasers, which were wet ground beef and beans on Toastmaster buns. 'True,' Jack said.

'So you're a quilter?' someone says to Brenda. 'Or should that be quiltmaker?'

'Either one,' Brenda says, feeling happy. 'Once at a party one of our neighbours introduced me to someone as "a quilter in her own right".'

'I just heard that Verna of Virginia was going to be here. Have you ever met her?'

'Well, no, but as a matter of fact – '

A man in a business suit tells Brenda, 'I'm what you call an accompanying person. Husband, that is. That's my wife over there in the white outfit. She's the crafty person in the family. Macramé. She was into macramé before it even started to take off. Now she teaches a class at the Y. It keeps her busy. Out of trouble. I'm in hydraulics. Just a small firm, two partners, secretarial staff. And we're doing our darnedest to keep it small. Things get so big and then they collapse on you. What's the joy in that? I was just reading this pocketbook, *Small is Beautiful*, and all the time I was reading it I was saying, right on, right on. Philadelphia's got a lot to recommend it, but who'd want to live here, right? Can I get you some more of this punch? I was just on my way over for a refill. Nice talking to you. Quite an affair, this.'

'No, it's true. Capricorns are more artistic than Geminis.'
  'Really?'

'I've been in crafts for eight years now,' a woman says. 'I learned when I was in the hospital. A therapist used to come in every day and give us instructions. Basic stuff, but I'd never learned to use my hands, so it was all new to me. I had had several electric-shock treatments and half the time I couldn't think straight, but my fingers at least could move. It was just like a dream when I look back on it. The yarn was just there in my hands, and this woman was helping my fingers to hang on to it. Some of the women hated it. They used to cry. One of them sat down in the middle of the floor and took off her shoes and wound the yarn around and around her legs. It was funny in a way. It took me about a month to finish my first piece. I kept falling asleep. But the second piece went faster, and the actual workmanship was a hundred per cent better; even I could tell the difference. They moved me to another unit and let me work as long as I wanted to on any one day. That was how I got started.'

' – the Crossland variation.'
  'But is it convincing?'
  'Yes and no.'

One woman asks, 'Say, do any of you know if they sorted out the mess with the rooms?'
  'I don't know,' Brenda replies. 'I haven't heard any more about it.'
  'Well,' someone volunteers, 'I heard the committee is going

to meet with the metallurgists in the morning. Of course, it's really the hotel management that's at fault.'

'But someone said the metallurgists were given the extra rooms because we got this room for the reception. It was some kind of deal they worked out.'

'Apparently *they* had to hold their reception downstairs in the Bavarian Cellar.'

'Really? Heavens, that's way down in the bowels of – '

'Nice atmosphere though. Informal. Conducive to conversation. This is really sort of overly formal.'

'That's for sure.'

Brenda's eyes sweep upwards, taking in the white scrollwork on the ceiling, the chandeliers, the Georgian moulding, the heavy blue velvet curtains caught back with curious gnarled hardware. An immense portrait of Benjamin Franklin hangs on one wall.

'Just look at the way he's peering down at us,' one of the women says.

'Those pink cheeks.'

'A great old man really. But that portrait makes him look like a country judge, not a man of genius.'

'Is it a true likeness,' Brenda wonders, 'or just a sort of idealized version . . . '

'He looks positively condemning, looking down at us guzzling up punch when we should be doing the early-to-bed early-to-rise deal.'

'A penny saved – '

'Was that one of Franklin's?'

'I think so. I get him mixed up with Proverbs.'

'Versatility. A real Renaissance man.'

'You know something, you never hear about Renaissance women, do you?'

'Versatility takes time. Who has time?'

'The whole picture is changing. I was reading this article in *Ms.* – '

'What I mean is, how much time does the average woman get to spend pursuing anything? She can't afford to make a false start and begin over again. If she's an artist of any kind, and I include crafts people in that – '

'Amen.'

' – then she's expected to do her stuff between loads of wash.'

Jumping through hoops just to find herself an hour or two a day.'

'That's changing now, don't you think?'

'I finally laid down the law and got myself a studio. What about you, Brenda?'

'Well – '

'A room of one's own. Good old Virginia. She had her head screwed on right.'

'But – '

'We really owe a lot to those early – '

'I sit down at that loom and catch myself thinking, maybe I should bake the kids some cookies. Or a pie. Some dumb thing like that. Ha.'

'I haven't made a pie in five years.'

'I've never made a pie.'

'Who needs pie!'

'Not me, that's for sure.'

'I sometimes think of that book *The Greening of America*, remember that? How he said something about handicrafts being a sign of spiritual resurgence in America.

'I love it. That's fabulous. I'm going to write that down.'

'Well, it's only a paraphrase. But it was something along those lines.'

'This punch is getting to me. I think I'll call it a day.'

'Me too. We've got the Keynote Address at nine sharp.'

'Early to bed, early to – '

'It's after one o'clock. I don't believe it.'

'And I was going to phone home. Check up on the family.'

'It's pretty late.'

'I suppose.'

'Have you got children, Brenda?'

'Yes,' Brenda says, 'two.'

'Me too. How old are yours?'

'A boy fourteen. And a girl twelve.'

'I'll bet you miss them already.' The woman who says this has a soft, faintly Southern voice, but the words hit Brenda like an electric shock. She hasn't thought of her children all day. Not once all day.

Room 2424. Brenda puts the key in the lock, turns it slowly, feels her heart contract. This is ridiculous, she lectures herself, she can't camp in the corridor all night. This is her room; she was assigned to it.

The room is empty. Verna's bed is empty, the sheets and blankets pulled up in a semblance of order and propriety. The table lamp has been left on; it projects a circle of yellow welcoming light onto the ceiling, almost as though it has been specially lit for her.

She is tired, exhausted; the rum punch has made her giddy, and so has the number of people she's met and talked to. Names, all those names, she'll never remember them all. She can wash her hair in the morning, she decides. Tomorrow she can borrow an iron from the chambermaid and press her other skirt. She can't wait to get into bed, to close her eyes.

And sleep comes with ease. Small, puffed clouds blow soundlessly past her. She thinks of Jack – not his face, but the density and smell of his body. She thinks of her children, asleep at home, not as they are now, but as they were when they were little – warm, sweet-smelling after their bath. She thinks of her quilts; somewhere in the darkness of this hotel her three quilts wait. *The Second Coming, The Second Coming.* She can move an imaginary finger along the raised centre piece, remembering the accuracy of edges and corners. She thinks of her red coat (small, worrying stain on collar), which is hanging down the hall in Barry Ollershaw's room. He will bring it to her tomorrow, he promised, and she has no doubt but that he will. The promise brings a flare of happiness. Faith presses; it has the weight of gravity; all is safe, all is well. She dreams of the pale-green artichoke heart, its leaves pushed apart, the sharpened oval of an almond embedded in its centre.

Chapter Eleven

SHE LOVED HER CHILDREN, OF COURSE SHE LOV[...] ren, her babies, Rob and Laurie. (Robert John [...] 1964, seven pounds, four ounces. Laura Jane B[...] 1966, one minute past midnight, eight pounds, Brenda's first thought when she woke up on Su[...] in an empty hotel room was of her children.

Six-thirty by the travel clock, but only five-thi[...] in Elm Park; Rob and Laurie would be sound asle[...] to sleep in on Sunday mornings, especially Rob, [...] in bed until noon if they let him – and more and [...] let him. These marathon Sunday-morning slee[...] his bedroom filled with evil smells – dust, sour b[...] comfortless air. This and the clutter of dirty socks[...] the bureau, and record albums, and old Sprite ca[...] depressed Brenda. He always punched in the sid[...] cans when he'd emptied them, an act which seem[...] compulsive and vaguely worrying, though sh[...] people did the same thing.

As recently as a year ago the walls in Rob's bedr[...] covered with triangular felt souvenir pennants _[...] Bears. The Wisconsin Dells. Cave of the Moun[...] Mich. Delavan, Wisc. Crystal Lake, Ill. They [...] cheap flimsy felt, cracked at the edges, crude[...] uneven ink, but they had brightened the room wi[...] and innocence, reminding Brenda of family trips [...] of days which now seemed less troubled.

Rob had taken the pennants down one Saturda[...] January, rolling them up and stowing them on h[...] And he had hung up in their place a small, frame[...] which he had bought with his own money — [...] money, he told Brenda when she questioned him[...] it in the window in the Westgate shopping mall[...] ately wanted it. It had cost $35, reduced from [...] Christmas sale.

she can't camp in the corridor all night. This is her room; she was assigned to it.

The room is empty. Verna's bed is empty, the sheets and blankets pulled up in a semblance of order and propriety. The table lamp has been left on; it projects a circle of yellow welcoming light onto the ceiling, almost as though it has been specially lit for her.

She is tired, exhausted; the rum punch has made her giddy, and so has the number of people she's met and talked to. Names, all those names, she'll never remember them all. She can wash her hair in the morning, she decides. Tomorrow she can borrow an iron from the chambermaid and press her other skirt. She can't wait to get into bed, to close her eyes.

And sleep comes with ease. Small, puffed clouds blow soundlessly past her. She thinks of Jack – not his face, but the density and smell of his body. She thinks of her children, asleep at home, not as they are now, but as they were when they were little – warm, sweet-smelling after their bath. She thinks of her quilts; somewhere in the darkness of this hotel her three quilts wait. *The Second Coming, The Second Coming.* She can move an imaginary finger along the raised centre piece, remembering the accuracy of edges and corners. She thinks of her red coat (small, worrying stain on collar), which is hanging down the hall in Barry Ollershaw's room. He will bring it to her tomorrow, he promised, and she has no doubt but that he will. The promise brings a flare of happiness. Faith presses; it has the weight of gravity; all is safe, all is well. She dreams of the pale-green artichoke heart, its leaves pushed apart, the sharpened oval of an almond embedded in its centre.

Chapter Eleven

SHE LOVED HER CHILDREN, OF COURSE SHE LOVED HER CHILD-
ren, her babies, Rob and Laurie. (Robert John Bowman, born
1964, seven pounds, four ounces. Laura Jane Bowman, born
1966, one minute past midnight, eight pounds, two ounces.)
Brenda's first thought when she woke up on Sunday morning
in an empty hotel room was of her children.

Six-thirty by the travel clock, but only five-thirty back home
in Elm Park; Rob and Laurie would be sound asleep; they loved
to sleep in on Sunday mornings, especially Rob, who would lie
in bed until noon if they let him – and more and more they did
let him. These marathon Sunday-morning sleeping bouts left
his bedroom filled with evil smells – dust, sour breath, chilled,
comfortless air. This and the clutter of dirty socks, and coins on
the bureau, and record albums, and old Sprite cans – all of this
depressed Brenda. He always punched in the sides of his Sprite
cans when he'd emptied them, an act which seemed to her to be
compulsive and vaguely worrying, though she knew other
people did the same thing.

As recently as a year ago the walls in Rob's bedroom had been
covered with triangular felt souvenir pennants. The Chicago
Bears. The Wisconsin Dells. Cave of the Mounds. Dearborn,
Mich. Delavan, Wisc. Crystal Lake, Ill. They were made of
cheap flimsy felt, cracked at the edges, crudely stamped in
uneven ink, but they had brightened the room with boyishness
and innocence, reminding Brenda of family trips in the car, and
of days which now seemed less troubled.

Rob had taken the pennants down one Saturday morning last
January, rolling them up and stowing them on his closet shelf.
And he had hung up in their place a small, framed Escher print,
which he had bought with his own money – his Christmas
money, he told Brenda when she questioned him. He had seen
it in the window in the Westgate shopping mall and immediately wanted it. It had cost $35, reduced from $50, at a post-
Christmas sale.

Brenda couldn't remember now why she had been so alarmed by the purchase of this print. Was it the amount of money – $35 was a considerable amount for Rob, who received only $5 a week for allowance – or was it the secrecy with which he had spent it? (He hadn't consulted them; he had simply gone out and bought it.) Now, a year later, whenever she went into his room to change his sheets – she seldom went into his room for any other reason these days – she paused and examined the print.

At first glance it looked like an abstract done in blacks and whites, but on close examination it revealed a flock of stately birds, seagulls, their wings outstretched, flying across the paper from right to left, veering upwards slightly. The spaces between the birds were white, and these spaces became progressively smaller as the birds approached the left margin, taking on, finally, the exact shapes of the birds themselves. It was a puzzle, a spatial question mark. There was a balance, she sensed, some mystery, precision, and something ironic too about the relationship between those birds and the small, airy, but distinct distances that separated them. Brenda could feel the suspended movement of their wings pressing like a weight on her eyes. The angle of ascent, not more than ten degrees, filled her with a curious, sweet melancholy. 'What does "covet" mean?' Rob had asked her not long ago, sitting at the dining-room table, writing a composition on mythology for school. She told him it meant wanting something that someone else had. 'For instance,' she told him, 'I covet your Escher print.' He had looked up, pleased. It had been almost painful for her to see how pleased and unguarded he had looked.

Laurie's room was larger, brighter, and tidier than Rob's, but a mistake. All that dotted Swiss, those ruffles; it was neat enough, but never quite clean-looking. That maple dresser, fake Ethan Allen, from their student apartment at DePaul, red and garish and covered with tiny scratches. Laurie had discovered the rolled up pennants in Rob's closet and had begged to have them; now they were thumbtacked on her rose-garlanded wallpaper. The arrangement was hectic and unbalanced. An old perfume bottle of Brenda's sat on Laurie's bedside table, stuffed with paper flowers, another cast-off. (Laurie was always rescuing things from wastebaskets, always spending her allowance at church bazaars or garage sales.) There were piles of comics on her shelves and sets of old Bobbsey Twin books with warped streaky covers. Miniature china animals in rows, miniature china jugs. Plastic pinwheels and whistles from cereal boxes. Bedroom slippers in dusty pink plush, a size too small. A pair of rag dolls propped on her pillow. ('I believe in dolls' – Laurie had whispered this solemn truth in Brenda's ear long ago when she was being put to bed.) There was a small rug on the floor which had been in the upstairs hall before they got the good beige carpeting. The radiator under Laurie's window needed painting; it oozed rust. Brenda promised herself she would get around to it in the spring. There was nothing in her daughter's room she coveted, nothing. No, that wasn't true. She coveted the view, which looked out onto the quiet width of North Franklin Boulevard. Despite the trees at the back of the house, electric wires and board fences and glimpses of alley disturbed the view. On the east side they were only feet away from Larry and Janey Carpenter's smooth grey stucco, and on the west their mock-orange bushes rubbed up against Herb and Ginger Morrison's hedge. Lucky Laurie at the front of the house had a wide, softly curtained view of elm trees (leafless at the moment), lawns, shrubbery, the street lamp across the street with its frosted glass, the dark, beseeching front doors of the neighbouring houses, one or two still silvery with Christmas arrangements. Lucky Laurie.

Brenda couldn't help wondering if Verna of Virginia had any children. She doubted it. There sat Verna's suitcase, a blue-and-red canvas carryall, zippered and jaunty, so different from her own. 'I am not the kind of person who looks in other people's suitcases.' Brenda said this to herself, feeling warmed by her virtue, but surprised at the same time that the thought had come to her.

Where was Verna anyway? Brenda could tell from the arrangement of sheets and blankets that Verna had not returned to the room. Where exactly *had* she spent the night? Perhaps there had been some change. She might have asked for another room. (An image of red buttocks flickered in her mind, brief as the light of a flashbulb.) But the suitcase was still here. It was a puzzle, even in an obscure way a rebuke. No, that was ridiculous.

She decided to have breakfast sent up. When she and Jack were on vacation and staying in a hotel, they always had breakfast sent up; it was one of the pleasures of travelling, they claimed. But it was always Jack who phoned room service. Which was strange, now that she thought of it, since she was the one who organized breakfast at home.

'Orange juice, bran muffins, and coffee,' she said into the phone, forcing her voice into briskness. (Ah, a no-nonsense woman, ordering herself a nourishing breakfast. A woman, alert and active, a woman who had certain expectations, who was accustomed to giving commands.) Brenda put down the receiver thinking: I am forty years old and have just phoned room service for the first time in my life.

Brenda knew, of course – she had known for years – that her life was out of joint with the times. Her richly simulated, commanding voice on the phone told her so, and so did the articles she read in magazines. Articles about women who set up their own law firms, women who conducted symphony orchestras, did photographic essays on Cambodia. Articles about women who lived alone in wilderness cabins and loved it, thrived on it, wrote books about surviving it. Articles about women who understood and provided for the needs of their bodies, who took as their due a satisfying schedule of 'screwing' – yes, that was the word for it now; only sweet Mrs. Brenda Bowman from Elm Park, Illinois, still referred to the act of love as the act of love. What a dumb sap she was, detained too long in girlhood, an abstainer from the adult life.

Only a week ago she had read a whole article on pubic hair, its importance, its differing types, how to look after it, how to augment it if necessary. There were women in the world, it seemed, who cared deeply about their pubic hair, and the thought of these women reinforced her feelings of estrangement. She had come to this awkward age, forty, at an awkward time in history – too soon to be one of the new women, whatever that meant, and too late to be an old-style woman. It was funny, she sometimes thought, or it was heartbreaking. She knew, on one hand, that it was idiotic to go out and buy a special cream rinse (a natural product made of pureed strawberries) to add lustre to her pubic hair, but perhaps, who knows, she was missing out on something. And she couldn't say fuck out loud; did that mean what she suspected it meant? (Probably not?) She loved her children, she loved her husband, but had seized, frantically seized, this chance to escape them.

And for this: a silent room, a solitary breakfast – cold muffins, bitter coffee, orange juice made from crystals. What a chump she was.

She thought of Jack's father, whose lament ever since she'd known him was that he had been too young to fight in the First World War and too old for the Second. (Though he *had* been made an air-raid warden during the second war and equipped with a prized flashlight and gas mask.) He had been 'cheated by time', he said, and she too had been cheated. Jack would call it historical accident, happenstance. There she had been, diapering babies, buying groceries at the A & P, wallpapering bathrooms, while other women – who were these women? – fought for equal rights, while a terrible war raged, while the country teetered on the brink of revolution. She had seen it all – but all of it on television and in the pages of *Newsweek*. A cheat. But probably she had chosen to be cheated. The coward's way out. Brenda could never make up her mind if she was the only one on the planet to suffer this particular species of dislocation or if the condition was so common it went unvoiced.

Frequently in the last year or so she has been struck with a sudden wish to freeze herself in time and announce to herself her exact location in the universe. Here I am, Brenda Bowman, boarding an aircraft for Philadelphia. Here I am, Brenda Bowman, sitting at a pine kitchen-table, filling out my tax form. Here I am, forty years old, the mother of two children, the wife of a historian, sitting on the edge of my bed applying Tawny Silk nail polish at three o'clock in the afternoon. My name is Brenda Mary Pulaski Bowman, I am forty years old, it is eleven-thirty at night, and I am engaged in the act of sexual intercourse, the act of love, with a man call Jack Bowman. Here I stand, a woman of forty, staring out of an upstairs bedroom window at a small patch of lawn (my own) in the state of Illinois in the United States of America in the . . .

Her pronouncements, rising out of moments that seemed to demand them, came as a comfort to her. They had the effect of running water, cooling and powerful. She could, with these utterances, draw precise circles around herself, observe the outlines of her body, the rhythms of daily acts which had previously been invisible. (Here I am sweeping my kitchen floor.) And she could cordon off, with remarkable clarity, certain areas of experience which had thus far eluded her. I have never been to Majorca; I have never owned any diamond jewellery except for my engagement ring; I have never been hospitalized for an illness; I have never been abandoned or down to my last cent; I have never been accused of a crime; I have never been told that someone hated me; I have never slept with a man other than my husband; I have never kissed another man since I was married, except Bernie Koltz, once, when he was drunk; I have never been really drunk; I have never until this moment picked up a phone in a hotel and ordered myself muffins and coffee.

Ah, but she had done it. And it had been easy, easy. Here sat the breakfast tray for proof. She could reach for a pencil, make a checkmark; she could say: I have just ordered myself a breakfast.

It was too quiet in the room, and for company she put on the television. Sunday morning. Nothing but cartoons and rosy-voiced evangelists. 'Ma Brethren – '

She turned the knob and found an educational programme for children, a farm broadcast sponsored by the National Dairy Association. 'Good morning, my young friends.' A farmer, looking more like a businessman in his coat and tie, was shown in close-up, his face tanned and nicely seamed as befitted a farmer. He was saying in a friendly, flinty way, 'Boys and girls, all over America cows are being milked.'

If Jack were here, Brenda thought, he would have laughed at this. It was the kind of statement he found funny. 'All over America women are hitching up their pantyhose,' he would say. 'All over America men are whistling Dixie and stepping into their jockey shorts.'

What was Jack doing now? Only seven-thirty. He would be asleep. Probably he had gone to the Carpenters' party last night. He had few close friends, but found it almost impossible to resist a party. He might wake up this morning with a hangover. If it was a bad enough hangover, he might be awake already, stumbling into the bathroom to look for the aspirin. He might even be downstairs, making himself a cup of instant coffee, rubbing the back of his neck, thinking he should put in a little work on the book he was writing about Indian trading practices. He might push that thought aside and switch on the television, instead, in an idle way and hear this same farmer saying, 'All over America cows are being milked.'

Would he laugh out loud in the empty living room? She doubted it. She couldn't imagine what it would sound like if he did. Twenty-four hours away from home and already she had forgotten what his laugh sounded like; amazing. It might be a good idea to phone home later in the day, just to see how they were getting along without her. On the other hand, a long-distance call presented certain small vexations. Should she phone person-to-person? What time would they be back from Dad and Ma Bowman's? And wasn't it a little neurotic anyway to phone home when she'd only been gone for twenty-four hours – a little bit flakey, as Rob would say. Flakey. She cringed when he said it.

A week ago Brenda had read a humour piece in the *Tribune* about the changing dialogue of the seventies. Certain expressions were out, it seemed, and others – new jargon words – were in. It was no longer fashionable to talk about one's identity; if you did you declared yourself a leftover from the sixties. It was no longer okay to talk about getting in touch with your anger or in touch with your feelings, and certainly not in touch with yourself. It was corny (oddly this was still an okay word) to talk about having a relationship, and especially corny it you were *working* at a relationship. The word 'trendy' was passé, and so was the word 'passé'. Only twelve-year-olds talked about having their own space. Both 'kitsch' and 'seminal' had had their season. If you went about shouting to the world that you had been deprived of certain 'life choices', then you were, without a doubt, mired in the hackneyed old early seventies and might never get out. You might run the risk, with your anger and your insistence on validity, of hitching yourself to a nostalgic chunk of time, like those old folksy sorts who still said 'neat' and 'terrif' and 'boy-oh-boy'.

Reading this article had made Brenda furious. It was shallow and coy, and, in a way, a betrayal. She had felt anger when she read it – real anger, not the kind you used or shared. But she had also felt a heartbreaking sense of exclusion. She had missed another decade, first the sixties, now this. For things *had* happened. Enormous shifts of perspective had taken place. Ideas had lived and died without touching the heart and mind of Brenda Bowman in Elm Park, Illinois, U.S.A., Continent of North America, *et cetera, et cetera*. She might never catch up now; she would spend her life in this perplexing cul-de-sac which time and circumstance had prepared for her. Brenda Bowman, forty years old, mother of Rob and Laurie Bowman, drifting, coping – should she grieve or rejoice? – responding, waiting, escaping occasionally (how pathetic!) to hotel rooms in secondary cities, ordering muffins and then regretting them, thinking of phoning home, wishing Hap Lewis had come, wondering if her husband Jack had heard that farmer on TV saying, 'All over America – '

A knock on the door. Brenda jumped. Surely not the chambermaid already. She brushed the crumbs from her robe. It might be Verna returning for her suitcase. She reached up and patted her hair.

No. She opened the door to find Barry Ollershaw, smiling nervously, smelling of aftershave, saying good morning (good mahning), and handing her a bouquet of flowers.

Chapter Twelve

'R OSES!' SHE SAID BY WAY OF GREETING.
Yellow roses. About half a dozen tiny blooms still tightly closed and looking to Brenda more like onions than flowers. How extraordinary! (And how expensive; the thought came to her unbidden.) 'These can't be for me,' she managed.

'Happy Sunday.' He smiled an eager, edgy smile.

'But –' Her hands reached out and felt the dampness of green florist paper. She became flustered, girlish; something was warning her, watch out. 'But why – ?'

He spread his hands. 'A girl was selling them down in the lobby. She was wearing a long dress and had one of those carts.' His eyes smiled. 'I couldn't resist.'

'Lovely.' Brenda poked a finger into the nested centre. There were soft-looking sprays of pale fern tucked in with the roses, giving off a humid, hothouse smell.

'Actually, ah, Brenda' – he seemed to be testing her name for accuracy – 'is it all right' – he glanced past her into the room – 'if I come in for a minute?'

'Well, yes, I mean come in.' She stepped aside, feeling not so much alarm as confusion. Flowers, expensive flowers, and so early – not even eight o'clock – and that racket coming from the television. 'I'm afraid I'm not dressed yet.' She backed into the room, clutching her robe, apologizing, 'I was being lazy –'

'Why not when you have a chance.' He was being kind. And careful.

'Just let me turn off the TV.' How had she managed to get muffin crumbs all over the table. She was as bad as Laurie. And coffee sloshed in her saucer too. And a wet bath towel on the chair; she never did that at home. 'Come in, sit down.'

She made a grab for the towel and twisted it awkwardly in her hands; what should she do with it? Then, regarding the flowers, she said, 'I should put these in water right away.'

'Here,' he jumped. 'What about this coffee flask? That should do the trick.'

'Oh, do you think – '

'It's just about empty. I could dump out the rest – unless you want it – and get some water.'

'It's terrible coffee anyway.'

'Oh?'

'Bitter.'

'Oh.' The word bitter hung between them. He nodded slowly. 'Hotels – '

Brenda reached for the coffee flask, bumping against his arm.

'I'll get it,' he said, and went whistling off into her bathroom.

She was left alone, listening to the water running, regarding herself in the mirror. This is crazy, she mouthed, and made a face at herself. She remembered she had left the bathroom in a mess, littered with – what? Stockings on the shower rail, talcum powder. Shampoo. Ban Roll-on. Her Second Debut in the large economy size. All the intimate equipment for her travel case dumped out on the counter, including, oh God, her new box of Tampax (always be prepared). What was that he was whistling in there? Something tuneless, whatever it was. 'Yankee Doodle'. She was reminded sharply of Jack's bathtub singing, which was modest, almost a mumble.

'There we go.' Barry Ollershaw settled the flowers on the writing table.

'They're really lovely,' she said again.

'I was wondering, ah, Brenda, if you were planning to go out this morning.' His voice had taken on a measure of shrewdness.

'Out?'

'Outside of the hotel.' He perched on the arm of the chair, waiting.

Brenda thought for a minute. 'Well, I don't know,' she said. 'We've got a talk at nine, the Keynote Address. And then a workshop at eleven. So I guess I won't be going out this morning. Why?

He gave a sharp sigh. 'It's about your coat, the coat you left in my room last night.'

'My new coat?' The word 'new' came out involuntarily.

'Was it new? Oh, God.'

'What happened?'

'I was going to bring it back this morning. If you remember.'

'I remember.' What was the matter with him?

'Well' – he paused, and his hands curled into fists – 'I might as well just tell you outright. It seems to have disappeared.'

'What has? My coat?'

'I'm sure it will come back. What I mean is, nobody stole it, nothing like that. It's just that I don't know where it is. At this moment. You haven't,' he asked brightening, 'brought another coat with you by any chance?'

'No,' Brenda said slowly. 'Just the one coat.'

'Oh.'

There seemed nothing to add.

'You mean,' Brenda said, taking a breath, 'that it was hanging there in your room last night, and this morning it's not there?'

'More or less, yes, that's what happened.'

'But the maid probably knows. Maybe she thought it needed pressing or cleaning or – '

'I've already asked her.'

'But,' and Brenda laughed more loudly then she meant to, a near cackle, 'a coat doesn't just walk away.'

'I think I do have an idea about what might have happened to it. The circumstances.'

'What?'

'I think it was just, well, borrowed.'

'But who – ?'

'It's awkward to explain . . . ' His eyes seemed to wander toward the arrangement of yellow roses, scowling, scrutinizing, questioning their presence.

Brenda waited. 'How awkward?' she said at last.

'Actually not all that awkward. I mean, there is a logical explanation. The thing is, well, the management asked me if I would mind sharing my room, since I had a double. You know all about the trouble with the overbookings – '

'Yes?'

'This was last night, when they asked me. Around midnight.'

'Midnight?

'So I said, sure, why not, it didn't matter to me.'

'And then what?'

'They told me another metallurgist, from, New York I think, would be coming. But I didn't realize he would be bringing . . . well . . . a friend for the night.'

'A woman friend, you mean.'

'Exactly. You've got it.'

'Did you meet her?'

'To tell the truth I haven't met either of them.' (Brenda liked the way he said 'eye-there'.) 'I was asleep when they came in. That must have been around two or so. I guess I woke up briefly when I heard them, but they didn't even put the light on, just stumbled around in the dark. I think they were fairly drunk. At least it sounded like it. And in a fairly amorous mood. So I kept discreetly turned toward the wall.'

'I can imagine.' Brenda was smiling and shaking her head.

'It was a fairly long and noisy performance. It made me think of you and what you ran into yesterday. God! And when I woke up this morning – I slept like the proverbial log in spite of everything – they had already left. And your coat – '

' – was gone too.'

'What I figure is, they must have gone for a walk or something. And just sort of borrowed your coat. I'm sure they'll bring it back. It could be back there now for all I know. I went downstairs and asked at the desk, but they – '

'Was that why you brought the flowers?'

'Well . . . '

'It wasn't your fault. About the coat.'

'I can't help feeling somewhat responsible – '

'I'm sure it will come back . . . Barry.' She tried out his name.

'I hope so.'

What an Irish-looking face he had – small, compact, with clear eyes and a mouth that closed with quickness. She wondered if he *was* Irish.

'I was afraid,' he was saying, 'that you'd be stuck inside the hotel all morning without a coat. Especially now with all the snow.'

'Snow?'

'You haven't seen the snow? It's been snowing all night according to the news.'

'I haven't even looked outside.'

She pulled the curtains, and there it was, everywhere. It was still falling; the sky was filled with heavy wet flakes. They drifted slowly past the window, reminding Brenda of bars of music, densely harmonic. Long rectangles of snow clung even to the blank glass office-building across the street (who would have thought there were places on that smooth face that could catch and hold these slim shapes). The smaller brick building next to it (a bank?) was softened by its white covering, the flat roof transformed to an untouched field, rural-looking, a farmer's pasture. The sky was surprisingly radiant, a sheet of photographic film, whitish-grey with a backing of silver, and far below Brenda could see the narrow street choked with drifts. This was a village lane. What had happened to the traffic, the flow of cars and buses and cabs? It had vanished, leaving this simple, bright river of white. A swarm of discs, human figures, moved toward what must be the front door of the hotel. Brenda, watching them, was reminded of iron filings, of an electromagnet, of Mr. Sloan at Morton High School, earnest and theatrical and prone to puns, giving a demonstration in the school basement. Brenda had been drawn to him, the herringbone of his jacket and the way his pack of Pall Malls stuck out of his pocket. He had only stayed a year; later another girl told her he was a 'homo' and so had been asked to leave. She hadn't believed it at the time; her innocence was stalwart and denying in those days, but probably, thinking about it now –

'Peaceful, isn't it?' Barry Ollershaw said.

'I should get dressed.'

'We were in Japan a couple of years ago.' (We? – his wife probably.) 'For another conference. There was snow falling right in Tokyo. Like this, these big flakes. And everyone just stopped and watched it. People sat all afternoon in restaurants, drinking tea and looking out of the windows. Someone told us it was a regular Japanese pastime. In the spring they sit and watch cherry blossoms, just watch them. And in winter – '

'It must be hypnotizing.'

'Sort of an art form, they say – '

'Meditation. A background to meditation.'

'Tranquillity.'

'It's the silence you feel. This thick glass – '

'With everything muffled and far away.'

'Chicago snow doesn't look like this.'

'Doesn't it?'

'Maybe it does, but I never really look at it. Not while it's coming down like this.'

'We're all too busy, I guess.'

'Rushing around.'

'I think children do.'

'What?'

'Stop. And really see things.'

'I think you're right.'

'You have children?'

'Two, a boy and a girl. You?'

'No.'

'Oh.'

'But I remember how when I was a kid I noticed things. I was telling you yesterday about how my mother made quilts, and even now, after all these years, I can remember exactly what the quilt on my bed looked like. Especially one jagged patch in the middle, sort of eight-sided.'

'Imagine.'

'It was some kind of scratchy wool, dark blue. I remember falling asleep with my fingers on it. When I think of all the things I've forgotten about. But I remember that patch, the exact shape and feel of it.'

'My husband's like that.'

'Jack?'

A pause. 'How did you know his name?'

'You said it yesterday.'

'Did I? I guess I did. Well, when he was young he used to have one of those wooden tops. Just an ordinary wooden top with a string. When Rob and Laurie were small he kept looking in stores for one just like it, but he never found one that felt exactly the same. He says he remembers just how it felt in his hand.'

'We don't have much snow in Vancouver. Maybe once or twice a year.'

'I didn't know that. I thought in Canada – '

'I suppose that's why I love snow.'

'Look at it. It's coming down even faster.'

'You can hardly see across – '

'I wonder how deep it is. From up here you really can't tell.'

'Strange isn't it, looking at the world from this height. What I mean is, weather hardly matters when you're up this high. It's sort of, well . . .'

'Abstract.'

'That's it. Abstract.'

'Maybe that's a bad thing in a way. Not feeling a part of the weather. Not needing weather.'

'The way farmers need it, you mean?'

'Something like that. One more thing taken away from us.'

'Peaceful though.'

'Watching it like this.'

'What else do you need when you come right down to it? Entertainment, television, who needs things like that?'

'We forget how to stop now and then and just look.'

'Popping pills. Running to shrinks. When all you have to do is stop and –'

'We're afraid of silence. A friend of mine says that. We feel we've failed if there's even a little pause in the conversation.'

'That's contemporary society. We feel we have to be communicating from morning to night.'

'Sometimes I think there's too much communication in the world.'

'And not enough time.'

'What we need is time to just . . . be.'

'Like this.'

'Just sitting. Looking at the snow coming down. '

'It's restorative.'

'It's so strange.'

'Yes.'

Brenda has never been unfaithful to Jack. In twenty years of marriage she has never once been unfaithful. When Bernie Koltz, a few months ago at a picnic, drunk on wine, cornered her and told her he adored her, had always adored her, she had not for a minute considered having an affair with him. She had taken his hand, patted it, offered to get him coffee from the thermos, told him he was sweet – which he was. For a week or two she recalled to herself, at odd moments, especially at bedtime, the exact way he had looked at her that day in the Forest Preserve and said, 'I adore you, Brenda.' But that was all.

Once, years ago, Dr. Middleton, Director of the Great Lakes Institute, said a strange thing to her. 'You have beautiful eyes, Brenda. They are eyes that could melt a man's heart. You'll think I'm being foolish, but sometimes I dream about your eyes.' Brenda had been astonished, puzzled, embarrassed. She tried to make a joke of it. 'Ah, Dr. Middleton,' she teased him in a daughterly way. 'I won't be fit to live with if you go on saying nice things like that.'

Another time she ran into Hap Lewis's husband, Bud, at Marshall Field's in the middle of the afternoon . She was on the main floor, buying socks for Laurie. He invited her out for a drink at a bar on State Street. After a bourbon and water he groped for her hand and told her she was a 'marvel'. He thought it was a marvel the way she had kept her figure. That she was a marvel of a mother to her children. He urged her to have another drink. He was sometimes subject to depression, he told her. He and Hap seemed to have little in common but the boys and the house. Brenda had some difficulty getting rid of him, and in the end invented a doctor's appointment.

Only a few weeks ago, at a party, she had met a travel photographer. He specialized in beaches he told her, going all over the world photographing beaches for hotel brochures. He suggested she drop into his studio one afternoon and see some of his work. He told her he was turned on by women who are intelligent and good listeners.

Brenda never considered having an affair with either Dr. Middleton or Bud Lewis or Bernie Koltz. Or the travel photographer – whose name she never did discover. She loved Jack, she trusted him. She knew all the creases and odours of his body. She was grateful and a little awed by his fidelity; many of the couples she and Jack knew were unfaithful to each other. But not them.

Now for the first time she felt she had stepped into faithlessness. So this was it! Not sex at all, but novelty, risk, possibility. She was sitting in a hotel room in Philadelphia, watching the snow coming down and keeping an elaborate silence – minute after minute passed in silence. The silence seemed to her to be pure, composed, and possibly dangerous. The longer it lasted, minute by minute, the more rarefied it became. (Later she would see it as miniaturized but undiminished.) This person sitting beside her – this man with his vivid Irish face and nervous hands – had surrendered to her, without caution or hesitation, his early memory of a particular eight-sided patch centred in his childhood quilt. Out of all his life, he had chosen that. There were things she would like to tell him in exchange. But not yet.

She thought of Jack at home in Elm Park, waking in the empty bed, reaching sleepily for the clock, already – though he didn't know it – betrayed.

Chapter Thirteen

MORTON HOLMAN IS WINDING UP THE KEYNOTE ADDRESS. His eyes glitter and pierce, sweep to the domed ceiling, dart downward to his wristwatch; he fixes his audience with a pleading high-pitched cry, begging them for just five more minutes.

'The history of craft is a history of renunciation,' he croons into the microphone. 'The pride of doing without. All of you here know the truth of that historic declaration: Less is More. But ladies, and I should say gentlemen, too, look around you and what do you see in the world today? We see the artifice of art, brought into being by a tasteless elite who' – he pauses, shakes his head with sadness, opening his mouth for air – 'an elite who, for all their philanthropy and their trusts and their endless advisory councils, are the greatest enemy of the true art. I speak, of course, of that art which grows from necessity. What a word that is – *necessity! Need.* I ask you, did we *need* paintings of Greek battles done by languid Englishmen idling in Italy? Porcelain *objets d'art* for the bedchambers of invalid kings? The odious fringes and tassels of novelty, and the equally odious insanity of vain pretension which fills this world of ours with non-objects – the unspeakable, untouchable horror of museum sculpture, for example. Ladies and gentlemen, the objects I've shown you today – and they will be displayed in the foyer this afternoon – the Shaker hayrake, the china doorknob, the New England weathervane – these objects demonstrate what the human imagination, tempered by stern utility and need, can produce. Sense and sensibility, to borrow a phrase. The human hand reaching out and touching what another human hand has fashioned. The subtlety of this doorknob, the way it fits the hand, its ability to rotate and create a secondary movement, a functional movement! I know I'm running out of time, but bear with me another minute please. These things must be said, ladies. And gentlemen. We can find, through this kind of tactility – I'm speaking of the doorknob – find what I believe to be a new spirituality. A sense of needful community. We must first know the maker, the craftsperson, and be able to trust his or her nearness, seeing him or her not as effete or ethereal – but I see I am getting a signal from your chairman and so must draw these words to a conclusion. In closing, then, I ask you to bear in mind, to carry away with you, the words of William Morris: sweetness, simplicity, and soul. A trinity for the honest artist, the man or woman not afraid of the label – dare I say it – the label of artisan. One who, in fact, rejoices in this acknowledgement of his or her utility in a world so badly in need of refreshment. I'm afraid I haven't had time to fine-tune these thoughts as I'd like, but I realize I am speaking to the converted, the very practitioners of these concepts, the men and women who carry their tools openly, unashamedly, and who leave the imprint of their own humanness on whatever they touch. I see I really must stop. Thank you for your kind attention. I am honoured, in my small way, to march beside you.'

'The old bore,' Susan Hammerman murmurs to Brenda over the noise of the applause.

'They say he's nothing but a pimp for the Gallery Naif in New York,' says Lottie Hart, who has arrived unexpectedly on the morning plane. 'How he wangled his way onto the programme I'd give my eyeteeth to know.'

' – nothing to say I didn't already know.'

' – still – '

'I thought he'd fine-tune me right to sleep for a minute there.'

'He's awfully inspiring though,' Lenora Knox whispers. 'About art and the sense of community and everything.'

'I didn't hear one word about needlepoint. I suppose he thinks needlepoint is too damned effete.'

'He does have a point,' Susan Hammerman admits, 'about us not taking a back seat to the so-called true and pure artists of the world.'

'Why the hell should we go around apologizing just because our stuff has a degree of usefulness.'

'He really does know his primitive Americana backwards and forwards. I read a write-up on him somewhere. In *Time*, I think it was.

'Shhh.'

'Now what?'

'God, not more speeches.'

Betty Vetter, trim in a blue wool pantsuit and with a flower in her lapel, is at the lectern, pounding for attention. 'Ladies and gentlemen, I've just come from the meeting of the ad hoc committee to look into the grievance about the hotel arrangements, and I'm happy to report to you that a tentative solution has been reached with the International Society of Metallurgists – '

'Boo – '

' – a tentative solution regarding space.'

There are cheers. Charlotte Dance, sitting in front of Brenda, raises a fist and looks around, grinning a toothy look of triumph.

Betty holds up her hand for silence. 'Forty of their delegates have agreed to double up, freeing twenty rooms for our members which' – she holds up her hand again – 'which just happens to be the exact number we need.'

More cheers. Brenda finds she is clapping furiously.

'Furthermore, they have agreed to hold their final banquet at six-thirty on Wednesday evening, if – no, wait – *if* we are willing to put ours off until nine o'clock. Can I have a vote on that?'

'Compromise!' a condemning voice calls out.

'Some of us have planes to catch.' Another voice.

But the vote is carried, and Brenda, raising her right hand, feels a swelling exhilaration. How quickly, how almost magically, solutions are found. What a remarkable thing agreement is. The world needs people like Charlotte Dance and Betty Vetter, people who know how to solve problems.

She says this later to Lenora as they make their way across the convention floor to the room where the first workshop is being held.

Lenora agrees. 'Of course, I myself am not political.'

Brenda is about to say that she is not political either, but she is interrupted by a man's voice calling her name. 'Mrs. Bowman. Are you Mrs. Bowman?'

'Yes,' Brenda says, and feels a wave of panic. Something has happened at home. The children. Jack.

'Excuse me, Mrs. Bowman.' The voice is smooth and practiced. 'Let me introduce myself. I'm Hal Rago from the Philadelphia *Examiner* and we're doing some coverage of the exhibition. Features kind of thing. Interviews. We'd like something real personal and down to earth, and I was just talking to a Mrs.' – he pulls out a card, turns it over – 'a Mrs. Hammerman. Who said you might be agreeable to an interview.'

'Me?'

'Sort of Midwest perspective, something along that line. We've already cased the East and the Northeast. They're in the can.'

'I don't know. I mean, I don't know what I could say, but I'd be happy – '

'Great. Terrific. Look, what about we meet at the Emerald Room – say this aft some time. Around three.'

'Emerald Room?'

'St. Christopher Hotel. Just a few blocks away. Nice atmosphere, the press sort of hangs out there, you know what I mean.'

'A few blocks away?' Brenda is thinking of the snow outside and the fact that she has no coat. Surely, though, she will have it back by three. But maybe – 'Could we maybe make it a little later? Say four?'

'You've got yourself a date, Mrs. Bowman. See ya, four p.m. Emerald Room. Just ask for Hal Rago.'

'What do you know,' Lenora says. 'You're going to be in the newspaper.'

Brenda thinks of telling her about the articles in *Chicago Today* and the *Elm Leaves Weekly*, and the radio interview on WOPA, but she resists, and says instead. 'I wonder what they mean by Midwest perspective.'

'The kind of regional-motif thing maybe. Like in the Southwest we've got this strong tie with the outdoors, and then the whole Navaho-Mexican influence. It shows up. You must have noticed that.'

Brenda shakes her head; she can't remember having had any thoughts which encompassed both quilting and the Midwest. Of course there was that one quilt, *Michigan Blue*; she could always talk about that. How does she feel about the Midwest anyway? Space. Cornfields. Rivers. Fertility. That was it, she could mention fertility. Or something like that.

A hand-printed sign on a door says 'Quilting Seminar'. More than twenty women – Brenda does a quick count – are gathered around a long table. A woman wearing the name card 'Reddie Grogan: Concord, N.H.' kicks off the discussion with a question about the place of nostalgia in the quilting tradition – how the sight of patchwork and appliqué free-associates with thoughts of home, hearth, warmth, the whole yesteryear sort of thing – and how this process enters into the basic aesthetic response of the public.

'But isn't this an enrichment?' someone suggests. 'A time-dimension thing, kind of a bonus, which gives a sort of creative head start – '

'But interferes, you have to agree, with the statement a particular piece is trying to make. Muddies the water, blurs the edges, dims the message – '

'A nostalgic quilt is a throwback,' a young woman calls out. 'Hacking out new forms is what it's all about.'

'I'm not talking about immersion, I'm talking about retrospective – '

'Listen,' a brave-looking woman in a tight sweater says, 'Do we as quiltmakers have to "aspire to cosmology"?' – she makes quotation marks with her fingers – 'I mean, *do* we? Can't we get back to making warm, attractive bed coverings?'

Laughter flows. Smiles all around. A sense of release. Brenda sits back, happy now, exchanging looks with Lenora Knox, who has put on a pair of rimless spectacles that pick up the light from the overhead fixture, making her look, for an instant, about a hundred years old.

'What sets quilting apart from other crafts is the built-in shiver of history.' Has she actually said this? She? Brenda Bowman? Yes. Amazingly enough, Brenda from Elm Park, Illinois, has spoken, and all around her women are listening and nodding. (It is Jack's phrase, 'the shiver of history' – borrowed from Flaubert, always scrupulously acknowledged. He uses it fairly often.)

'But is it holding us back? That's what I want to know. I don't mean consciously, I mean unconsciously.'

'Is that supposed to mean – ?'

'A hand reaching from the past, a restraint in the end. Unless, that is, we recognize it for what it is.'

'The Mexican tradition – ' Even Lenora is jumping in now.

'But do we actually know where our patterns come from?' someone is asking. 'Is it possible to say that some forms are legacies from the past and others are original and innovative?'

'You mean like some are just kind of made up?'

'They're all made up, aren't they? When I'm cutting something out with a pair of shears, I'm making a new form.'

'I don't think so,' Brenda is saying. She is thinking now of *The Unfinished Quilt* at home. 'Certain forms are basic. I mean, take the circle.'

'The mandala,' someone contributes knowingly.

'The what ?'

'How can you get away from a circle? It's not just a traditional form, it's more basic than that even.'

'Mythic.'

'The shape of the world, a boiling pot.'

'A baby's mouth.'

'Or a . . . what do you call it . . . you know what I mean . . . '

'Yes.'

'But do these things ask for definition? I mean, do we have to put a name to them?'

'No,' Brenda says. 'We don't even have to think of them. They come out of our fingers.' What has she said? Does she know what she's talking about? Does she believe it? Yes, she does.

'You mean you're saying that art is anti-intellectual. The old instinct thing working it all out?'

'Well' – she feels trapped now – 'what I meant was more of a – '

'I think I know what you mean. I think you're saying we have to trust our hands. That sometimes our hands are a move or two ahead of our brains.'

'Yes,' Brenda says. 'Like typing. The fingers just know where the keys are.'

'I see what you're getting at.'

'Interesting. I never thought of it like that. Comparing it to typing. I always make these elaborate patterns first – '

'Always worrying about what it means. Does it make a statement or does it not make a statement.'

'Me too.'

'Instinct and spontaneity, they're like flip sides of a coin.'

'Whereas the deliberate suppression of memory or nostalgia – '

'I like Brenda's phrase better, the shiver of history.'

Brenda looks around the table. What intelligent women these are! She feels a surge of love for each of them. One of them is jabbing at the air now, saying something about the juxtaposition of time and matter.

Time and matter. In her mind Brenda sets these works carefully aside. She will have to tell Jack . . .

Chapter Fourteen

BRENDA WAS NINETEEN WHEN SHE MET JACK BOWMAN. IT happened during a cold Chicago winter. She can remember that at the end of March that year there were snow flurries; the wind off the lake carried with it particles of ice and dirt and shook the coats of the young secretaries and office clerks, lifting them unexpectedly as these young women descended from their buses in the early mornings.

Somehow Brenda had found a typing and filing job at the Great Lakes Institute on Keeley Avenue in the Loop. There had been an ad in the paper: Experienced Typist Needed. Dr. Middleton himself interviewed her. He offered her tea. A window in his office looked down into the small, green chilliness of a park, sparely symmetrical with stone benches and shrubs and statuary. On one wall of his office Dr. Middleton had a number of dark, oily landscapes, and on another an arrangement of wooden figures. 'Iroquois,' he said to Brenda in a cold, lonely voice. On his desk was a photograph of a woman with smooth blonde hair pulled back from a lean face. That must be his wife, Brenda said to herself. 'My wife, Anne,' Dr. Middleton said in a voice suddenly thawed into warmth. Brenda was amazed at the way he said, 'My wife, Anne'. She had never heard anyone, except perhaps Cary Grant, speak so delicately about a woman.

'Do you mind, Miss Pulaski, if I inquire as to why you are considering leaving Commonwealth Edison after only four months?'

Brenda hesitated. One hand went to her mouth. What should she say? That she wanted to find more interesting work? Something more challenging? Or the truth: that she was suffering unspeakable and undreamt of loneliness in her first job, sitting all day in a long, shadowless room with thirty other girls, all of them typing away, under the savage overhead lights, clack-clacking all the day long. A week earlier, riding the bus to work, her coat gathered tightly around her, tears had sprung into her eyes. Why? And in Dr. Middleton's office it was happening to her again; her throat was suddenly tight with tears, her eyes filling. She lifted the teacup and held it hard against her lips.

'Perhaps you just wanted a change,' Dr. Middleton said after a moment, and at that Brenda managed to nod.

There were only four of them – Brenda, Glenda, Rosemary, and Gussie – in the Great Lakes typing pool; it was one of Dr. Middleton's jokes that they constituted not a pool at all, but a pond. Glenda was red-headed, big-busted, wide-hipped. She powdered her broad nose with Charles-of-the-Ritz loose powder in a shade especially blended for redheads. Her sweaters and blouses were in tones of pink and copper. 'Arlene Dahl says we' – *we* meant all the redheads in the world – 'should stick with the pinks and the coppers.' She wore a girdle which had been specially made for her in the corset department at Field's, and she was saving her money for a pair of custom-made shoes. 'Face it,' she said, 'every foot is different, right? At Billings the doctor swore he'd never seen an arch like this.'

Rosemary. Rosemary was thirty and had speckled skin and watery eyes. She was given to dim, helpless, endearing confessions of mortification. 'There I stood, blushing like a *beet*' or 'Well, I just about dropped dead on the *spot*.' She had been engaged for two years and wore a zircon. When would her wedding take place? It was discussed endlessly. But there were problems. Art wasn't ready to settle down; he lived with his mother and father in Skokie; it was hard to find a decent apartment; besides, he was Jewish and expected her to convert.

Gussie Sears was twenty-two and had a brace on one leg. Polio. Her face was dark, skeletal, and ugly, but despite this she was married. She had been married for almost a year to a shy, ugly youth named Franklin Sears, who worked for an insurance company on LaSalle Street. Brenda and Glenda and Rosemary saw Franklin Sears every day, for at five o'clock sharp he would arrive at the Great Lakes Institute, red-faced and winded from his walk, to take Gussie home on the El. At lunchtime he phoned Gussie or else she phoned him. 'It's hard,' Gussie told Brenda one day in the washroom, 'for us to be away from each other all day.'

The words, shyly uttered, had fallen on Brenda's ears like revelation. That love could be like this, so strong that it brought pain. And was it really possible that love came even to those who fell short of physical beauty, whose bodies, untaught by Arlene Dahl and Charles of the Ritz, were simple, shallow vessels of hair and bones and skin? How could passion rise from so much flatness? But it did, it did! Gussie *longed* for Franklin; by mid-afternoon she was tapping her pencil and watching the clock. And Franklin's slack and reddened flesh clearly longed for Gussie. His long legs hurried into the typing room at five o'clock, and his awkward hands shook as he helped Gussie into her woollen coat. This sensual excitement seemed to Brenda grotesque, a little laughable, but also dazzling.

From the first day she loved working at the Great Lakes Institute. She relaxed. She felt at home. The terrors of Commonwealth Edison faded fast. She loved her partitioned desk drawers, with their paperclips and pencils and extra typewriter ribbons. And she loved Rosemary and Gussie and Glenda. Hours spent together in the typing pool knit them together within days into a tough, jokey sisterhood. They lent each other nail polish and Kleenex, they discussed their mothers, they conspired tenderly against Dr. Middleton. They covered for each other; they trusted each other. On payday they went to Roberto's around the corner and ordered platters of spaghetti or lasagna. They were the four fish in Dr. Middleton's pool and felt themselves to be worthy and cherished.

Only Gussie stood slightly apart, and this, Brenda perceived, was because she, alone of the four, was married.

Married! It was another state of being, a state that was sealed like an envelope in its inviolability. The state of marriage was secret and safe, a circle of charmed light beyond the horizon of the easily capsized now.

Glenda and Brenda and Rosemary probed for details. What did Gussie fix for dinner? Had she tried doing pork chops the new way with condensed cream-of-mushroom soup? Had she tried her hand at making cloverleaf rolls? What about a budget? Did she and Franklin have a budget? Of course they must; so much for entertainment, so much for groceries. Did Gussie think spray wax was as good as paste wax? What did Gussie and Franklin do in the evenings? Did they watch TV? In the furniture line, did they like Early American better than French Provincial? What about goals and ideals? Were they hoping to get their own automatic washing-machine eventually? Saving for a house? Was a Hide-a-Bed a sound investment for a young couple? When they had children, would Gussie quit work and stay at home with the kids? Sterling or silverplate?

Brenda and Glenda and Rosemary hungered for these details. (It was 1957.) Even more, they longed to know, but didn't ask, whether or not Gussie had a supply of pastel nylon nightgowns and if she took the brace off her leg when she went to bed – of course she must! And how it had felt when . . . well . . . the first time? Did it hurt? How often did they do it and did they turn the lights off and did Gussie use a douche after?

Gussie, poor Gussie, smiled at the questions about cloverleaf rolls and paste wax; her pale, uneven lips parted; it seemed a miracle that her teeth weren't broken. 'Well,' she would say, puzzled, letting the 'well' drift off like cigarette smoke, 'well, I don't exactly know.' She was clearly baffled by their interest. These domesticities seemed not to have occurred to her. Franklin was planning to finish off his accounting course at night school, that much she volunteered. On Sundays they drove out to Sycamore to visit his family. They saved Green Stamps – but in a haphazard way, half the time forgetting. And occasionally, in the summer, they had attended the concerts at Grant Park. (At the mention of the Grant Park concerts, Brenda and Glenda and Rosemary had beamed and nodded. It seemed the right thing for a young couple to do, educational and romantic, and was free besides.)

But about the colour of her kitchen cupboards, Gussie was oddly unforthcoming. ('They're just painted, sort of yellowish.') She seemed not to know much about the new spray wax or very much about shelf paper or bleaching agents. At work she was quietly industrious, an excellent typist with a tidy desk top. If Dr. Middleton had a special job, something he wanted done quickly, he always gave it to Gussie. Her small, wiry body, straining forward, pressed the typewriter keys with energy and knowing; there were days when she typed right through the coffee break, leaving Brenda and Glenda and Rosemary to go off on their own to the cafeteria and speculate, endlessly speculate, about the intricacies, the mysteries, of married life.

Brenda herself could not understand her new mania for domestic details. Certainly it was not the domesticity of her own life that had ripened her for this; she and her mother still lived in the same old apartment in Cicero, over the dry cleaner's, where they had always lived. Dust continued to settle in a friendly way on her mother's sewing machine and on the living-room radiator; the refrigerator in the kitchen still whined its old tune, and its stale, metallic-smelling shelves held salami, herring, a carton of milk, a net bag of navel oranges. The wiped oilcloth on the kitchen table was weighted down, as it had always been, by the pink-and-white sugar bowl and the salt shakers in the form of twin squirrels. All of this comforted Brenda in a vague way; none of it interested her.

It was the domesticity of the newly married that enchanted her, its crisp, glazed magazine aura, rising out of the whiteness of weddings and opening like a play onto rooms paved with Armstrong flooring. Basket chairs with corduroy cushions. Café curtains on brass rods; Brenda, in those days, sometimes dreamed about café curtains. And what else? A Duncan Phyfe coffee table in front of the couch; a white padded wedding-album brought out for visitors to see. Carpeting on the stairs, and a staggering of small, framed flower prints. In the bedroom: coloured sheets, a dust-ruffle, perhaps a canopy. Brightly toned towels in the bathroom, stacked on open shelves – such riches – and little cakes of scented soap in a glass apothecary jar. She wanted an organized linen cupboard. She wanted to plunge with a brave face into low-budget entertaining, to put the whole of her heart into steaming casseroles of beef Stroganoff and, for desert, frozen lemon pie with graham-cracker crust. She wanted it all, all of it: a vacuum cleaner with a set of attachments, a spice rack of carved red maple, a doorbell that chimed – all of it.

Years later at a party given in her honour – she had just won her first award – someone asked her why she had married so young. She replied with a truthfulness that surprised even her. 'I wanted to have a pink kitchen,' she said. 'I was *dying* to have a pink kitchen.'

In those days, Jack, a history major, was in his senior year at DePaul, and was doing his Special Project on the French explorer LaSalle. One morning in late March he turned up at the Great Lakes Institute to look at an old survey map. Dr. Middleton greeted him warmly enough, shaking his hand and expressing interest in the project – 'We need young men like you in the field' – but was clearly anxious to have him off his hands. 'Miss Pulaski here, Brenda that is, will look after you,' he assured Jack.

Brenda led Jack down the hall and around the corner to the map room. It was kept locked, and she struggled for a moment with the key.

'Here, let me.' He stepped forward. He had lean hands, rather hairy (but in a nice way), and a plaid shirt. The door opened at once, making a creaking noise that encouraged them to turn and smile at each other.

He told Brenda about the Special Project. 'It's a sort of thesis, you might say, only they don't call it that except in grad school.'

At that time Brenda didn't know what a thesis was, and she had never been in the map room before. It felt dry, and was filled with air which seemed too thin for health. The walls were entirely lined with locked drawers and cupboards, all painted an unglinting metallic green. She examined the keyring Dr. Middleton had given her; she regarded the cupboards. 'Eenie, meenie, miney, mo,' she said inanely.

She unlocked a drawer and stepped aside. Jack began to extract maps, one at a time, taking care to hold them at the edges, not to bend them. She noticed that his plaid shirt was made of the kind of cotton flannel no one wore any more. The cuffs were soft with wear, almost colourless, and the sight of them touched her deeply.

'Here it is,' he said, holding up a map.

'Are your sure?' It seemed impossible that he could have found it so readily, and in the first drawer she'd opened.

'Absolutely. Here, you can tell by the markings at the bottom.'

She looked and saw a wavering line of unreadable script. 'Oh.'

'I really appreciate you helping me like this.'

She felt she should explain. It was pure luck, she said, that she had opened the right drawer. She'd only been at the Institute for a month and had never been in the map room before. It was another girl, she explained, Rosemary, who usually looked after visitors. Before coming to work at the Institute she had worked at Commonwealth Ed. But it was so big. There were so many girls.

She was babbling. She could hear herself babbling, and was acutely aware of a small, red coldsore on her upper lip. He was staring at her oddly, as though she might be crazy.

A bad beginning.

Nevertheless, he asked her to lunch. 'There's a place around the corner. Italian. Do you like Italian food?'

'You mean Roberto's? I love Italian food. Last week, on payday, we – '

She stopped herself in time.

She loved his face, even though it struck her as being overly wide and rather blank. This effect of blankness was false; he was, at twenty-one, waiting only to be unlocked. (Brenda thought of the shut drawers in the map room.)

At Roberto's, remembering his worn shirt-cuffs, she ordered vegetable soup, thirty-five cents, the cheapest thing on the menu – and a grilled-cheese sandwich and told him about how she had found the job at the Institute, how nervous she'd been during the interview, how she had almost spilled her tea in her lap. 'Oh, it was so funny,' she said, almost believing it.

His glance, which at first seemed withheld, opened an inch. He had wide, sleepy-looking eyes. She saw him taking in the blue curves of her angora sweater and saw something which might have been surprise break over his face. How had she done this – surprised him like this?

He told her about the explorer LaSalle, and, in a slow, thoughtful voice, he admitted that he had chosen the topic because a professor had suggested it. Not much work had been done on LaSalle's last journey; it was open territory, so to speak.

His words had the quality of being chosen rather than spilled, and Brenda sensed a consciousness as carefully mapped as a coastline. Nevertheless, she felt she could say anything to him, even something shocking. His hands on his fork and knife carried the peculiar density of someone who was waiting to be shocked.

'This is delicious,' Brenda said, finishing her soup and starting on her grilled cheese.

He wanted to order a bottle of wine.

She looked at her watch; she was worried, she said, about being late getting back to the Institute. 'And besides,' she added, 'wine for lunch isn't my cup of tea.'

Or at least this is what Jack, when he reminisces about their first meeting, claims she said.

She cannot imagine saying anything as witless as this. But she is not absolutely sure, and doesn't like to spoil what is one of Jack's favourite stories – a story which reflects badly on her, she thinks, but hints at an innocence she would like to claim.

She would marry him. The thought came like a streak of lightning cutting swift stripes on sleepy darkness. She would tell Jimmy Soderstrom, who had been taking her out all winter, that she had met someone else. She wouldn't have to go into details. She could be gentle and vague; it would be easier on the telephone. She would miss him, his shyness, his difficult courtesies, and especially his eager hands groping under her winter coat, searching over the softness of her sweater front. Oh, she would miss that eagerness, that quick snuffle of breath against her neck, that powerful moment when she would, safely, gently, push him away.

Years later she saw Jimmy Soderstrom on Roosevelt Road when she was going to visit her mother. He was stepping out of a small sportscar, slamming the little door in an energetic and familiar way. They stood talking for a few minutes, and she had been astonished at how easily he had talked – he was a car salesman, Chrysler – he who had been so tonguetied in the old days.

Everything changes, or at least everything seems changed. Looking back, Brenda finds it difficult to believe that, when she first went to work at the Institute, Dr. Middleton had been only forty years old, younger than Jack is now. Incredible. And she knows now that when this younger Dr. Middleton pronounced the words 'my wife, Anne', he spoke not with affection but with grievous exhaustion. She had no idea then how much people had to pay simply to endure.

Once a year now she has lunch with Gussie and Glenda and Rosemary. They have these annual lunches during the week or two preceding Christmas, always meeting at a table in the Fountain Room at Field's and always ordering something light like tuna-fish salad or the fruit plate.

None of them works at the Institute now. They are all married. Glenda, in fact, has been married twice; her first husband was an alcoholic. Once he socked her in the jaw; once he broke two of her ribs. And even so, she had gone back to him.

Rosemary, at last, had converted to Judaism and, at last, married Art, and now they live with their young daughter in a tiny, stone-faced house in Berwyn. Art, an industrial engineer, is prey to bouts of unemployment; once he was without a job for two years and four months.

And Gussie? Gussie and Franklin Sears live in a rambling old house in Sycamore, Illinois, fifty miles from Chicago. Franklin has had rheumatoid arthritis for years, and despite occasional remissions, he is more or less bedridden. (Yes, Gussie confesses, there are bedpans.) To keep the family going, Gussie has a bookkeeping job with a local lumberyard and, in addition, she serves as secretary to the Sycamore School Board. When she takes the bus in for the Christmas lunches, she brings snapshots of the two children, a boy with dark hair and glasses, and a little girl, blonde as an angel and strikingly beautiful. Gussie is always the last to arrive, and she comes in, exuberant at having a day off, slipping out of her coat, and saying in a single rising breath, 'Franklin sends all of you his love.'

When Brenda thinks back to her typing-pool days at the Institute and to the time when she first met Jack, she cannot believe in her own luck. How confidently, but how blindly, she had allowed herself to drift along, a lazy swimmer adrift in a dangerous sea. What was it she had wanted then? What, besides the pink kitchen, had she asked for? Nothing much, it seemed, only something glimpsed from the corner of an eye, an image of shelter and its scanty furnishings. What did she know then of ecstasy? Nothing.

But anything can break the fragile arc of fortune, anything. There are casualties everywhere; Brenda is always running into them or hearing about them. She has been one of the lucky ones, and in her leather handbag she carries charms to protect her: snapshots, a tarnished French coin, her mother's old thimble, a newspaper clipping announcing Jack's appointment to the Elm Park Heritage Committee. Even her keyring jingles with good fortune, promising provision, enclosure, safety.

Chapter Fifteen

'ARE THERE ANY MESSAGES?'
'For?'

Brenda, standing at the hotel desk after lunch, finds her breath stuck dry as as nut in her throat, although she couldn't have said why. 'Room 2424.'

The harried desk clerk scowls, turns, then hands her a single folded slip. 'Just this.'

It's from Barry Ollershaw, a scribbled message on hotel notepaper. 'Brenda (dash dash) No coat yet, but I'm getting warm. Will keep in touch. Regards (dash dash) Barry O.'

Brenda holds the note in her hand and feels herself lifted by an unexpected sensation of buoyancy, a sudden lightening of the air in her lungs. Her throat relaxes, breathes. Getting warm, Barry Ollershaw has written – as though the two of them, she and Barry, were cheerful conspirators let loose in the Franklin Court Arms, a couple of children off on a scavenger hunt. (Brenda shuts her eyes for an instant; a film-strip, softly coloured, shunts into view; she and Barry composed in their chairs on the twenty-fourth floor of this hotel, watching the silent snow drift past the window to land somewhere out of sight.)

'I hope it's not bad news,' Lenora Knox whispers. Brenda has forgotten about Lenora.

'No, not really.' She can't bring herself to meet Lenora's anxious, probing eyes.

'Not your kiddies, I hope,' Lenora inquires.

Her children. Rob and Laurie. 'No.' Brenda shakes her head. Why is she smiling like this? Like a crazy woman. She feels her face pulling back, ready to split in two. She looks at the floor and bites down on her lower lip.

'When I'm away I always worry about the craziest darned things,' Lenora is saying, folding her granny glasses and stowing them in the depths of her felt bag. 'Like maybe the kids locking themselves out of the house or forgetting their lunches or something. Once – '

114

Brenda refolds the note, creasing the length of it with her thumbnail and tucking it in the side section of her bag. Hmmm. She gives the bag a pat, appreciating anew the silkiness of the soft bulging leather. Should *she* leave a note for Barry? Tell him not to worry? Tell him *she* will be in touch?

'You know,' Lenora says, 'we really should keep in touch, you and I, Brenda. When this is over, I mean. Like, who knows, maybe you'll get to New Mexico one of these days, for a visit. Like on a trip to the Grand Canyon or Mexico or something like that. Of course, the Grand Canyon's in Arizona, but that's only one state over from us. Have you ever been out there, to the Grand Canyon? They have these packhorses you can rent by the day – '

'Pardon?' Brenda says, pushing her hair out of her eyes. Why is Lenora talking about the Grand Canyon?

'Or at least we should exchange Christmas cards once a year. That's one good thing about Christmas cards. It may be commercial and all, but it's the only way to keep in touch.'

'Yes,' Brenda says enthusiastically. The fountain in the middle of the lobby sucks and gurgles as though someone is tinkering with its pump. Yes, there is a workman, bending over it, reaching an arm into its stainless-steel innards. It spouts suddenly at his touch – a whooshing sound that makes her feel lighthearted and generous. She *will* leave Barry a message. Why not? It is only common courtesy to reply to a note. (Years ago Brenda served as Corresponding Secretary to the Woodrow Wilson P.T.A.; recently she was asked if she would consider filling the same office for the Chicago Craft Guild.) It wasn't fair to have Barry Ollershaw worrying about the loss of her coat; he didn't come all the way from Vancouver, Canada, to worry about her red raincoat, did he? It wasn't his fault it vanished.

'Heavens, Brenda, I just hope I haven't put my foot in it.'

'Your foot?'

'I mean, mentioning Christmas cards just then. I mean, you could be Jewish for all I know. Or – '

'No, I'm not, we're not. Jewish that is.'

'Last year I quilted my Christmas cards. You just use cotton percale and tissue paper and just a little snitch of rickrack. My husband said I was just plain out of my head, just plain up a tree, but I found this pattern in *Quilter's Quarterly*. I could send it to you if you're interested, or maybe – '

Brenda is thinking; why not suggest to Barry Ollershaw that the two of them get together for a drink? She calculates quickly: the newspaper interview with Hal Rago is at four; it would have to be later, maybe after the President's Dinner, she couldn't miss that; or would that be too late? It might be after eleven, but the bars would still be open and there wasn't a law that said she couldn't –

''Course the silly things took me ages to do. Ages. Allen and I usually send out seventy-five cards in all, so you can imagine. But the postage was the same, that was a good thing – '

Yes, she would leave a note. The curious, peaceful levity she was feeling would stabilize the pen in her hand, enable her to slash at the paper like a schoolgirl. Greetings, she would write in a jaunty, jabbing backhand. She would be cheerful, buoyant, splashing the page with large loopy letters, and she would sign her name simply 'Brenda' – so that it rose at the end like a banner or a silk scarf floating – 'Brenda'. She would dash a line or two beneath it – make it firm, joyful, unhesitating, girlish – 'Brenda'.

'The thing is, they're kind of a keepsake in a way, if you know what I mean. At least that's what everyone kept telling me.'

'Lenora?'

'Yes, Brenda?' Lenora's eyes swim blue. Pure blue. Innocent blue.

'Lenora, do you have a piece of paper by any chance? Any old thing will do. I have to leave a message for someone.'

The main exhibition hall can be reached directly from the hotel by way of a lengthy underground concourse lined with gift shops and travel agencies and lingerie boutiques. (One of these, The Underneath Shop, catches Brenda's eye as she and Lenora pass.) Today, since it is Sunday, most of these stores are locked up and darkened by iron grills. Here and there along the way there are narrow underground avenues darting off in other directions, and these are signposted: Parking Garage, Theatre Complex, Museum Entrance. This, Brenda observes, is a complete underground city, all of it sealed off from the weather, and all of it as brilliantly lit as the out-of-doors. It would be possible to stay a week or a month in Philadelphia and never have to set a foot outside. Philadelphia backyards and fences and houses – where were they? They must exist. They had to exist. But outside this central underground trunk everything seemed reduced to supposition. It was even possible to imagine that there were no people above ground, no noisy population with fixed habits of restaurants or buses or jobs or favourite grocery stores. Only the visitors really exist, convention- goers, herds of metallurgical engineers and thronging needlewomen. The only people are *us*, Brenda thinks. She looks at Lenora and smiles.

Chatting, peering into windows, they walk for what seems a mile or more down the bright terrazzo-floored tunnels. Arrows in primary colours point all along the way to the Exhibition Hall. And there it is at last, a polished space opening before them, acres of unencumbered space, reminding Brenda of a gymnasium constructed for giants. The trusswork is exposed, and skylights high overhead let in natural light – though it is light that seems filtered and carried from a great distance, varnishy yellow light spreading a haze of seriousness over the vast, settled indoor air. The whole space hums with light, or is that the distant electric buzzing of ventilators? Probably.

'Hey, we're not open yet, ladies.' A uniformed guard, arms folded on navy-blue chest, blocks their way.

'We just wanted to look around.' Lenora says this in her high, sweet, reasonable voice. 'Would that be all right?'

'It says seven o'clock. Look in the paper. Didn't you see the paper? The show opens at seven.'

Lenora persists. Her little mouth goes straight as a coin slot. 'But you see, we're the exhibitioners. My friend here and I just want to check on our own displays.'

'The orders I got – '

'I've come all the way from New Mexico in the southwest United States.' Brenda recognizes the timbre of Lenora's voice – she has friends (Leah Wallberg, Sharon Olsen) with similar voices, voices that carry the sweetness of implacability.

The guard moves aside. 'They told us not to let anyone in here. How'm I supposed to know – '

'Thank you,' Lenora says pleasantly, and breezes past him.

There is the needlepoint section. There is the macramé section. There is a section devoted to Leather Arts, a subsection for Beadwork. But the largest section is set aside for quilts; the quilts, in fact, fill all of the east end of the hall. Brenda has never seen so many displayed at once. Even in the Chicago Craft Fair, which is the biggest fair in the Midwest, there are never more than thirty or forty in any one year. Here there are hundreds, perhaps even a thousand. To save space, each one has been suspended on a large, swinging frame that reminds Brenda of the display racks for Oriental rugs she has seen at Marshall Field's. It is necessary to view the quilts one at a time, turning the hinged frames as though they were pages in a book. Some of the quilts are still being hung by a team of young workmen in clean white overalls.

'Isn't this just . . . the most thrilling . . . ' Lenora bangs the side of her head with her fist. 'I can't believe it.'

'Yes,' Brenda says, awed.

'I mean to be shown. Here. With,' she jerks her arm in the direction of the quilts, 'with all these. The thrill.'

'I know what you mean,' Brenda says.

The quilts, they discover, are hung alphabetically by the quilter's last name, and Brenda and Lenora start at the far right in order to stay out of the way of the workmen's ladders. 'Look,' Brenda cries. 'These are Verna's. Verna of Virginia.'

'Your mysterious roommate.'

'Yes.'

'My heavens, Brenda, just look at this.' Lenora's hand plucks at the binding of Verna's quilt. Her voice has shrunk to a despairing whimper.

'I know,' Brenda actually wails.

'How does she do it?'

'Those colours.'

'Nerve, I guess. Just plain old nerve.'

'And workmanship.'

'Workpersonship,' Lenora giggles.

'The trapunto work! Those leaves!'

'Are those leaves?'

'The curve of them. And what's she used in the corner there? I don't believe it. It looks like denim.'

'It is denim. Old denim. Faded.'

'Marvellous.'

'Incredible.'

'The whole thing just sort of floats off, doesn't it?'

'Like the sky, like in the Southwest – '

'Or water – cool like water.'

'I guess you probably heard the Metropolitan Museum in New York City – '

'I *know*.'

They move along.

Lenora has bought two of her prize quilts for competition, *Fiesta* and *Terracotta*. The orange radiance of *Terracotta* wrings from Brenda an involuntary cry of delight. 'Why this is really wonderful, Lenora.'

'I sort of like *Terracotta* too, but my husband says, when it comes right down to it, that he really prefers *Fiesta*. Allen has this weakness for – '

'*Terracotta* leaps right out at you. You could put your arms around that central panel. Really, Lenora, I mean it, it's absolutely wonderful.'

And it is wonderful. In the centre stand a stalkless flower frazzled by its own heat and a ring of brittle birds with snapping jewelled eyes and cruel beaks. Wonderful. Brenda has to restrain her incredulity. On the other hand, why shouldn't Lenora Knox of Santa Fe, New Mexico, be able to create a work of art that shimmers with originality; and no doubt about it, it *was* original to sew a wide band of velvet, black velvet, around the edge of the hot, kindled centre panel like that. (Brenda thinks of a plain casket filled with dazzling primitive treasures.)

'It did get the ribbon at the State last year.' Lenora confides this in her soft, forthcoming voice. 'I was just so surprised, well, just bowled over really.'

Brenda's quilts *Clairvoyant* and *Lakeside* have been hung in place, and one of the workmen, standing on a stepladder, is easing *The Second Coming* onto the metal frame.

'My goodness,' Lenora says, 'my goodness, Brenda, you've really got talent.'

Lenora's lozenge eyes open wide, but Brenda detects something vacant in the words, as though she and Lenora are locked now into a kind of ritual of too-generous praise. She thinks of telling Lenora about *The Unfinished Quilt* at home, but stops herself. Lenora doesn't want to hear about *The Unfinished Quilt*. Brenda knows this. She knows because of the bright little sparrow of cynicism that sits on her shoulder now. It's been there for a while now, this sparrow. One year? Two years? It's hard to pin such things down. And equally hard to accuse the little fellow of specific damage. But he (he?) does chirp in her ear now, a fracturing peep-peep, posing cocky questions('But what is this for?') or throwing into doubt such steady, accustomed things as praise, condolence, sympathy – even, at times, truthtelling.

Lenora rattles on and on. 'I mean, Brenda, they are just absolutely gorgeous, all three of them. I'll just bet a dollar you're going to take home a prize. And especially with that one. *The Second Coming* did you say it was called?'

Brenda is watching the workman struggling with the top corner of the quilt. The irregular border makes it hard to attach it to the frame. ('Shit,' he is muttering into the cloth.) She is remembering how she and Hap Lewis had lifted this same quilt just two days before and carried it to the window in her workroom.

A sharp longing for home strikes her, and she yearns for her backyard with the stillness of elm and oak and leafless hedge, for Hap Lewis with her rich, nutritious laughter, for the hanging plants leafing out, even for the children's voices below, arguing, yelling, but making the walls vibrate and breathe. *The Second Coming* seems lost in this enormous exhibition hall. Brenda would like to carry it away, off to her hotel room, put it on her narrow bed, lie down on its bracing squares of yellow. (Infantile, she upbraids herself.) Why *is* she so tired?

But she can't allow herself to be tired; she has an appointment at four o'clock at the St. Christopher Hotel, and it is after three now.

'Excuse me,' she says suddenly to the man on the ladder. 'Excuse me, but that's my quilt. I'm Brenda Bowman.'

'Yeah?' He looks down at her blankly.

'Well, look, I need it for a little while, okay?' (At home Laurie annoys Brenda by ending her sentences this way: okay?)

'I dunno – '

'I need to do a little more handwork on it, a few stitches. I'll bring it right back.'

'Do you think that's wise, Brenda?' Lenora worries.

'Yes.' Firmly.

'You gotta have it back before seven,' the man on the ladder says. 'Doors open at seven and we got to be done and outa here.'

'Oh, I'll have it back way before seven,' Brenda promises. 'I just thought I'd – '

'Suit yourself,' he shrugs. 'It's your blanket – you can do what you want with it.' And he lets it go, dropping it light as a parachute into her outstretched arms.

Chapter Sixteen

THE AIR OUTSIDE THE HOTEL WAS MOIST AND BRILLIANT, and the snow, which had stopped falling at last, lay melting on the sidewalks. Brenda, stepping through the wide bronze doors, congratulated herself for having brought along her winter boots.

The Second Coming was fastened beneath her chin, held in place by a large safety pin. Worn on the bias, with one corner tucked under, it fell warmly around her, reaching as far down as her knees. Lucky for her she'd decided to use light dacron batting – never mind what the purists said – and lucky, too, that she'd designed it off-centre, so that the bright elongated blocks showered in a circle from her shoulder; it might have been designed for this very purpose. Of course, it was awkward having to clutch it closed from the inside, but once she got used to it –

Only four blocks to the St. Christopher, but they were long city blocks. The doorman at the Franklin had pointed the way. He offered to get a cab for her, at the same time gesturing at the hopelessness of this, but Brenda had waved the idea aside. She needed fresh air, she needed time to herself, she felt feverish, and her eyes smarted with excitement. The doorman's glance lit on her cloak; the glance turned into a slow-tracking look of surprise, then open admiration, then a plump, courtly stepping aside to let her pass. 'Madam,' he crooned, and released into her face a puff of cologne and whiskey.

Outside the wind was brisk and reviving, and Brenda's hair, blowing straight across her face, seemed restored to richness, a richness lost to twenty-four hours of dry indoor air and to private metabolic eruptions (her approaching period, now three days late). Overhead the narrow sky fitted between the intricate roofs of buildings, topping them with blue and gold. I am not walking, Brenda said to herself; I am striding along. I am a forty-year-old woman, temporarily away from home, striding along a Philadelphia street wearing a quilt on my back. I am on my way to –

Two women at the corner, bundled in scarves, heads bent against the wind, looked up as she passed. Brenda floated a smile over their heads, and heard, as a reward, the drifting word 'gorgeous . . . '

Ah, *gorgeous* Brenda Bowman, striding along, or rather, being borne forward on rails of blue oxygen, her boots kicking out from the brilliant folds, punching sharp prints in the wafery layer of snow. Ms. Brenda Bowman of Elm Park and Chicago, gliding along, leaving a streak of indelible colour on the whitened street and trailing behind her the still more vivid colours of – what? Strength, purpose, certainty. And a piercing apprehension of what she might have been or might still become. Her shadow, which she could not help but admire, preceded her down the sun-struck street. She was, for once, splendidly detached from shop windows, posters, scrawled graffiti, the eaten snow around fire hydrants and lamp posts. Forty years of creeping, of tiptoeing, of learning to walk down a street like this. Forty years of preparing – a waste, a waste, but one that could be rectified, if only she could imagine how.

There was something epic in her wide step, a matriarchal zest, impossibly old. She was reminded suddenly of The Winged Victory of Samothrace.

When they were in France four years ago, she and Jack had made a point of going to the Louvre to see The Winged Victory. ('You can't go all the way to Paris and not see The Winged Victory,' Leah Wallberg had instructed them at the surprise bon-voyage dinner she and Irving had given for them.)

But a few days later, across the Atlantic and standing on the grand staircase in the Louvre directly before the statue, she and Jack had felt bewildered. Was this all there was?

'Well,' Jack said at last, 'considering it doesn't have a head or any arms – '

'Leah said to look at the drapery,' Brenda reminded him. 'And the way the figure is striding through the stone.'

'Hmmm.'

'She said to look at the legs. The legs seem to know just where they want to go.'

'I suppose so,' Jack said. He was a man with a gift for resisting disappointment.

123

'She said to concentrate on the wings and legs,' Brenda persevered, 'and sort of try to fill the rest of it in mentally.'

'I suppose it does have a *kind* of power,' Jack decided, and, in fact, he carried back to Elm Park and to Leah and Irv Wallberg the message that he and Brenda had glimpsed a very real power in The Winged Victory. ('Didn't I tell you!' Leah cried, eyes aglow, fingers pointed skyward.)

Brenda clutched at her cloak; the wind was colder than she'd thought, especially at the intersection, where it whirled and swept unpredictably, slapping at the skin of her neck and cheeks and lifting her hair straight up; the granite foundations of office-buildings wailed as the wind struck their sharp corners. In an hour or less the sun would be down and the air would be even colder. Why should she stand waiting, shivering, for the light to turn green? There was hardly a car to be seen. She stepped off the kerb. Bravely. With stateliness. The cape swirled around her knees. Inside her head she was smiling.

Years ago she had made her son, Rob, a Superman suit for Halloween. He must have been eight or nine at the time, a more excitable and passionate child than he was now. He had put it on and immediately run out into the backyard with the red cotton cape flying behind him. Brenda remembered that he was also wearing a pair of old blue tights, hers, and that they sagged ludicrously at the crotch and knees and ankles. But he seemed purely unaware of any imperfection. 'You know,' Brenda had marvelled, watching him through the kitchen window, 'he really thinks he *is* Superman. Just look at him.' Jack, coming to the window to look, had smiled. 'Clothes make the man.'

Together they watched as their son tore back and forth across the grass, leapt over the flower bed with its brown tangle of dead chrysanthemum heads, his arms outstretched. 'Up, up, and away,' they heard through the storm window, a wild cry, surprisingly high-pitched. He whirled and soared and in a minute was over the bushes into Miss Anderson's yard, grabbing for a branch of her oak tree, swinging widely, and dropping with an inspired pounce into her leaf pile. Brenda watched him, shaking her head. 'Now he'll catch it,' she said, unable out of pride to tear herself from the window. She saw Jack's mouth go slack with love. 'Superman himself,' he said tenderly, and his eyes filled.

Miss Anderson next door was a witch, a fact well known to Brenda's children and to the other children in the neighbourhood. Miss Anderson's was the only house that they approached on Halloween night with thrilling terror, though year after year she met them, amicably enough, on her front porch, wearing her soiled robe and dropping wrapped caramels into their open sacks. Her reputation for witchcraft derived chiefly, Brenda supposed, from one of her eyes, which sagged shut, yellowed with chronic ulcers, and from the long black coat she liked to wear, a coat from the late forties or early fifties, absurd, flowing, out of style, and made of a shiny, elegant material like taffeta. She wore this old coat year round, even when stalking up and down the back alleys of south Elm Park on her annual spring mission.

This mission was to plant hollyhocks in the small waste spaces that lay between neighbourhood garages and board fences and garbage cans. Here, in packed earth already captured by tough stands of dandelion and plantain, she scattered the seeds early on May mornings. Everyone knew about these expeditions – it was common knowledge – and once Brenda, up early and carrying out the garbage, had actually seen her with her own eyes. The sight had formed a lasting impression, like a moment frozen in an old newsreel. There came Miss Anderson, striding lankily down the alley in her rustling coat, a cotton scarf tied on her head and a cloth bag of seeds hung round her neck. There was no laborious bending, no meticulous placing of the seed – of course her eyes had been failing for years – just a willful, arrogant, almost random sowing of them. Her black-sleeved arm reached into the bag, withdrew, and hurled handfuls of seeds into the thin dirt.

A surprising number of these hollyhock seeds took root, and though Miss Anderson died two years ago, the long fuzzed stalks and delicate, frilled blooms persisted remarkably. The same could not be said of Miss Anderson's memory, for after her death, which occurred so swiftly and cleanly that Brenda cannot remember the exact cause, the house was sold to Larry and Janey Carpenter, who gutted it from top to bottom, dug up the garden, and built a handsome cedar deck, the first of its kind on Franklin Boulevard. Brenda found it hard to believe, and somewhat unfair, too, that a human personality, especially Miss Anderson's, could be so quickly and thoroughly obliterated. Occasionally Hap Lewis, out of cheerful sentimentality, reminisced about 'Old Cactus Cunt', but the younger couples on the block have hardly heard of her. To Brenda it is surprising that no mythology has grown up around her, given the peculiar coloration of her habits; even Rob and Laurie seem to have forgotten her name, referring to her, as they still do from time to time, as that old lady in the coat, or simply, The Coat Lady.

But this afternoon the thought of Miss Anderson and her vigorous, purposeful back-alley striding spoke to that part of Brenda she kept unexamined. Shouldn't she have tried to get to know her a little better when she was alive? The black coat and the eccentric preoccupation with hollyhock propagation had seemed, then, to make her impenetrable and unknowable, and her age had made her seem, to a younger Brenda, not worth bothering about.

But it might have been interesting, and perhaps even profitable, to discover what mysterious childhood shaping had determined that Miss Anderson would be old, relentless, and, in some strange way, content. Something historical had predetermined that straightforward gait. Something historical, too, had touched her mildly with madness. Everyone had a history, after all, everyone – even Miss Anderson, even Brenda's son, Rob, even that nameless classical beauty (complete with head and arms) who posed thousands of years ago as the model for The Winged Victory of Samothrace.

It was one of Jack's beliefs that she, Brenda, had no sense of history. What he meant, of course, was that she lacked his own vivid pictorial sense of a world in which he had never lived; she lacked even an interest in it. It was true enough, she had to agree. She knew, furthermore, that Jack pitied her for this disability, though he had never said so in so many words. He pitied her in much the same way that she pitied him for his seeming inability to learn foreign languages.

For her it had been different; she grew up speaking and understanding Polish, and was even said by an old friend of her mother's to have a cultivated, rather aristocratic, accent – though she could never account for that. And her old high-school French had stayed with her; four years with Mlle Wilson at Morton High School and she, even today, could pluck out a verb whenever she wanted to – which was seldom, she admitted, but it did happen. Coming down the stairs in the morning to make breakfast, the word *descendre* sometimes dropped, pale as an opal, into her consciousness. When she shopped for groceries at the A & P, the old vocabulary lists – *betterave, haricot vert, laitue* – popped up in her head, alphabetized, the irregular plurals carefully indicated, *pruneaux*.

Ah, poor Jack. When they were in France it was she who ordered their meals and arranged for their sightseeing buses, while he, hands behind his back, stood numbly locked into the everydayness of English. She had made, for his sake, careful, patient translations, which he received gratefully and with equal patience, but even so she felt he was being cheated and unfairly humbled. The flatness of the English words broke her heart, and particularly since Jack seemed innocent of any loss.

But he did possess that which she didn't: an historical sense, a sense of the past, or, more accurately, a sense of personal connection with the past. Jack, in Paris, had walked the old revolutionary quarter – he loved the French Revolution – dazed with happiness and so shut into meditation that he went for minutes without speaking, except to stop, consult the Michelin Guide – the English version – and ask Brenda, 'Do you realize that on these very cobblestones – ' or to exclaim, 'It was right here, under this arch – '

She tried to see a portion of what he saw, but couldn't. No, she could not imagine the brutal romance of peasants approaching in their rags. The eighteenth century was shut to her, and so was the nineteenth. No, she couldn't even picture Simone de Beauvoir sitting in a particular café with her note-book open on a table; no, she could not visualize the Allied armies marching up the Champs. It was her nature to resist the images of the past. But what Jack perceived as failure on her part was only the other side of her talent for calling a spade a spade, her bondage to facts and to the present moment.

Still, she felt it was not entirely true that she lacked a historical sense. In a way, her ability to perceive history whole was greater than Jack's, more detailed and more securely fastened to the springs of cause and effect. Jack was a romantic, and condemned to the broad stroke; his historical happenings were purpled with a flood of anonymous blood. History was a monster machine, a John Deere harvester, gathering everything into a hopper.

What he didn't seem to grasp (as Brenda did) was that history was no more than a chain of stories, the stories that happened to everyone and that, in time, came to form the patterns of entire lives, her own included. That some of these stories were dark (her mother's terrible and sudden death) and others drenched with light (the random inexactitude of her love for Jack and the children) – this made little difference in the end. These stories rose out of mystery, took shapes of their own, and gave way in good time to newer and different stories. It was all so simple, it seemed to Brenda; at other times it seemed not simple at all.

For some of these stories were as tentacled as the most exotic vegetation, reaching back impossibly far. Mlle Wilson at Morton High had encouraged Brenda to go to DeKalb State (where she herself had gone) to study to be a French teacher, but Brenda's mother Elsa wanted her to be a secretary so she wouldn't have to be on her feet all day (as she had to be). And so Brenda *had* become a secretary, going to work at the Great Lakes Institute, where she met Jack Bowman (out of the blue) and began the longest story of her life.

Some of Brenda's stories – more than she liked to admit – found their spaces in the improbable future. And one of these came to her now, on her way to the St. Christopher Hotel. It went like this: she and Jack might find themselves in Vancouver, Canada, for a historical conference perhaps – not really so unlikely – and she might be doing a little shopping in one of the department stores and suddenly see a familiar face. Why it was Barry Ollershaw, of all people! She would go up to him, touch his arm, surprise him with her voice. 'Do you remember . . .'

Or she might be sitting at a table with a man (face blurred) and he might place his fingertips on the inside of her wrist, the softest part of her body, and trace the faint cording of veins all the way up to her elbow. He might reach out and run those same fingertips across her lips and eyelids and then – the little table whisked from view and replaced with a width of soft grass – then he might lie down beside her, leading her out of this story and into the next one.

This kind of story, which seemed to her denser than a mere fantasy, might be told with differing annotation, depending on the imagined listener. 'How could I refuse?' to her mother's large eyebrows. 'Why not?' to Hap Lewis's open mouth. 'Life is short,' to her children's puzzled gaze.

One thing was certain. These imagined stories never ended as stories in books did, with telling declarations of arrival: ' – and then she realized – ' or 'It came to him suddenly that – ' Instead they ended somewhere on their own descending curvatures, simply run out of fuel or deprived of interest, or, as frequently happened, interrupted by the exigencies of real life and the return to the true and ongoing story that pressed as tightly as clothing against the skin. The street, the hardness of the pavement, the snow turning blue in the fading light.

And there it was, the St. Christopher. Old, ornate, with dark, wet stonework and leaded-glass doors and lights like rubies burning inside. Four o'clock exactly; the sun almost sunk, and Brenda stamping snow from her boots and beating out a poem on the brass grating of the vestibule. O snow, O Love, O Victory.

Chapter Seventeen

T WO HOURS LATER BRENDA WAS DRUNK. DRUNK AS A SKUNK, as Hap Lewis would say. Or zonked, as her husband Jack would say. Larry Carpenter next door would say, in his pompous, fake-British way, that she was ripped. She was blotto, her son Rob would say, also fried and frittered (or did that refer only to drugs?). She was stewed, sauced, pie-eyed, blitzed, and potted. She was lushed out, pissed to the eyeballs, Oh good God, Oh Christ, son of Mary.

It had happened so fast. She couldn't account for it. (Atmospheric pressure? Coursing hormones?) She had entered the St. Christopher Hotel, found the Emerald Room, and there, at the dark table in the corner, saw Hal Rago of the Philadelphia *Examiner* with a cigarette burning in his fingers. 'Hi there, Mrs. B.,' he greeted her.

Mrs. B.? The off-hand familiarity was wrenching, and seemed to certify her terrible ordinariness. Her housewifeliness.

She sat down and eased the quilt from her shoulders, *The Second Coming*, her transforming cape, now re-transformed into ridiculous improvisation. Kitsch.

'Hey, you dropped something,' Hal said loudly, and dived under the table for the safety pin. 'This yours?'

The ceiling of the Emerald Room was a depthless black, starred with hard little lights. The speciality of the house was something in a tall green glass called Irish Squint, and Hal Rago had clearly downed several before Brenda arrived. 'Try one,' he leered.

'I'll have a brandy,' Brenda said. She had a sudden, seething desire to be unaccommodating.

'Brandy it is.' He stuck a finger in the air to summon a waiter, and lewdly licked the butt end of a felt-tip pen. 'Then shall we get down to business?'

'Why not?' Brenda returned, heartened by the glassy minerals in her new voice. Gone was the full-spirited woman striding through the snow. Poof. The weight of twenty years had fallen in on her, along with the spectre of middle age, with its faked allegiances, its betrayals, its bodily leakages, and its secret pods of flesh and sour smells. Winged Victory – Ha! She shook her hair roughly back and downed her brandy.

'Atta girl. Just the thing for a lousy day like this.'

She glared at him, and he immediately signalled the waiter for another.

With grief and without the aid of mirrors, she saw herself: a woman with a flimsy comic-strip name – Brenda. She had never mastered her cuticles. She was missing two back teeth. She had stretch marks on her stomach and her neck was wrinkled, *wrinkled*. She would never again be able to command ardour; she was a fool.

Hal pulled out his notes; stared at them lengthily, as though trying to draw some restorative sobriety from what he had written earlier. 'Maybe you could tell me how you got your foot into the craft business,' he suggested.

'I can hardly remember,' Brenda said. The brandy was working its magic. She smiled at Hal Rago, her Princess Look as Jack called it.

'You're from Chi-Town, right?'

'Right.'

He made a note. 'Midwest perspective, they want. Jesus, who thinks up these crazy angles? So what have you got pithy to say about the Midwest?'

'I don't really know.' She drank deeply.

'You grow up on a farm or something like that?'

'Cicero, Illinois. Over a dry cleaner's.'

'Cicero, Christ! Isn't that where the one and only Al Capone – ?'

She nodded.

'Jesus, that's a tough place, Cicero, a real tough place.'

She was beginning to like him. 'Where'd you grow up?' she asked sociably.

'In Pennsylvania. On a farm.'

They roared with laughter.

He told her a long, pointless joke about a Pennsylvania farmer going to New York for the opera season, and followed it up with a rambling anecdote about the young John O'Hara.

She told him why she was wearing a quilt instead of a coat.

He asked why it was called *The Second Coming*, and she told him how she'd seen the neon sign on a West Side Chicago church. '"The Second Coming Is at Hand." It sounded pithy,' she said with a burst of wit.

He told her about his Italian grandmother and how she'd wanted him to be a priest.

She told him about Mlle Wilson wanting her to be a French teacher. She even spoke a few words of French for him. And then a little Polish.

He had told her how he'd got fired from his first newspaper job (an involved story about interviewing a corpse).

She told him about how she'd met her husband in the map room of the Great Lakes Institute.

He told her about his divorce from a girl named JoAnne. This story, which had many chapters, took a long time to tell. It was a tragic story – JoAnne turned out to be a nymphomaniac – but it must have had some funny parts too, for later Brenda remembered downing several fierce little glasses of brandy and wiping away tears of laughter.

He took her elbow at last and put her in a cab. 'This has been beautiful, Mrs. B.' He said this through misted eyes. 'And you are one beautiful lady.'

She said goodbye to his large, hard, red face and managed to pronounce for the taxi-driver the words 'Franklin Court Arms.'

About the ride to the hotel she remembered nothing, but she did dimly recall passing through the lobby, where crowds of people passed like waves across the wide carpet and where the splashing of the fountain affected her with extreme nausea – which she managed to contain until she got up to the room.

She woke several times. Once the phone was ringing and ringing; the sound seemed to radiate from the dark walls, a bright fluorescent electric blue circling each separate ring. Her eyes and ears burned. At least twice she stumbled to the bathroom to pour glassfuls of water down her parched throat. Later, toward morning, she opened one eye and observed a woman lying back against the pillow on the next bed. She was smoking a cigarette. For a minute Brenda, hypnotized, watched the glowing red tip and the long, strenuous releasing of smoke.

Then she fell into a deep sleep which lasted until the fierce buzz of her travel clock announced eight o'clock.

Chapter Eighteen

'I DISGUST MYSELF,' BRENDA WAS SAYING, LEANING BACK on the pillow.

'Shhhh. Drink this.'

'I'm going to float away if I do.'

'It'll do you good. What time did you say you took an aspirin?'

'Three aspirins. Eight o'clock, I think. When the alarm went off.'

'You could probably have another one now. It's after eleven.'

'Eleven o'clock! I've missed the theory session on appliqué. *And* the English Quilting Workshop. Or maybe that's this afternoon. And the worst thing was missing the President's Dinner last night.'

'What you need is rest.' Barry took the orange-juice glass from her and handed her a wet facecloth.

'I can't tell you how embarrassed I am. I must look awful. This room must smell like – '

'Why don't you go back to sleep. I'll give you a call at two or so. You should be ready for some solid food by then.'

'Never.' A shade dramatic.

'You'll be surprised.'

'Barry.'

'What?' His hand rested on the bedspread like a weight placed just so.

'I really want you to know something. That this has never happened to me before. I don't know why, but I want to assure you that I've never thrown up all over a bathroom and passed out and made a complete fool of myself – '

'Don't – '

'It really is important to me – I don't know why – that you don't go home to Vancouver thinking – '

'Shhhh.'

'This is my first real . . . disgrace.' She pressed the cloth to her forehead. The word disgrace had a puzzling richness to it. She felt dismayingly theatrical, but didn't know how to stop.

'Is it really? Your first disgrace?'

'You sound amazed.'

'I am.'

'Why?'

'Why? Well, must of us have disgraced ourselves fairly often by – ' He paused.

'By this age? Say it.'

'By this age then.'

'Well . . . ' She was thinking.

'Well, what?'

'Well, once when Jack and I – Jack's my husband – '

'I know.'

'We were invited out to Highland Park, to Dr. Middleton's for dinner. He's the head of the place where Jack works – '

'And?'

'This was years ago. Back in the days before I didn't know enough to be nervous about going to dinner there. I remember they had endive, which I'd never seen before.' Brenda smiles faintly, starting to enjoy herself. 'And English trifle, which I'd never even heard of. But I managed to take all this in my stride. And when we were finally saying goodnight, I was feeling so cheerful and lively and happy to be at the end of that evening that I sort of swung my coat on. And in the process knocked over this little figurine they had in the hall. Which turned out to be some kind of ancient pottery.'

'Irreplaceable, I suppose.' Barry's eyes smiled.

'Not quite pre-Columbian, but almost. I found that out later. It was awful. Jack almost died. Dr. Middleton had tears in his eyes – real tears – picking up the pieces. Of course they were all very polite. Jack said that naturally we'd pay for it, and they said they wouldn't hear of it, it was their fault for having it there by the front door. Which it was in a way. But you can imagine how I felt.'

'Yes.'

'There was just no way to compensate for something like that. For years I kept inviting them to our house and hoping they'd break something of mine, but of course they never did.'

'Do you want the curtains left open? The sun's right in your eyes.'

'I know. But that's what I need. To suffer.'

'Sackcloth and ashes.' He smiled down at her.

'I suppose.'

'You're not the first person in the world to have too much to drink, you know.'

'I just thought of something else. Another awful disgrace.'

'Tell me.' He perched on the air-conditioning unit, his hands grasped around his knee.

'It was just after we'd moved to Elm Park. Before that we'd been living in a student apartment downtown and this was sort of our introduction into the middle class, you might say. I guess all my disgraces are social disgraces.'

'Go on.'

'Some people in the neighbourhood gave a little party so we'd meet everyone. It's that kind of neighbourhood – very friendly, without being chummy. Robin and Betty Fairweather – they're divorced now, as a matter of fact, just last year – they were the ones who gave the party for us. It was on a Sunday afternoon, just drinks and cheese and olives and so on. And they had hired a man to serve the drinks and pass things. And I'd never been to a party where someone had been hired to help. So what did I do but introduce myself to this man. He was wearing a white jacket and everything, but I never even thought he might be a waiter. "Hi, I'm Brenda Bowman." I actually said that – and stuck my hand out to shake hands with him.'

'And that was your worst disgrace?' Barry shook his head.

'Well, in a way, but I suppose it doesn't really count as a disgrace. Because, by some kind of miracle, there was no one else standing there at that moment. No witnesses, I mean. So no one ever found out about it except for this waiter and me. As a matter of fact, this is the first time I've told anyone else about it.'

'Not even – ?'

'Not even Jack.'

'Why not, I wonder.'

'I don't know. Jack would probably just laugh. Now, that is. But then – well, we were younger then. And I don't know, sometimes we don't always laugh at the same kind of things.'

'I know what you mean.'

'What was your worst disgrace?'

He was sitting leaning against the wall with one knee drawn up. This posture seemed in some way to invite intimacy. He considered the question gravely, and then said, 'I suppose it would be the same as for most men. A sexual failure of some kind.'

'Oh.' She shut her eyes. 'I shouldn't have asked. It's none of my business. I'm terribly sorry.'

'Why be sorry?'

'I must still be a little drunk. Rattling on like this.'

'You're looking, well, not so pale. As before.'

'Thank you. I mean thank you for looking after me like this. The orange juice and aspirin and everything. And taking the quilt over to the Exhibition Hall for me this morning. I was probably sick all over that, too.'

'Just a little.'

'Ooooohhhhh.' She groaned into her hands.

'I sprayed something on it. You had something in the bath-room – '

'Spray-Net.'

'I think so.'

'I deserve this.'

'Anyway, they said it was in plenty of time. The judging isn't until this afternoon some time. Three o'clock I think they said.'

'You know, I can't believe this.'

'What?'

'Here you are, all the way from the West Coast, attending a professional conference, and you spend your whole morning running around with a filthy quilt smelling of someone's vomit you hardly even know – '

'I've known you forever.' He said this lightly, with a twist of a smile, only slightly mocking.

'You don't believe in former lives, do you?' Brenda asked.

'No.' Apologetically.

'Good. I don't either.'

'My wife says I haven't got an occult bone in my body.'

'Neither have I. I don't even read the Horoscope in the *Trib*.'

'I don't even open fortune cookies.'

'You're purer than I am. I open them but I don't believe them.'

'I've often wondered how people get like this. Like us.'

'So have I. I think we're born this way. A special race of people. The race that calls a spade a spade.'

'A deprived race maybe.'

'Why deprived?'

'Think of all we miss. All the excitement. An extra dimension.'

'Probably. But would you have it any other way?'

'No.'

'She was here last night.'

'Who?'

Brenda nodded at the other bed. 'Verna. My roommate.'

'Ah, Verna the post-virginal.'

'At least I think she was here. I woke up and saw a woman lying in bed smoking a cigarette. I think it was about five o'clock.'

'You could have been dreaming. Or – '

'I don't think so. And the bedspread does look a little bit rumpled, don't you think?'

'A little.'

'I shouldn't be keeping you,' Brenda said. 'I know you probably have something or other to do.'

'I should let you get some sleep. But, look, is there anything you'd like before I go?'

'I can't thank you enough – '

'Don't.' He stood up and closed the curtains. The cessation of sunlight came like an absolution.

'I feel like a child being taken care of,' Brenda said.

He stood in the dark for a moment, not saying anything.

'Is it really the worst thing?' Brenda said. 'Sexual failure?'

'I think so.'

'Worse than the failure of love?'

He considered. Brenda waited with her eyes shut.

'I'll have to think about that,' he said.

Chapter Nineteen

B RENDA CAN HARDLY BELIEVE WHAT SHE'S HEARING. IS THIS
woman serious? Yes, she is.

Dr. Mary O'Leary, Guest Speaker: creamy high forehead,
bluish highlights in thick auburn hair, a suit of heavy wool
cloth, a voice springy with authority. And she appears to have
the right credentials. Brenda reads about her in the programme:
Radcliffe (Major in psychology), the Sorbonne, then a Ph.D. in
Art History from Stanford. Her topic for today is Quilting
Through the Freudian Looking-Glass: A New Interpretation.

Can it be true what she's saying? Is it possible? All around
her, Brenda sees women, and one man, nodding agreement,
nodding approval, listening. Dr. O'Leary, a stack of note cards
in hand, touches on the best known of traditional quilting
patterns, naming them lightly, as though they were as familiar
to her as the names of her children or her oldest friends. The
lecture is accompanied by slides projected on an overhead
screen. Slide one: the Star of Bethlehem clearly representing an
orgasmic explosion, though it has also been viewed as an
immense, quivering vulva. 'Women in pioneer America sup-
pressed their sexuality as society demanded, but ecstasy found
a channel through circumscribed needlework.'

Slide two: the well-loved Wedding Ring quilt, symbolizing
the enclosed nature of femaleness. Next: the Double Ring quilt,
which, instead of breaking through that enclosure, merely
amplified it. Then the traditional Fan quilt, quietly mocking
male ontology – Brenda is not sure of the word ontology – with
its dull, unrelenting repetitions; Dr. O'Leary sees this mockery
as being subtle, punitive, and filled with pain. The Log Cabin
quilt, the most telling, the most incriminating of quilting patterns, presents a seamless field of phallic symbols, so tightly
bound together that there is no room at all for female genitalia.
The multiple phallic images suggest penis envy on one hand
and fantasies of gang rape on the other.

And finally, the ironically named Crazy Quilt, offering early

American women a sanctioned release from social and sexual stereotyping, and, in the hands of the most daring, an expression of savage and primitive longings. Dr. O'Leary has made a detailed study of the shapes in these so-called crazy quilts; the presence of many triangles suggests irresolution, perhaps even androgyny. Breast shapes, interestingly, outnumber phalli, but Dr. O'Leary and her assistant are hesitant about drawing premature conclusions. It may be that women were defending and proclaiming their femininity; or, and this seems more likely, they may have been expressing infantile needs which had not been satisfied. As for the present-day revival in quiltmaking, Dr. O'Leary interprets it partly as apologia, partly as retreat from responsibility, and partly a continuum of what it has always been, a means of exercising control over a disorganized and hostile universe. End of lecture.

From the audience there is scattered applause at first, which then grows; there are even a few cheers. But Brenda, who knows herself to be capable of serious acts of capitulation, does not clap at all. She is caught, silent, between stunned bewilderment and boiling laughter.

'Claptrap,' Dorothea Thomas from Lexington, Kentucky, says. 'Poppycock, every word of it.'

Brenda smiles, thinking of how she will relate these comments to Hap Lewis and Leah Wallberg and Andrea Lord when she gets home. ('And she actually said poppycock, just like Ma Perkins used to.')

Dorothea Thomas, who is considered to be the Grandma Moses of the quilt world, continues. 'Sometimes I wonder why the devil I bother coming to these things when all there is is talking, talking, talking, and about the craziest farfetched things. The Star of Bethlehem is the Star of Bethlehem for Pete's sake. That's what it *is*.'

'You don't think that, on an unconscious level, it symbolizes – '

'Fiddlesticks.' ('And she actually said fiddlesticks!')

'But the Log Cabin quilt – ?'

'One of the prettiest quilts around. My own mother – and this was way back in 1902 or 1903 – had a Log Cabin quilt, made it with her own hands, and if you'd have known my mother – of course she died in 1919 – you'd know better than to think she had thoughts like that in her head. Rape and so on. She was too darned busy raising kids and washing and sewing and keeping chickens and ducks and I don't know what all else to sit around worrying about rape. She was always sewing – the way that woman could sew. Made all our clothes, even for the boys, their pants and shirts, and she ended up with all these itty-bitty scraps, so what did she do but sit herself down and did like women in the country did then. She made this beautiful Log Cabin quilt; I still have it in my possession. No electricity, not back in those days, just the kerosene and the light from the fireplace, and that's how she put all those pieces together. Then, for the quilting part, she had her friends. The friends that woman had! Not my father, a good man but he didn't hardly have a friend to his name, sort of kept to himself, quiet man, hardly talked. But my mother, what a difference, the house was always full, relatives, sisters, friends just stopping by, there was always coffee, I can't remember a day when there wasn't coffee hot on the stove, and there they'd sit. They had sewing baskets they'd take around with them when they visited, always had a little handwork on the go, darning, mending, embroidery, crotchet work, you name it. And the way they'd laugh, they'd laugh about anything, old times, old memories, gossip I suppose you'd call it, but nothing bad that I can remember, by that I mean nothing unkind. I was always there, at least that's how I remember it, just a little thing, seven or eight years of age, no one ever said run along and get lost. They'd hand me their basting threads to straighten out, and then they'd use them over again, imagine! Oh, I used to love it, just being in that front room when they sewed and laughed, it was wonderful. I'd stop and think of my father out there in the barn, doing chores all by his lonesome – it got freezing out there – and think how lucky I was to be inside with my mother and my mother's friends, just sewing away and laughing and telling each other stories.'

Dorothea Thomas's speciality was story quilts. She was famous for them. Some of her story quilts were on permanent exhibition in public galleries, and others had been sold to movie stars; Paul Newman and Joanne Woodward were said to own several. Last year she was written up, with photographs, in the Lifestyle section of *Time*, where she was quoted as saying: 'I like a pretty design as well as the next person, but it's got to tell a story.'

Brenda met Dorothea Thomas at the afternoon workshop on Narrative Quiltmaking. Thirty women (and two men) crowded into the Freedom Room at the end of the convention floor and listened to Mrs. Thomas, seventy-eight years old, chin sunk between the roughened roundness of cheeks, talking about her craft. By a story, she told them, she didn't mean anything long and complicated with lots of turnings like TV soap operas or *Gone With The Wind*. Just something with a beginning and a middle and an end. She'd done fairytale quilts and folktale quilts, but the ones she liked to do best were based on plain old everyday family stories.

As a demonstration, she showed her quilt *Prize Squash*, asking Brenda and Lenora Knox, who were sitting in the front row, to hold it up so everyone could see. It was rather small, a child's crib-cover, divided into four sections. Sometimes, she explained, she divides her quilts into eight or twelve sections, depending on how long the story is. The top left-hand square of *Prize Squash* showed the simplified outline of a boy on his knees, dropping a seed into the ground. The picture was composed of primitive colours and shapes, half patchwork, half appliqué, and all of it was tracked with whimsical stitchery – the young boy's overalls were held up with cross-stitched suspenders, and the seed held in his hand was a glowing triple French knot worked in silky thread. In the second square the boy was standing measuring with sunburned hands the height of a young green plant. The third square – Mrs. Thomas leaned over and pointed a bony finger at the bottom left-hand corner – was entirely filled with the swelling yellowness of squash, and the fourth panel showed the boy facing forward, a blue ribbon on his chest and an upturned hand holding a clutch of glistening seeds.

The story, Dorothea Thomas said, was a true one, based on her son Billy, now a man of fifty-five and the owner of a doughnut franchise in eastern Kentucky. When he was a boy, they had lived in the country, and he had raised, one summer, a prize Hubbard squash. 'One thing I know, for sure,' Mrs. Thomas told the roomful of listeners, 'is that if I live to be a hundred and ten, I'm never going to run out of stories. All I do is dig out the old picture album, and something jumps up for me every time.'

She has done birthday quilts and wedding quilts and even quite a few funeral quilts; the funeral quilts for some reason are the most sought after of all. One of her first designs – she began quilting seriously at sixty – was the life story in eight panels of a family pet, a she-goat named Ruthie-Sue. 'I just loved telling folks about that crazy old Ruthie-Sue of ours, the way she used to knock her head up against the back porch when she wanted attention and eat my morning glories, and the way she'd roll over on her back like a puppy dog – it seemed like she thought she *was* a puppy dog – and on real hot days she'd go crazy and start nibbling on the tyres of the half-ton truck we had at that time. Everyone was always asking me how Ruthie-Sue was getting on, everyone I met. One day I just thought, why the heck don't I make a quilt about it all? So that's just what I did.'

Brenda listened, thinking of stories – her own stories, or rather the stories she shared with Jack – stories too trivial even for family albums; the time Rob locked himself in the bathroom and had to be rescued through the window; the time Laurie, seven years old, figured out how to put the lawnmower back together again. And the time Brenda's mother got mugged down on Wabash with only thirty-one cents in her purse. The time she and Jack were snubbed – or thought they were snubbed – by a waiter at Jacques's. The time in France when they saw a man on a bicycle carrying a bottle of wine under his arm; the bicycle hit a stone, throwing him over the handlebars, but he leapt up like a gymnast, nimbly saving the bottle in the nick of time, and making the sign of the cross in the air, a wonderful silent movie of a story.

When they tell these stories to friends (as they sometimes do) Brenda never says to Jack, 'Please don't tell that old story again,' and he never says to her, 'We've all heard that one.' They love their stories and tacitly think of them as their private hoard, their private stock, exquisitely flavoured by the retelling. The timing and phrasing have reached a state of near perfection; it's taken them years to get them right. It seems to Brenda that all couples of long standing must have just such a stock of stories to draw upon.

In fact, when Robin Fairweather divorced Betty Fairweather last year and married a twenty-four-year-old beautician named

142

Sandra, the first thing Brenda thought about was that she would never again hear that wonderfully funny tale about Robin and Betty's 1953 honeymoon spent next door to a pet shop in Akron, Ohio. Robin, aged fifty now, with a jiggling belly, would have to start all over again building up a fund of tellable stories (and somehow Sandra, with her contact lenses and flat rear-end, seemed an unlikely repository). What a loss it all was, Brenda thought, all that shared history down the drain.

How could people bear it?

After the workshop Brenda went up to Dorothea Thomas and said, 'I can't tell you how much I've enjoyed this. It's wonderful to meet someone who's so sure of what she's doing. I could sense, while you were talking, that you don't have any doubts. I think most of us do, from time to time anyway.'

'Well, an old bag like me' – Mrs. Thomas said this in a firm voice, her large teeth shining – 'I just do what I can do, and that's all there is to it, I guess.'

'I saw your *Corn-Planting Quilt*. At the Art Institute show last year in Chicago.'

'Oh, that one! Boy oh boy, I'd like to get my hands on that one again. It's all wrong, the last two squares anyways are all wrong. As soon as it got sold I figured out what it was that wasn't right, what I should have done. Then, well, it was too late. That's how it goes.'

'It seemed to work for me,' Brenda said in her awful voice, her phony voice.

'The thing is,' Dorothea Thomas went on, 'I used to think stories only had the one ending. But then, this last year or so, I got to thinking that that's not right. The fact is, most stories have three of four endings, maybe even more.'

'I don't think I – '

'You've got your real ending, plain and simple. You know, the way things really happened. That's the ending I've been putting in my quilts all along. And then there's the ending a person's hoping for, the one he's got his fingers crossed for. That's real, too, in a way of speaking. And then there's the ending he's scared to death is going to happen. And worst of all – and don't we all know it – there's the way it might have been if only – '

'You mean the road not taken?'

'Good heavens,' Mrs. Thomas cried, 'that just exactly what I mean, what you just said. I like the way you put that now. The road not taken.'

'Oh, that's not my phrase. I think it was Robert Frost who – '

'The road not taken, I'm going to remember that. Keep it in mind for the future. All my new quilts, the ones I've been doing this fall and winter, they've all got two or three endings to them. 'Course they're getting bigger and bigger, kind of superduper king-size now, and still growing and growing. Some folks don't like them so much as they did. Too big to put on a bed for one thing. And kind of confusing, I guess. They like them like a picture book, just one ending, nice and simple. The people in New York that look after the selling for me say these new ones I've made, they're not so popular. Harder to sell, you know. They say they're not really primitive art any more, not like they were. But what the heck, I say, I'm not going to start fussing at my age about what people say, I could be dead next year, I could be dead tomorrow.'

'We all could,' Brenda said.

'You're so young, you're like a girl still, a young girl with your life ahead of you. My what I'd give . . . ' She stopped, pressed the palms of her hands together, shook her head.

Moved, Brenda vowed to be sterner with herself. But kinder.

Chapter Twenty

THE ART SCENE by Hal Rago

CHICAGO WOMAN SEES
PIONEER CRAFT AS ART FORM

Attractive Brenda Bowman hails from the American Midwest, but she's a long long way from being your stereotype image of a rural, cornbelt quiltmaker. Ms. Bowman is an urbanite to the core, a Chicagoan by birth, a quilter by profession.

Even the coat she was wearing yesterday as she battled her way through a Philadelphia blizzard was a handsome example of her work, a rich, vibrant collage of purples and yellows.

'I got into quilting accidentally,' Ms. Bowman confessed in an interview yesterday. 'A few years ago I went out to buy my daughter a new bedspread, and I was so floored by the prices that I decided to make her one instead. I had a few odds and ends of material around the house — luckily I was brought up by a thrifty mother who taught me to sew — so I cut out some squares and stitched them together and — presto — there was my first quilt. Some friends encouraged me to sign up for a design course the next winter at the Art Institute, and that was the beginning of the whole thing.'

Brenda Bowman hasn't looked back since. In the last four years she's made and sold dozens of quilts, and this week she's in Philadelphia attending the National Handicrafts Exhibition. Examples of her work are on display at the Exhibition Centre which opened last night to record crowds. Quilters and other needlework artists from coast to coast have converged at the Franklin Court Arms for a few days to discuss their crafts and compare their wares.

Asked if she could define the particular invigorating essence of the American Midwest, Ms. Bowman replied succinctly, 'Fertility, a tradition of fertility.' The warm, empathetic Brenda Bowman, mother of two teenagers, went on to discuss the connection between art and craft. 'Art poses a moral question; craft responds to that question and in a sense provides the enabling energy society requires.'

(Tomorrow Hal Rago talks to tapestry-maker
Lily Sherman from Tallahassee, Florida)

'Cheer up,' Barry Ollershaw said over the potato-and-leek soup. 'It's really quite a nice write-up.'

'It's awful,' Brenda said, spooning up soup. She was ravenous.

'Attractive, warm, empathetic. Nothing wrong with any of that.'

'I can't believe I said all that pompous junk about art posing questions. And the fertility thing. I don't even know what I mean.'

'I followed you all the way to enabling energy and then – '

'It's all hogwash, as Dorothea Thomas would probably say.'

'Succinctly put. '

'I'm being kind to myself. It's really worse than that. It's pretentious hogwash.'

'I think you're being too severe.'

'Another funny thing, even though he didn't mean it literally, was the part about never looking back. Because it seems to me I spend half my time looking back.'

'Do you? That surprises me.'

'Poor Lily Sherman, whoever she is. I suppose she's going to get the Emerald Room treatment too. Maybe I should look her up and give her fair warning.'

'I imagine it's too late by now.'

'The one consolation is that I don't know a soul in Philadelphia. And no one in Chicago's going to read a word of this. The worst part, when you think about it, is that dumb "presto" stuck in the middle. Did I really say presto? I probably did, I vaguely remember. I should go stick my head in a bucket of water.'

'Have some soup instead. How are you feeling?'

Brenda, cheerful, hungry, sitting at a candlelit table in a corner of The Captain's Buffet, felt removed from the feebleness of human complaint. She folded Hal Rago's column in two and smiled at Barry. 'I'm feeling better than I deserve. Fine, in fact.'

'Who's Dorothea Thomas?'

She liked him for asking; and for getting the name right. 'Dorothea Thomas? She's a prize quiltmaker from Kentucky, almost eighty years old. I met her today for the first time. She makes me think it might not be too bad, growing old.'

'Do you really fear it?' Barry asked her. (He was good at questions.) He lifted the wine bottle, asked her with his eyes if she wanted some.

'I'd better not.' Brenda shook her head at the wine. 'I must be a little afraid of getting old, because every morning I get down on the floor and go through this exercise routine. The Air Force exercises. Which I hate. All the time I'm bending and stretching I think to myself, all this just so I'll be spry when I'm seventy.'

'So do I.'

'What?'

'Air Force exercises.'

'Oh.'

A silence dropped between them. It came without warning. The waiter came and took away the soup bowls and brought hot platters of paella. Brenda placed a fork into a piece of scallop. It tasted of parsley and browned garlic.

The silence obstinately refused to lift. Brenda felt suddenly overly large and clumsy. What was she doing sitting across from this man? His hands, slender and more agile that her own, held the knife and fork in a way that she recognized as being European. What was she doing eating an intimate dinner with this stranger, surrounded by the romantic claptrap (another Dorothea word) of candlelight, wine bottle, solicitous service, soft piped music; what did she think she was doing anyway?

Perhaps he was thinking the same thing; how had he let himself in for an evening like this? She watched him chase a shrimp to the rim of his plate. He sat looking intently at a piece of tomato, then divided it in two. A delicate man with precise gestures. Perhaps a little prissy. She remembered the way he had said, when they first met, that he was nuts about quilts. An odd thing to say, now that she thought about it. Why exactly had he invited her to dinner anyway?

What had joined them earlier, her reaction – overreaction – to finding Verna in bed with a man, her lost coat, the falling snow, now seemed insubstantial, used up. They were just two people adrift, nothing more. Barry had a lead on her coat; the metallurgist sharing his room was called Storton McCormick, he was from New York, and apparently he had been called back suddenly. But he was due to return to Philadelphia in the morning. He was giving a paper, in fact, in the afternoon, and Barry hoped to speak to him afterwards about the missing coat.

'I really would appreciate that,' Brenda said. 'You're sure it won't be too awkward?'

'Not at all,' Barry said, and fell silent.

After a minute he cleared his throat and went after the shrimp once more.

She should have gone with Lenora Knox and Lenora's roommate on the Philadelphia-by-Night bus tour.

The rice was cold, microwaved. She swallowed and heard, self-consciously, the sound of her swallowing. ('An urbanite to the core' – the phrase rolled down her throat like a marble.)

There was an arrangement of wet roses on the table; her paralysed eye hung on a single petal beaded with water. Shouldn't she be better strung together at this age, able to cope with silence gracefully? But this wasn't like the silence she'd shared with Barry yesterday morning as they sat in her room watching the snow come down. This was silence wrenched into being by the weight of occasion (an invitation: Barry on the phone asking her to join him for dinner; a date for heaven's sake, ridiculous word). The schmaltz of candlelight and soft music put a burden of expectation on her – and on him too she supposed – asking the question What is this leading to?

The waiter hovered. 'Is everything all right?'

'Fine,' they chorused.

Brenda felt immobilized, as though eating and chewing and swallowing were all she was capable of doing. There must be social questions she could ask. What? He had mentioned Japan. Do you do much travelling? Any good restaurants in Vancouver? Sports? Hobbies? How were your meetings today? (Too wifey, that last one.)

The wine was a deep red, soft-looking, probably very dry. His eyes seemed locked to the level of his glass.

What was the matter with her? Did she really think this pleasant, civilized man was softening her up for seduction? She had friends – Betty Corning, Kay Wigg – who were always thinking so-and-so was after them, looking them up and down, undressing them with their eyes. It happened to women in their forties, this kind of self-delusion.

What a bore she was. She imagined Barry Ollershaw recalling this evening, how he'd hoped for a cheerful dinner out and instead got stuck with dullness and silence. Maybe she was still hung over. Or premenstrual. Or both.

Or maybe she was feeling guilty. Would he tell his wife he asked a woman to dinner? Would she tell Jack? The question struck her forcibly, and so did a vigorous protestation: why shouldn't a man and a woman, meeting by accident, share a meal? It happened all the time (but never before to her).

The waiter was back. 'Would you care for dessert?'

He thinks we're husband and wife, Brenda thought.

Barry ordered Dutch apple tart.

'I couldn't eat another thing, ' Brenda said in a pinched voice. (Warm, empathetic Brenda Bowman.)

The tart was a lean triangle covered with a trail of cream. 'You're sure you wouldn't like some?' Barry asked politely.

'I'm sure.'

'Really?'

'Yes.'

'Brenda.' He pronounced her name in a quiet, tired voice. And reached across the table to cover her hand with his. His own was trembling slightly; the sight of a raised vein on the back of his hand touched her, and, to her relief, she abruptly broke the silence.

She began to talk, rushing from one thing to the next, telling him finally about Dorothea Thomas's stories, how Dorothea had discovered that stories have more than one ending.

Barry, still covering her hand, listened, tipped his head to one side, said yes, it was true, he could see that plainly, but was it wise to overcomplicate that which was simple and straightforward?

'But what choice does she really have?' Brenda asked, comfortable with the feel of his dryish hand on hers. 'Even at her age she can't go on pretending. It's like a primitive painter who's discovered perspective and shading and all the rest.'

'She could shut her eyes; keep her life simple.'

'Do people do that? I'm not sure they do. Or that they can. I can't. And I'd like to, believe me. I used to be happier than I am now.'

'Of course no one can recover innocence. When it's gone, it's gone. But most of us, I suppose, pretend.'

'You too?'

'Sure.'

'Give me an example,' Brenda said happily.

'Coffee?' the waiter again.

'Coffee?' Barry asked Brenda.

'Please.'

'Where were we?' He turned to her.

'Pretending things are simple when they're really not.'

'You asked for an example.'

Brenda nodded.

'This isn't a very happy example.'

She felt reckless. 'Go on.'

'It's about children.'

'Children?'

'The other day you asked if I had any. Do you remember?'

'And you said no.'

'But I do – that is we do, my wife and I. One child. A daughter. She might be dead. She probably is dead. We don't know for sure.'

Brenda wasn't sure she'd heard right. But, yes, she had. 'What happened?' she said slowly.

'She went over to Europe when she was eighteen, when school was out. Hitchhiking we think, although she had a rail pass. She started with a friend, but that didn't last long.'

'And then what?' The pressure of his hand increased.

'No one knows. They started in England. We think she was in France for a few weeks. Someone remembered seeing her, or someone who looked like her anyway, near Notre Dame in Paris, and she was talking about going to Morocco. That's all. There's never been any trace – nothing, no postcard, nothing.'

'How could that happen? How could someone disappear like that?'

'It does happen. And not just to us. We keep a running ad in the Paris *Herald Tribune*, a come-home ad, once every two weeks. There're lots of them, a column of them. "Come home, all is forgiven," that sort of thing.'

'That's awful, awful.'

'When it happened – when we realized she was lost – I went to France and spent a month looking for her, talking to the embassies, to the French police. But where do you begin? It was hopeless.'

'When was this, when she disappeared?'

'Four years ago now. She was eighteen. She'd be almost twenty-two now, if she's alive.'

'What time of year was it, when you were in France?' It seemed important to know.

'Easter. I flew to Paris on Easter Sunday.'

She wanted to cry out, 'But that's when Jack and I were in Paris.' Instead she said, 'Oh Barry. I'm so sorry. About your daughter. Not to know, that must be the most terrible part.'

'I suppose that's what I meant about pretending. It may be an act of dishonesty on one's part, but it's simpler – less painful anyway – just to say, if someone asks, as you did, that there are no children. Simpler than explaining and thinking about what might really have happened. My wife and I, it's as though we're in training to learn how to be a childless couple. It's harder for Ruth than for me. She blames herself. She can't bear it. It's changed her utterly.'

'I would die,' Brenda said, meaning it.

'You probably wouldn't.'

'I would.'

The waiter arrived with more coffee and a plate of chocolate mints. 'Brandy?' he asked.

'Nothing for me,' Brenda said.

'Nothing more,' Barry said.

With solemn faces they regarded each other. Then Barry brought her hand to his lips, kissing her fingertips.

Chapter Twenty-One

THE NEW SEXUAL FREEDOM HAS NOT TOUCHED BRENDA, THOUGH it has touched almost everything and everyone around her. She and Jack know several couples who have made, after many years, new arrangements which accommodate each other's private longings and needs. Bernie Koltz's wife, Sue, goes away occasionally for weekends without Bernie. 'Sue's out of town this weekend,' Bernie will say to Jack, letting the phrase sit out in the open like a plum on a plate, daring Jack to knock it off. 'Does *he* go "out of town" too?' Brenda asked Jack once. Jack didn't know for sure, but suspected he did. He must. 'I certainly hope so,' Brenda said emphatically. She had never liked Sue Koltz much.

When Robin and Betty Fairweather split up a year ago, Betty went to Puerto Rico for a week to lick her wounds and had sex one night in her hotel room with a man whose name she never did discover. 'Robin's playing his little games, why shouldn't I?' She'd said this to Brenda on her return, without a trace of guilt or sorrow or self-reproach or shame. 'And this guy was more of a man in bed than his royal highness Robin Redbreast ever was.'

Bill and Sally Block's daughter Lucy, seventeen years old, is living in Wheaton with a thirty-six-year-old-man, and Sally has recently been out for a visit, helping Lucy make curtains and wallpaper a bathroom.

Brenda's oldest friend in the world lives the life of a high-priced hooker. Rita Simard, later Rita Kozack, still later Rita LaFollet, went through grammar school with Brenda, and then through high school. Before she was twelve she had the breasts of a woman. She now lives in a sparkling glassy North Shore apartment, paid for by a number of out-of-town businessmen.

Larry Carpenter next door tells stories at parties which involve acts of fellatio, sodomy, and copulation with geese. Brenda, listening to him, remembers her mother's idea of a rowdy party joke: look down your blouse front and spell attic.

The world has changed, she admits it. Her own son, barely

fourteen, has a stack of *Penthouses* under his bed. A neighbourhood party, one she and Jack luckily missed, apparently dege-
nerated – reports were garbled – into something of a free-
for-all.

Janey Carpenter, sunbathing in her backyard last summer,
remarked to Brenda how worn out she was – fucking all night
long, it got to be too much.

Calvin White, who works at the Institute with Jack, has
moved in with Brian Petrie, who also works at the Institute, and
Brenda suspects they are living as lovers.

Last year Jack and Brenda stayed in a new hotel in San
Francisco where there was a vibrating bed which ran on
quarters, also soft-porn movies which could be had for $6.50,
also a notice slipped under their door one morning which said
'Dianne, Expert massage, any hour.' 'It's too much,' Brenda had
burst out. 'I feel like I'm drowning in sex.' Jack had given her his
Groucho leer – 'How can there ever be too much sex?' Later,
though, he said, 'But I know what you mean.'

Ease, openness, a tearing down of rules. It had all taken place,
and it seemed to Brenda it had happened overnight. Marital
fidelity had become a thing of the past, the word itself antique,
and as embarrassing as certain companion words like husband
and household.

Not long ago Brenda discovered a scrap of paper in Jack's
shirt pocket on which he had written 'Fidelity 15'. Fifteen what?
she'd wondered. The word fidelity gnawed away at her for
days, and its curious attached number opened up several
possibilities, none of which she wanted to dwell on. Several
times she thought of asking Jack about it, but held back. The
contents of pockets were private. (And Jack, to his credit, never
went into her purse or dresser drawers.) The enigma was
abruptly solved when he told her one morning he was thinking
of buying a Fidelity Trust savings certificate at fifteen per cent
instead of their usual government bond. She had felt a dismaying flood of relief – dismaying because she trusted Jack, she
always has. And he trusted her.

Before they were married Brenda and Jack talked frankly about
sex. It was the spring of 1958; the *Ladies' Home Journal* had
recently done a series of interviews on the current state of sex in
America.

Premarital sex. It was risky. Should they chance it? Yes, Brenda said, though she dreaded, feared, the act itself, the ballooning pain exploding inside her; she didn't believe in the mere tablespoon of semen, it must be more than that. And she dreaded the knell of finality, for once this act was accomplished, what was left in her life? But she was strongly tempted; she wanted to see what it was all about, all this fuss.

No, Jack said, they'd waited this long, they could wait another month or two. It was hard to explain, difficult to justify, but the old myth of respect for the virgin bride persisted beyond logic. *The girl that I marry will have to be / As soft and as pink as a nursery / The girl I call my own.* Et cetera. Besides, he knew what sex was. He had gone steady with a fellow student named Harriet Post for a year; Harriet had been reckless and sensual; she had owned a diaphragm since her eighteenth birthday. She was quick and passionate, according to Jack, and sometimes impatient with him. More than once, he confessed to Brenda, he had felt himself a mere instrument in her arms. She had badgered him, hurried him; 'Now,' she had cried, 'hurry up for the love of God.'

Jack and Brenda, one damp night before their marriage, sitting in Jack's father's car, had related to each other versions of their sexual histories. Kissing, yes, Brenda admitted; and a little feeling around. Above the waist though, and on top of clothes. Except once, with Jimmy Soderstrom out at the Forest Preserve. He had undone her bra and kissed the tips of her breasts; she had felt ridiculous, but faint with pleasure.

Jack, in turn, told Brenda about his relationship with Harriet Post. He had broken up with her, said goodbye, but a kind of gratitude lingered. She had taught him something about women.

Both Jack and Brenda had believed that marriage stood a better chance if the male had had some previous sexual experience. This was verified by a set of graphs in a book they read.

The name of the book was *The Open Door: A Marriage Guide for Moderns*. They bought it shortly before their wedding, a solemn purchase, and poured over its pages. There were chapters on foreplay, climax, afterplay, premature ejaculation, impotence, and frigidity. There were cross-sections on a penis and its attached testicles, of a vagina and its linkage with the womb and the ovaries. Graceful swollen passages, these, imprisoned in the lower portions of human bodies.

The mystery of life was that a tentacle of rigid flesh could be inserted into an answering vessel. This was what all the songs, poems, and Bob Hope jokes were about. A mystery, a joy, which in a matter of weeks would be theirs.

It hurt terribly. He had been guilt-stricken at the pain he inflicted on her – but not guilt-stricken enough to stop. 'Bite my shoulder,' he whispered to her in the darkness that night. She hadn't wanted to; she shrank from pain. She didn't want to hurt him; but she felt it was only polite to do as he requested. The circle of teeth marks on his upper arm lasted the whole of their honeymoon.

She had married him for his face, its puzzled withdrawn look of readiness. She hadn't banked on his body, especially its darker, hidden areas where the skin was coarse, folded, reddened, covered with hairs. It took getting used to.

She had expected the act of love to be accompanied by the clear, piping tones of an alto clarinet, but she heard only something guttural popping in Jack's throat.

Everything was spoiled. If only they could go back to what they had had before; those delicious, endless hours of kissing in Jack's father's car, the clean, solicitous feel of his tongue nudging at hers, and his grateful sighs as she stroked him through his cotton chino pants.

She had read too many articles, many of them damaging. A man wants to experience the feeling of a woman surrendering to him. But how was she to *express* this message of surrender? The timing of the climax was crucial. Was she moving her hips too much or not enough? She was constantly thinking, evaluating, planning, counting, asking herself what was the next move? And the next?

She worried about – was tormented by – the thought of Harriet Post.

In the motel room in Williamsburg where they spent their honeymoon she woke in the mornings depressed and sticky, her embroidered batiste nightgown a dishonoured roll at the foot of the bed. The jelly in her diaphragm gave off a sweetish, unwholesome perfume. Her legs ached. She imagined years of aching and soreness ahead for her.

And there came Jack, again, approaching her after his morning shower, his eyes soft, never to be so tender again, bringing her, again, the anxious, trembling gift of his love.

They had been married for three years when she asked him abruptly one night if he was circumcised. He had collapsed with laughter on their bed. He couldn't stop.

'Well,' she said coldly, a little hurt, 'are you or aren't you?'

'You honestly don't know?'

'How would I know? What would I compare – ?'

'Yes, yes,' he managed to moan between gasps.

'Yes what?'

'Yes, I'm circumcised. Yes.'

She couldn't help laughing too. He was so grateful for her innocence, by now so diminished as to be scarcely visible.

While not literary, Brenda had an ear for a phrase. Once she read, 'For certain of us, the colour of passion burns brighter.'

Did it for her? No. The thought hacked at her heart. But by an enormous effort of concentration she had been able to imagine a flame of sorts. It swayed before her eyes, a blue-footed, gold-tipped flame, growing steadily more brilliant, rising out of the palpable, solemn stillness of flesh.

She had surprised Jack with her new-found energy. She felt him falling back, stunned.

So this was what all the fuss was about. This rich enjoyment.

On alternate Sunday nights when they go over to the Lewises' to play bridge with Hap and Bud, she and Jack come home and dive into bed like troupers – he out of gratitude, she suspects, for not being married to Hap Lewis, and she thankful for having been spared the dark, groping, large-knuckled hands of Bud Lewis. On these nights they are especially generous with each other, languorous, assured, creative – what a lot they owe to Bud and Hap really.

Brenda wonders at times if Jack is aware of this almost laughable connection between their Sunday-night bridge games and the sharpness of their sexual love. She herself noticed it first years ago, and now she waits for it. The nights when she and Jack win at bridge are especially bountiful. Several times she's been on the verge of mentioning this to Jack, but is afraid that by drawing attention to the phenomenon, they will be robbed of what they've accidentally been given or what, in a sense, they've earned.

During the days of the Vietnam war, Brenda once overheard a discussion between Jack and his friend Bernie Koltz. Jack made the observation that because the strictures of modern society had effectively removed most issues of right and wrong, the war presented to many Americans the first serious moral choice they were ever called upon to make.

Bernie had disagreed. What about loyalty, he asked. Loyalty constituted a moral issue, and loyalty in the form of marital fidelity was a fact confronted by almost every adult. (This discussion took place two or three years before Bernie's wife, Sue, began having lovers.)

Jack had conceded that Bernie might be right; but he sounded to Brenda doubtful.

Was Jack faithful to her? Yes, she was sure he was. Despite Harriet Post – how that name was incised on her brain – she felt he was monogamous by nature,

Once, though, about two or three years ago, he had gone to Milwaukee to give a paper at the Milwaukee branch of the Great Lakes Institute. He had been away a week, staying in a room at the Milwaukee Hyatt. He seemed to her, on his return, to be newly gifted. His hands and mouth, especially his mouth, had learned a new sureness. She thought of asking him if something had happened in Milwaukee – she could make a kind of joke of it – but resisted.

Brenda sometimes thinks: I had a mother who came out of nowhere. *I* came out of nowhere. Surely that's mystery enough for anyone.

But it wasn't. Her children were secretive and ultimately mysterious. And when it came to Jack, there were larger, deeper mysteries. There are areas of his life, she realizes, that will remain unknown to her, areas as large as football fields.

She has her secrets too. Once, years ago, when she was painting her bedroom, she stood on a stepladder and saw carved into the moulding over the door frame the words 'Jake Parker, builder, 1923'. She thought of telling Jack about it, but never did. He would overprize it, lead friends upstairs to see it. She kept it to herself: Jake Parker, young, muscular, audacious.

It seems an innocent secret and in no way a betrayal. She and

Jack, by luck, and by the sheer length of time they've been together – twenty years is not to be sneezed at these days – have come in silence to certain understandings. The distances between them are delicately gauged, close to being perfect.

How fortunate they are. Only a fool would throw away this kind of rare good fortune.

Chapter Twenty-Two

BRENDA HAD SIGNED UP FOR THE NINE O'CLOCK WORKSHOP on Ethnic Stitchery, but when morning came she decided instead to spend the hour shopping for a new nightgown. She remembered seeing a lingerie speciality place in the shopping mall. The Underneath Shop. She and Lenora Knox had walked by it the other day and remarked on its name. Lenora told Brenda that there was a similar boutique in Sante Fe called The Bottom Line, and Brenda said there was one in Chicago called Sky with Diamonds.

The thought of buying a new nightgown had come to her late last night after she had said goodnight to Barry. They had turned outside her door and unexpectedly embraced. They collided awkwardly, and held on to each other for a long, unmoving minute, Brenda's face pressed against the clean sharpness of Barry's shirt collar. Her arms tightened on his neck, holding not just him, but his lost daughter, too, and the whole void left by her absence, including the agony of guilt that gripped and 'utterly changed' that person he mentioned in passing, his wife, Ruth. What did it mean anyway to be 'utterly changed'? The thought was frightening, unthinkable. She could not imagine it.

She had run herself a long, hot bath and had lingered in it a good half-hour, her brain numbed in the slow steam. Then she got out, dried herself with particular care, under her arms, between the toes, and pulled her pink flannelette nightgown over her head. With the side of her thumb she touched the place on her cheek where Barry's dry shirt-collar had pressed.

Sleep was slow to come. Her old nightgown should have been softened by wear, but wasn't. It scratched around the wrists, and Brenda pushed impatiently at the sleeves. She had never liked this kind of granny gown, but the Elm Park house was draughty in winter; the furnace was outdated and the old storm windows fitted badly. She and Jack talked from time to time about putting extra insulation in the attic, but Jack kept postponing it. He protested the drifting away of his dollars into unseen corners of the old house, and resisted, too, the violation brought about by clumsy, scratchy batts of fibreglass or rock wool. (He loved poking his head up through the trapdoor in the bathroom and gazing at that spare dusty space, narrowly braced with lines of dim light and shadow.)

Brenda remembered that she had bought this pink nightgown on sale. She recalled exactly what she paid for it – twelve dollars. That was three years ago at a sidewalk bazaar in LaGrange. She didn't even like pink, especially not this ripe watermelon shade – what her mother used to refer to as Goldblatts' pink.

Her face, restless on the pillow, pulled into sharp, scolding relief; what was she doing wearing an itchy faded pink nightgown anyway? Unaccustomed anger nudged at her and kept her from falling asleep.

In the morning she climbed out of bed, still tired and still scolding herself. 'What do you think you're doing in that get-up, sister?' (Hap Lewis's borrowed voice.) 'That lace has had it, for God's sake! That elastic's right out of the sleeves, no wonder it's itchy. Time to throw this rag away, kiddo.'

She yanked it over her head, rolled it into a ball, gave it a wicked twist, and dropped it in the wastebasket.

Verna's bed, calm, unslept in, seemed indifferent to her rage, and Verna's suitcase rested at peace on the floor where it had been since Saturday. Or had it been turned around? Possibly.

It came to Brenda that something serious might have happened to Verna – she had a fleeting image of a body jammed in an air shaft. Perhaps she should just mention to Betty Vetter – no, that was ridiculous. Verna, she imagined, was a woman capable of travelling lightly. No nightgown at all, not even a toothbrush. Verna of Virginia. Lucky, free, uncluttered, transparent, invisible, talented Verna.

At The Underneath Shop Brenda was the first customer of the day. A cheerful salesgirl – about twenty, Brenda estimated – her front teeth slightly parted, showed her where the size twelves were, and Brenda carried an armload into the fitting room.

First she tried on a white, double-nylon full-length gown with a pleated ruffle around the hem. No, white might be all right in summer with a tan, but not now. Also, there was something a touch too Elizabethan about it, reminding Brenda of *The Duchess of Malfi*.

Next she slid a black and silky sheath over her head. It fell down around her body with a sibilant swish, then pressed and clung like a licking of lips. A fragile fan of lace lay across the bosom, and a thin halter-strap held it up – but bit into her collar bone. Nice, but painful to wear, and a little short; it stopped awkwardly at the mid-calf – what they used to call ballerina length when she was in high school.

After that she tried a creamy Anne-of-Green-Gables concoction in a material that looked like lawn. It fell from a wide yolk, transparent, but without being tartish. The long, bell sleeves were edged with antique-looking cotton lace, lovely. Perfect, in fact. No, it was too wide across the shoulders. No wonder – she peered at the tag – a size sixteen. (Thank God she wasn't a size sixteen.) She removed it carefully, gratefully.

Then a spruce-green affair composed of long, intricately fitted gores. It was made in France, and was beautifully finished. Brenda, hissing through her teeth, thought: this is it. It was beautiful. She examined herself sideways in the mirror. No. Too tight across the bust.

A purple satin with shoulder ties looked falsely theatrical.

So did the orange chiffon: more *Duchess of Malfi* – a dress for a giver of curses.

There was a silky spiderweb of a gown in café au lait, which fit not too badly and made her shoulders look soft. But a brown nightgown was a brown nightgown. No.

Maybe something in a print. But the full, gathered nightie – this kind of gown could only be called a nightie – looked worse on her than the one she'd thrown away. (She wondered if the chambermaid had emptied the wastebasket yet.)

A slim lavender wisp, the colour of a winter sky, looked more like a slip than a nightgown. And she couldn't go around holding in her stomach all the time.

'What exactly did you have in mind?' the salesgirl asked, sticking her head in.

'I'm not really sure,' Brenda said. She was stepping into a yellow brushed-nylon. It dragged heavily from shoulder to hem. Awful. All she needed was a candlestick. It even had buttons.

What did she want?

In the fitting room next to her a woman was trying on a bra. Brenda could tell by her stern voice that she was a determined shopper. The salesgirl was helping her do up the hooks. 'Well,' came the woman's voice, broad and powerful over the partition, 'how's it fit in back?'

'A little tight,' the answer came. (Brenda imagined an immense, moulded bosom – a solid, fused front that pushed forward as though directed by a nervous system of its own.)

'What I want – ' the woman boomed, then paused. 'What I want – '

Brenda listened. The salesgirl listened. The nightgowns on their plastic hangers listened.

'What I want is better separation.'

'Ah,' came the soft, immediate, girlish reply. 'Well, if *that's* what you want . . . '

'That's what I want.' The voice came down like thunder.

Brenda left without buying anything. She told herself she had lost the habit of wanting. It was no one's fault but her own; through lack of practice she had simply forgotten how it was done, how to open her mouth and say: I want. Perhaps she had never really known how to say it. Wanting required more than the force of sentence parts; it needed a kind of dogged, deliberate stamina she had been spared. It grieved her to think of the time she had expended on wasteful errands. A passionate search for towels for the powder room, for the perfect recipe for spinach quiche. These tasks seemed devised to sound out her own authenticity; and almost always she walked away – like this – light as air, empty-handed.

Back in the room she rescued the nightgown from the wastebasket and hung it on a hanger, smoothing out the shoulders, running a finger down the disintegrating lace, giving it a tug, which might have said either: 'Who cares?' or 'Hello, old girl.'

She felt herself stretched with happiness. Something fortunate was happening to her.

Ten-thirty. Time to meet Barry in the lobby.

She sniffed; the room smelled of cigarette smoke. Verna's zippered case smiled up at her with grinning metal teeth.

Chapter Twenty-Three

BETWEEN ELEVEN AND ELEVEN-THIRTY IN THE CONSTITUTION Room, Barry Ollershaw presented a paper on *Chlorine-Assisted Leaching of Uranium Ores*. Brenda sat in the fourth row, listening, observing. Unfamiliar terms – radionuclide and thorium and radium 226 – sailed past her, words that seemed rectangular and solid, with syllables securely riveted and lightly rusted like ingots long stored in a vault. She wondered if he was in the middle of his talk or getting close to the end; there seem no recognizable signs, no foothold to keep her on course.

When the applause came she was taken by surprise. It was so vigorous, so generous. Barry, relaxed now and catching her eye over the lectern, shuffled his notes back into order and leaned forward comfortably on his elbows.

There were a number of questions from the floor. The men (and one woman) who asked the questions seemed filled with benign earnestness. 'Have you considered the effect of – ?' 'Should future research take the direction of – ?' 'In your opinion, Dr. Ollershaw – ?' *Dr.* Ollershaw!

An elderly man in the front row, lean, snowy-headed, with a beak of a nose, rose with the help of a pair of canes and commented at length in a sweet quavering scholarly voice. His remarks were greeted with roars of laughter and thumping applause. This gathering, Brenda saw, was a small world of its own, stocked with its private jokes and beloved personalities. Oddly, it satisfied her to know that Barry, whose existence had seemed contingent on her own – *her* rescuer, *her* confidant, *her* comrade from the twenty-fourth floor – was clearly a part of this specialized world, recognized and listened to and agreed with. An absurd flame of pride fluttered within her.

His replies were deferential, carefully worded. He was not unlike Jack, she saw, in that respect.

Last year in San Francisco she had gone to hear Jack deliver a talk on patterns of Indian settlement in the Middle West. He had spoken for an hour, glancing only occasionally at his notes.

Exactly when and from where had he acquired this relaxed fund of material? She hadn't realized he knew this much about settlement patterns. 'You never told me all that about family cohesiveness in tribal societies,' she accused him afterwards.

He'd countered mildly, reflecting a little of her look of surprise. 'It's not that interesting.'

The truth was she had never really understood Jack's profession, never quite comprehended how a historian spent his days. Jack's office at the Institute was a tidy cork-lined box, his chair a squeaky swivel model. There he sat, day after day, reading, turning over papers, making notes; and for this he was rewarded with a salary, plus medical benefits and a guaranteed pension plan.

How were all those hours filled? – she had often tried to imagine. They must contain something, some level of daily substance. But what? When Rob and Laurie were babies she had occasionally phoned him at lunchtime – in those days he took a sack lunch; they had just moved in to the Elm Park house and needed every penny to make the mortgage payments. 'What did you do this morning?' she would ask, picturing how he must look, relaxed at his desk, unwrapping his sandwich, polishing his apple on his knee, staring at the leaves of his single philodendron.

His answers were vague, at times even evasive. 'This and that' or 'just collating some new stuff' or 'checking a few references'. Her own tasks at that time were tedious but sharply defined; by noon she had done a load of laundry, swabbed a bathroom floor, made up the formula, baked a cake, and vacuumed the living room. Jack seemed to her to be almost romantically idle.

Later she realized this was because of the nature of what he did. Historians didn't solve existing problems. They set the problems themselves, plucking them out of the banked past like prize jewels, and then played with them for years on end.

Jack had been working for three years now on his book about the Indian concept of trade and property. From time to time she's helped him with the typing and the sorting of notes, and she understands in a general way what the scope of the book is to be. What she hasn't been able to say to Jack is that she finds the project bewildering in its purposelessness.

Of course she could be wrong. It might be that dozens of

scholars in the field were waiting for exactly this kind of comprehensive study. Perhaps it *was* destined to fill a serious gap. Perhaps it would shed new light on old, perplexing, unanswered questions.

She doubted it though.

There was a time when she might have questioned Jack about it; now, after three years, it seemed somehow too late – particularly since she suspected he shared some of the same doubts.

Three years, and he was still in the middle of Chapter Six. In the last year he'd hardly worked on it at all; there were other projects, he said, claiming his attention. Dr. Middleton, in his sixties now and only a few short years from retirement, was pushing more and more administrative work his way. Jack's outline and notes for the book sat in his old briefcase or lay scattered on his desk. It was difficult to work at home, he said. Laurie was always barging in. Rob played the radio so loud it carried to every corner or the house. The phone was constantly ringing at weekends. The downstairs den where he worked was chilly; he talked about getting a little electric heater and had even looked at a few models at Wards one Saturday morning. Brenda suggested that he move his desk to a corner of their bedroom where it was warmer and where the light was better. She felt, as she made this suggestion, a brief blush of guilt, having taken the guest room herself – easily the brightest room in the house – for her quilting. On the other hand, needlework required good lighting, natural light if possible; and she used the room far more than he ever would. She was, in addition, more serious than Jack about her work.

She found this last – the fact of her seriousness – astounding, for in the beginning Jack had been the serious one, the one whose work had taken precedence. She had, in those days, shushed the children so he could read; she had zipped them into their snowsuits and taken them out for long walks in Scoville Common on Saturdays so that Jack could work on his papers. Her husband was a historian; once she had loved the sound of that word. He required for this quaint pursuit an envelope of quiet protection, and this she could provide, could joyfully provide.

And now she wanted to provide something more. She wanted – had tried, but courage failed her – to release him, let him off the hook. She wanted to tell him to forget about writing this book if he honestly felt it was a waste of his time.

She had given some thought as to how she might broach the subject. A Sunday morning would be best, while they were still in bed. Their Sundays, a relic of student days, were relaxed and easy. Often they woke up and made love while the sun streamed in, striking the white of the walls, rebounding to the surface of the blue-and-green quilt, touching the soft sides of Jack's face and the curve of his closed eyelids.

'Listen, Jack,' she planned to say. 'Just because you've invested three years in this project doesn't mean you have to sweat it out to the end.'

Or 'Listen Jack, no one's jumping up and down and demanding that you finish this book. Why not quit and try something you've got some faith in?'

'Listen, Jack,' she could say, giving a little laugh so he wouldn't think she lacked faith in him, 'Listen, love, your heart obviously isn't in this thing.'

The trouble with saying this was that she didn't know what his heart *was* in. Perhaps there was nothing, nothing at all. And she was fearful of letting the light fall on what might be a width of emptiness.

Chapter Twenty-Four

THE NIGHT BEFORE, AT DINNER, BRENDA HAD ASKED BARRY Ollershaw exactly what it was that metallurgical engineers did.

'Why don't you sit through a session in the morning,' he'd suggested. He was giving a paper himself, he said, on uranium ores. 'It'll be deadly dull,' he warned 'but it might give you an idea of what it's about.'

Today, sitting across from Brenda in the hotel coffee shop, he bit into a club sandwich and said, 'Well, didn't I warn you?'

Brenda admitted she hadn't understood a word. 'But when I looked around at all those other people, they seemed absolutely . . . well . . . rapt.'

He chewed happily. 'It did go better than I thought it was going to.'

'You're positively basking,' Brenda accused.

'We all need a bask now and then.'

Brenda agreed, but said, 'I wonder why we do. Why we need to be rewarded, I mean. You'd think we'd outgrow it somehow. At least, I'd like to think so.'

'You'd think so,' Barry said. 'Especially once you've had a glimpse at how artificially the reward system usually works, how really false most honours are. How they cater to our weaknesses and – ' He stopped and shrugged.

'I dread the announcement of the quilting prizes this afternoon,' Brenda told him. 'I'm excited by it, but I dread it more. It doesn't make sense, does it? It's even degrading in a way to have to go through it.'

'Would you have worked as hard on your quilts if there hadn't been a competition?'

Brenda thought for a minute, then said, 'Maybe. Yes, I think so.'

'You're one of the lucky ones.'

'Would you have written the same paper if you hadn't been invited to read it in front of all those people this morning?'

'Probably not. That is, I'm always working on something, but there's a certain excitement about actually presenting it. I'm sure it's a vanity thing.'

'Deep down we're all shallow,' Brenda said. 'That's what a friend of mine, Hap Lewis, always says.'

'I suppose your husband, Jack, is into all this too.' He pronounced Jack's name slowly, as though it were a difficult word in a foreign language, letting it expand warily like a collapsible drinking cup.

'Into what?'

'Writing papers for conferences and so on.'

'Jack? Yes, he does. I was just thinking this morning about a paper I heard him give last year on Indian settlement patterns. It was strange, but all the time he was on the platform talking, I had the feeling he was someone I hardly knew. Here was this middle-aged man, this authority for heaven's sake. His voice, his gestures, his face looking out from behind the microphone, everything, it all seemed so different.'

'It probably made a difference to him, too. Having you there in the audience, I mean.'

'I doubt it,' Brenda said. 'I think he just slipped away. Into his other self, as it were. His working self, the history part of him.'

'It made a difference to me,' Barry said, 'when I looked up from my notes and saw you sitting out there. In that green blouse. A woman in a green blouse. I felt twenty-five years old, not fifty.'

'Really?' Brenda said, absurdly flattered.

'I'd like to buy you a present this afternoon.'

'A present!' She put down her sandwich and stared.

'Why not?'

'I can't let you buy me a present. Why should you anyway? Because I went to your lecture? I wanted to go to your lecture.'

'You saw that elderly gentleman sitting in the front row this morning?'

'With the white hair and the two canes?'

'That's Professor Denton. From Cornell. Emeritus now. He came up to me this morning and handed me an envelope with an honorarium in it. Completely unexpected, I might say, and extremely generous.'

'Found money,' Brenda smiles over her coffee. 'Part of the reward system we were just talking about.'

'What I'd like to do with it – now don't interrupt me – is to take you shopping and buy you a coat.'

'A coat?'

'Yes.'

'Barry, you're not still worrying about my coat?'

'I am, yes.'

'But it'll turn up. I'm sure it will turn up. Didn't you say what's-his-name, the man sharing your room, is going to be here this afternoon to – '

'Storton McCormick. He's cancelled. Professor Denton just told me. He's left word that he won't be able to speak this afternoon. And he hasn't been back to the room at all. Not that I know of.'

'But he's bound to turn up eventually. He hasn't checked out officially, has he?'

'No, but no one's seen him.'

'It's only Tuesday – '

'And meanwhile you're stuck in this hotel without a coat.'

'But everything I need is right here: the exhibition centre, all the meetings, everything.'

'You haven't seen a thing of Philadelphia. This is a remarkable city, full of – '

'I can always see Philadelphia some other time.'

'And how exactly do you think you're going to get home to Chicago without a coat. If it doesn't turn up by Thursday, Brenda, what in hell are you going to do? Wrap yourself in the shower curtain? It's cold out there. This is January.'

'*Listen* to me a minute.'

'What?'

'In the first place, I lost the coat, not you.'

'The point is – '

'The point is, I'm not worried about it, so why should you be. Thursday's a long way off and – '

'The point really isn't the coat at all. I'm just wanting to buy you a present.'

'The roses, you've already – '

'A real present.'

'But why on earth should you – ?'

'Because you came to my lecture in your green silk blouse – '

'Polyester.' She said this sternly, a matter of keeping the record straight.

169

'And listened to me ramble on last night; and you held my hand – '

'I'm forty years old,' Brenda said.

'You're also lovely – '

'And married.'

'And married.' He brought his fingers together. 'That's the rub, I suppose.'

She tried to laugh. 'I'm not sure what you mean by rub.'

'It's against the law to buy presents for married women, I suppose.'

'It's not that at all. As you perfectly well know. It's just that it would make me feel . . . ' She hesitated. 'Make me feel rather . . . '

'Obligated,' he supplied.

'Exactly, yes. Obligated.'

'Even if I assured you – I can't of course very well go down on my hands and knees here in the coffee shop, not without making a scene – but even if I assured you from my heart that no obligation is attached to this wish of mine – '

'I know that. I really do know that. But the uneasiness would be there, on my side. It's difficult to explain, but I wouldn't feel easy about your giving me a gift like that. In fact, you don't know this yet, but when lunch is over, I intend to wrestle you for the cheque.'

'I'm loving this, you know.'

'Arguing with me?' she smiled. 'About buying a coat?'

'Sitting here. Eating a club sandwich. Sitting across a table from a nice woman.'

'I'm loving it too,' she said, surprising herself. 'I really am.'

'Brenda Bowman. Quiltmaker. Urbanite to the core. You bring a tear to my eye.'

'Truly?' She looked; his eyes did look faintly misty. On impulse she touched his sleeve.

'I love sentimental scenes,' he confessed, taking her hand. 'I even cried in *Mary Poppins*.'

So did Jack, she was about to confide, but didn't. Instead she said, 'Can I ask you a question?'

'Anything. As long as it's not about metallurgical engineering.'

'It's about something you said last night. About your wife.'

'Ruth.'

'About her being . . . ' Brenda fumbled for the exact words. 'I think you said she was utterly changed.'

'Yes.' He let go of Brenda's hand.

'How did you mean? Changed how? In what way?'

'Every way there is to change. She's lost herself. You'd have to know how she was before – '

'How was she?'

'Lively. Active. She did research at the university; she's a botanist. Or was. She played tennis like a pro.' He spread his hands. 'Now she doesn't do anything.'

'Nothing at all?'

'Of course, she's heavily tranquillized most of the time. But even so – '

'Oh, Barry – '

'And, of course,' his voice changed key, 'of course we no longer love each other.'

At this Brenda felt no surprise; she'd expected this for some reason. 'Not at all?'

He bore down hard on each syllable. 'Not at all.'

'Not even – ?'

'Not spiritually, not psychologically, not physically. It happens sometimes. So we've been told. When a child dies, the parents, or one of them anyway, blames the other.'

'What do you do?'

His voice sounded, for the first time, harsh. 'What do you mean, what do I do?'

'How do you cope with it is what I mean.'

'If you mean what do I do with my time, I work hard. I work at weekends; I work nights. I do a fair amount of consulting, and that requires travelling. I've got three or four research projects on the go. I swim, sail a little; we have quite a number of old friends – '

'But what about . . . ?' She hesitated, not sure what she was asking.

'It you're asking me am I faithful – and I think you are – the answer is no. I was faithful though – don't stop me, I want to tell you this – I was faithful for the first year and a half. Which is a long time, I think you'll agree.'

'I do agree, yes.' Brenda nodded quickly, cringing to hear how facile she sounded.

'She's been hospitalized twice,' he went on. 'She can't be left on her own. Right now her sister is staying with us. Which is why I was able to get away to this conference. Which is why I'm able to sit here, boring the hell out of you with all this depressing tale of mine.'

After a minute Brenda said, 'What are you going to do this afternoon?'

'I'd hoped to take you shopping. But that . . . seems to be out.'

'Why don't you come with me to the Awards Ceremony. It's at three o'clock, in the Exhibition Hall. There are hundreds of quilts. And all kinds of other things. You'll love it.'

'Will I, Brenda? Yes, I think I will.'

Chapter Twenty-Five

'**B**RENDA BOWMAN, I'VE BEEN LOOKING HIGH AND LOW FOR you.'

It was Susan Hammerman, waving her arms, making her way through the crowd. On her forehead shone a fine, glistening, happy mask of perspiration. 'At last I found you.'

'Susan, this is Barry Ollershaw. Susan Hammerman. Susan's from Chicago too. She's a weaver.'

'Hello, Barry. You did say Barry? You a quilter too?'

'Well, no, I – '

'Oh, sorry, I didn't notice your name card. So – you're one of *those*.'

'I'm afraid so.'

'Anyway, Brenda, I just wanted to congratulate you. When I saw your name up there with an honourable mention, I just about – '

'Thank you.'

'I think we can really be proud of good old Chicago today.'

'We just got here, I'm afraid. Did – '

'Lottie's got an honourable too, in macramé, and I guess you must have seen my name – '

'No. What happened?'

'Second prize. I nearly flipped. I mean, two years in a row, how lucky can you get.'

'Congratulations,' Barry said.

'Why, that's wonderful, Susan.'

'I'm feeling crazy. There goes Lottie now. I've got to catch her while I've got the chance. Nice to meet you, Barry. See you, Brenda. Isn't this the wildest?'

'Brenda Bowman, *there* you are.'

'Barry, this is Betty Vetter, the organizer of the whole thing. Betty, this is Barry Ollershaw.'

'Aha! One of the infamous – '

'Afraid so.'

'Brenda, can you tell me where Verna is? I've been looking all over the place. I've had her paged and everything.'

'I haven't seen her. In fact – '

'The first-prize winner and she's not even here to accept her ribbon.'

'Have you asked – '

'I thought of making another announcement over the loud-speaker, but there's so much noise in this place I don't know if it'd do any good.'

'I was going to ask *you* about Verna, Betty, because the truth is – '

'Look, would you be a pal and help me out? When they call out her name, if she doesn't respond, would you mind getting up there and accepting for her? Just say a word or two, you know the sort of thing. I know it's asking a lot – '

'Me?'

'You're her roommate. I mean, it's sort of appropriate, if you know what I mean.'

'But I don't even know – '

'You're a honey. Honestly, you're a honey. I'll see you later, okay?'

'Brenda, for goodness' sake, where've you been hiding yourself?'

'Lenora! I'd like you to meet Barry Ollershaw. Barry, this is Lenora Knox, another quilter.'

'How do you do, Lenora.'

'To tell the truth, I've got a splitting headache. With all this noise. What branch are you in?'

'I'm with the metallurgists – that other group – I'm afraid.'

'Oh. I don't have my glasses on or I'd have seen your name card. I was looking for you this morning, Brenda. I thought maybe we could have lunch together today, but – '

'What about tomorrow?'

'Well, I don't know. I'm giving my workshop tomorrow. On the Genre Quilt. It's about animism. That's when – '

'Oh. That sounds interesting.'

'I almost forgot. Congratulations for your honourable mention.'

'Thank you. I really was surprised.'

'I guess you've probably heard the rumours going around about the judges.'

'No, what rumours?'

'Morton Holman. Someone pointed out – but it was too late – about the conflict-of-interest thing. Apparently it's going to be looked into. For next year.'

'I see.'

'And Dorothea Thomas. She's marvellous, just marvellous, as a craftsperson she's one of a kind, but when it comes right down to the nitty-gritty of judging – '

'Yes?'

'She's just . . . well . . . you know. As someone was pointing out, new blood is what we need. And better regional distribution – '

'I suppose so,' Brenda said.

'Hey, it's Mrs. B herself, isn't it? How's Mrs. B. feeling today?'

'Barry, I'd like you to meet Hal Rago. Hal, this is Barry Ollershaw.

'Great to meet you, Barry, just great.'

'Good to meet you, Hal. I read your piece on Brenda in the paper yesterday.'

'Terrific, terrific. Well, you're going to be reading more about her today.'

'Oh, no,' Brenda said.

'Yeah, I got the list of winners last night, and we've got a nice news piece in the afternoon paper, sort of zeroing in on the whole caboodle of winners. Say, you don't happen to know this Verna of Virginia, do you? Thought I'd take her out for a liquid supper; do a spotlight thing on her for tomorrow.'

'I'm afraid I can't help you with that, Hal.'

'No one seems to know where the hell she is. Probably one of your shy, retiring types. Too bad. When she finds out she's missed out on some free PR.'

'Yes,' Brenda said.

'Hey, what do you know, someone's got a newspaper over there now.'

'Today's?'

'Looks like it.'

'Let's ask – '

'Can I just have a look at that, do you mind?'

'What page is it on?'

'Well, what do you know! An art story on the front page.'

'Will wonders never cease.'

'About time.'

'Jesus.'

'Look at those pictures.'

'Not bad.'

'What are you laughing so hard about?' Brenda asked Barry. He was doubled over. 'I can't stop. I can't stop.'

'Let me see that again. I don't see what's so funny about that.'

'The headline,' he gasped. 'No, not there, the subheadline.'

'It's just a headline, that's all.'

' "Second Coming Gets Honourable Mention". '

'Well?'

'And you don't think that's funny?'

'Well,' Brenda said, 'not particularly.'

'It's wonderful. It's priceless.'

'I don't – '

'And the best part,' he wiped at his eyes, 'the best part is he probably didn't even intend it to be funny.'

'Hmmmm.'

'Wonderful, wonderful.' He was off again, hanging on to a post for support. 'Wonderful.'

'Hmmmm,' Brenda said again, smiling at him, feeling weak with happiness.

Chapter Twenty-Six

At seven o'clock, from barry's room, brenda phoned home to Elm Park and talked to her children. It was Laurie who answered.

'It's Mom, ' she shrieked. 'She's phoning long distance. Hey, Rob, get on the upstairs phone, it's Mom.'

'How are you, sweetie?' Brenda held the phone in both hands and saw in soft-focus her twelve-year-old daughter, Laurie, with her round face ashine, rosy with its own heat, and her soft mouth open and eager – heartbreakingly eager.

'Guess what, Mom, I made a Caesar salad. And Bernie – he was here for dinner – he said it was the best he ever tasted.'

'Bernie was there for dinner? That's nice. When was this?'

'Hi, Mom.' It was Rob on the extension. He sounded sleepy, dazed, cool. 'How're things in Philly?'

'It's been really – '

'Did you hear about the snowstorm?'

'You mean – '

'It was in all the papers, on TV – '

'We got eleven inches last night, Mom.'

'Ten inches.'

'Eleven it said in the *Trib*. You should've been here. We had a real white-out. And no school today, they were all closed, and this huge big tree over at Scoville – '

'No one even went to work,' Laurie said. 'Hardly anyone – '

'Everything was closed, all the stores and everything. Even the gas stations – '

'No one could get their cars out, you couldn't even open the garage door, there was so much snow.'

'How's Philadelphia?' Rob asked in his adult voice. 'What's it like?'

'Well, it's – '

'How was the plane? Did you get airsick?'

'You know I never get – '

'The snowplough hasn't even been down Franklin yet. It's done Holmes and Mann, but not Franklin. That's because – '

'It's over my head,' Laurie squealed.

'How could it be over your head,' Rob said, 'if it's only ten inches?'

'Between the Carpenters and us, I mean. It's all piled up, you should see it. You should've seen us jumping off the garage roof today, the whole neighbourhood – '

'It's a record. Since 1942 this is the most snow ever. Not the most snow in total, but the most inches in the shortest period of time.'

'How's Dad? Is he – ?'

'They're going to have it on radio tonight, all the stations, if the schools are going to be closed again tomorrow. They haven't decided yet.'

'The grammar schools are closed,' Laurie said, 'but not the high schools.'

'Where'd you hear that? Not on the radio.'

'Someone told me.'

'I bet.'

'You're getting along okay though?' Brenda asked.

'Yeah, we had hamburgers last night. Dad got them somewhere. He got home late because of all the snow. The Eisenhower was closed. It's the first time in history it's ever been closed, that's how bad the snow was.'

'They showed this man on TV who got a heart attack shovelling out his car.'

'He's going to be okay, though, they took him to the hospital.'

'Who? Who had a heart attack?'

'This guy on TV. Nobody we know.'

'How're Grandma and Grandpa? Did you go over on Sunday?'

'Yeah.'

'They're fine.'

'Where's Dad? Can I talk to him a sec?'

'I think he's still at work.'

'Yeah, he is.'

'I thought you said everything was closed today, all the offices.'

'What?'

'Because of the snow. You said everything was closed and no one went to work.'

'Yeah, but I think Dad went to work. He went somewhere.'

'How's Philadelphia, Mom? Did you see the Liberty Bell yet?'

'No, but I got an honourable mention. For *The Second Coming*.'

'Hey, that's neat.'

'Is that the one with the flower thing on it?'

'No, that's one of the other ones.'

'Neat.'

'I'd better go, kids. I'll see you on Thursday, okay ? You're sure everything's okay?'

'Did you say Thursday?'

'Dad knows. It's on the bulletin board. The flight number and everything.'

'We're going to try and borrow a snowblower tomorrow. Remember the Pattersons? Next to the McArthurs. They've got a snowblower.'

'Listen, kids, give Dad my love, okay?'

'What?'

'She said give Dad her love.'

'Oh, love, that's what I thought she said.'

'Okay, we will.'

'Don't forget.'

'Forget what? Oh, okay.'

'Goodbye, kids. See you Thursday.'

''Bye, Mom.'

'I really do miss you both.'

'We miss you too, Mom.'

'So long.'

Chapter Twenty-Seven

OH, SHE LOVED THEM, LOVED THEM. FOR A MINUTE SHE kept her hand on the receiver, unwilling to lose the connection of love between herself and her two children.

'Well,' Barry said from across the room where he was pouring gin into glasses. 'Is everything all right?'

'Everything's fine,' Brenda said, and, a little giddily, turned and reached for the glass he offered. 'It's just that it's humbling when you realize that your children cope perfectly well without you.'

'Deflating?' He sat down on the bed and took a sip of his drink.

'No.' She sat across from him. 'No, it's sort of amazing.'

What amazed her was that, in the four short days she'd been away, she had completely forgotten what they were like. How selfish they both were, Rob and Laurie. But how purely and transcendentally selfish. Their self-concern glowed like some primitive element, bright and more fiercely than radium. And the intensity of their attachment to the present moment – to the trivia of weather records, the drama of their unfolded stormy day – touched her to the heart. This simplicity, this openness to sensation – they wore it like an adornment. The contamination of boredom would come, no doubt, no doubt – but not yet.

Oh, she loved them. And only days ago she had found them unlovable and unloving. Why was that? she asked Barry.

He was in a philosophical mood. 'I suppose love comes in waves. Like sound waves and lightwaves and everything else in nature. Blowing hot or cold. On again, off again.'

'It shouldn't though,' Brenda said, determinedly righteous. 'What about steadfast love? You know,' she gave a short laugh, 'the sustaining flame.'

'You mean what we all want? And what we think we deserve?'

'Maybe we don't really want it all the time.'

'Maybe not. I suppose it's a fantasy to think we can love

anyone with that kind of consistency. It might even kill us, getting loved back like that. Like being bombarded with a ray gun.'

Brenda set her glass on the night table. 'It may be true, but I hate to believe it.'

'So do I. But put to the empirical test, I can't think of anyone who's loved someone else unceasingly, unstintingly, and at full force, day in and day out. Maybe in literature or pop songs – '

'My mother maybe. Of course, I was the only one she had. But aside from her – '

'Aside from her?'

'I suppose love does fail from time to time.'

'It lapses anyway,' Barry said. He finished off his gin.

'That's a better word, yes. A lapse of love.'

'And you and . . . ' He avoided the word, making a circle with his empty glass instead, 'you and . . . ?'

'Jack,' she said, helping him out, anchoring his question with matter-of-factness.

'You and Jack then.' His tone was elaborately cynical, but a little shy. 'I suppose it's been all steady flame for you. No lapses or anything like that.'

'I don't know,' she said with great care. Her hand, flat and sensible on the bedspread, spread wide. 'I suppose we've been . . . fairly . . . '

'Lucky?'

'Well, yes. Mainly anyway.'

He asked if she wanted more gin. She shook her head.

'Lucky Brenda,' he said, letting the word float on the air between them.

It was almost true, about the steadiness of the flame. But not quite. Four years ago Brenda had wakened one morning in her blue-and-white bedroom and looked at her sleeping husband. Jack's face in repose had been blank and shuttered and unfamiliar; she said to herself, or rather to the white walls, 'I don't love him any more.'

Minutes later he woke up, turned off the alarm, and reached for her through her newly forming haze of sorrow. They performed the motions of love, and Brenda registered with awful chilliness: now he's going to do this, now he's going to do that. When he took his shower afterwards, she stayed in bed thinking: now he's washing his neck, now he's standing on one foot soaping his toes. Now he's stepping out and stealing secret, prideful looks in the mirror, patting his stomach, cocking his head intelligently to one side, mumbling under his breath.

He came damp and powdered into the bedroom and saw her still in bed. With unforgivable nonchalance he asked her, 'Aren't you getting up this morning?'

It had fled. Love was gone. The world was spoiled. For months she had no idea what to do. There was, in fact, nothing she could do. Trapped in her own reputation for sunniness, she had to carry on as though nothing had happened. She could only pretend.

Jack, though, seemed not entirely taken in by her pretence. She caught him looking at her oddly, searchingly. A penny for your thoughts, he said to her far too often. He took her out to dinner at Jacques's in the middle of the week for no reason at all. He urged her to sign up for an evening class. He took her to see a rerun of *Laura* at the Arts Theatre, where she endured the soft pressure of his hand on her thigh. He even – she found this out much later – had a long, confidential talk with Brian Petrie at work about the advisability of psychiatric counselling for her. (Brian, who had been through the mill himself, advised against it.)

In the evening, when they were alone, he urged her to talk about her mother, who had died in the fall.

Of course! Of course. How like him to think that that was the problem: her shock at her mother's sudden death and her anger at the doctor who might have prevented it. Her withdrawal, her dullness, her easy daily tears and compulsive shopping – all this he laid at the blameless door of her mother's death. His eyes, as he tried to draw out her feelings, were so sad and so injured that she longed to run from the room.

During that winter Brenda slept woodenly beside this shallow, presumptuous stranger and allowed him to believe. His patience, his solicitude, his stroking hands – especially his stroking hands – would drive her mad, but she let him believe anyway.

When he went to work she sat in the kitchen, trying to imagine why she had committed her life to this empty human being. She resurrected her nineteen-year-old self and marvelled at the temporary illness that she had mistaken for love. One morning she sat at the kitchen table for two hours without moving, and out of her mouth came a strange, loose, whimpering sound that refused to yield to tears.

In the spring they went to France. He surprised her with the plane tickets, bringing them home one night along with an itinerary. Was it for a conference, something he was researching? No, he said, it was a vacation, just the two of them. Her heart plunged at the thought – just the two of them. She loathed herself in the role of neurotic, grieving woman, and resented him for inventing that role, for making her into an invalid who had to be jollied out of thoughts of her dead mother by being taken on an expensive vacation to France.

The first week went badly. The fervent sightseeing dragged on her energy. Their day at Versailles lingers in memory as an ordeal, wordless and odourless; they had wandered for hours, dully, through dull rooms; the Hall of Mirrors was a blur of smudged surfaces, sending back to them uneven images of disappointment.

Jack's efforts to interest her in the Gobelin tapestries – he arranged to go on a day when the lecture was in French, not English – had seemed to her to be staged and sacrificial and pathetic, and she resented the doses of gratitude she expended on him for his small acts of thoughtfulness. At meals, sitting in Paris bistros, she dutifully laced her fingers with his and despised him for the readiness with which he responded.

Then they rented a car and drove to Brittany, which was a wild place, wet and reeking in the countryside, prim and dusty in the towns. Through the windshield of the little white Peugeot they watched clouds pile themselves above along rises of land – clouds sooty brown and curled at the edges like soufflés set out on platters of air. It was beautiful; she forced herself to admit it. The sun that fell on the slaty rooftops seemed an older, wiser cousin of the American sun. In the country its pale light fell through the green lace of branches onto narrow fields of mustard and clover, and the shadows brought to mind the blue, intricate pattern of a cloisonné vase in their bedroom at home, a wedding gift from Dr. and Mrs. Middleton; when Brenda mentioned this to Jack, he nodded, as though the same thought had occurred to him simultaneously.

The eiderdowns in the chilly hotels smelled of mildew; the beds were cold and tipped towards the centre, causing them to cling to their separate sides, divided by Jack's respect for her terrible grief and by her failure to admit to him that she no longer loved him.

The food was extraordinary. Brenda, who had never eaten kidneys in her life, couldn't get over the delicacy of veal kidney flamed in cognac and served with mustard sauce; she ordered it three nights in a row, and Jack sat across from her, watching this indulgence with hope.

One day, on a narrow back road solidly hedged with green, their Michelin guidebook directed them to a small humped country church made of moss-green stone. It had rounded windows, very small and high up, and a thick oak door which swung open to a damp cave of darkness. But when they dropped a one-franc piece into a metal box, an electric light snapped on, revealing for three ticking minutes an ancient painting on wood over the altar: a scene of villagers in medieval dress, their bodies healthy and rounded with thankfulness. These people were carrying baskets of fruit and vegetables into a church, and, astonishingly, the church in the picture was *this* church – the church they stood in, only when it was new. The roof was a painted square of clean, yellow thatch; the walls were built of newly quarried whitish stone; the sky was fresh and alert; and the slightly elevated ground around the church looked newly levelled and surrealistically aglow.

When the electric light clicked off, they were left again in darkness, but now the darkness pulsated with colours. Brenda could see the arched roof of the church with its graceful timber-beams, the smoky stone of the old walls, and, beside her, the framed whiteness of Jack's face. She dared to put her arms around him, and they both, as though given permission, began to cry. It seemed to Brenda that at that moment they were one person, one body.

Her long nightmare, the loss of love, had inexplicably dissolved. Love was restored, for whatever reason. Jack, perhaps, was persuaded that the grieving process had come to its natural end – and perhaps it had, for Brenda was never able to unwind completely the complicated strands of that winter's despair. Looking back, it seemed to her to be a time of illness; she had been assailed by a freak visitation, and preserved the knowledge that it could happen again.

She thought of sharing this revelation with Barry. It would in a sense help right the imbalance between them: his unfortunate life and her lucky one.

She decided against it, if for no other reason than that it seemed a betrayal to pronounce aloud what had been resolved in silence. 'We've been fairly lucky, yes,' she was able to tell Barry Ollershaw, gazing across at the crease in his trousers, transfixed by the polished toes of his black oxfords.

'Well then,' he said, a little shortly, 'you've been exceptionally fortunate.'

To be kind she added, 'Of course, there've been ups and downs.'

'Of course.' He touched her hair.

There was a short silence, and then she asked, 'What time does your plane go on Thursday?'

'You mean Wednesday. Tomorrow.'

'Wednesday? You're going to be here until Thursday, aren't you? Aren't you?'

'I'm going to Montreal from here. I thought I told you, Brenda. I'm sure I told you. Tomorrow afternoon, around two.'

She sat back, dazed. 'You did tell me, but – I just assumed – I mean, the banquet for the metallurgists is tomorrow night, isn't it? And I just assumed – '

Barry was talking, moving around the room, making himself another drink, saying something about meetings and a government contract, people to see in Ottawa, an appointment hastily arranged and with great difficulty.

She shook her head in disbelief. 'I'm just surprised,' she said. 'I just took it for granted. I just assumed.'

Chapter Twenty-Eight

THEY DECIDED TO GO FOR A WALK SINCE THE EVENING HAD turned mild. Barry wore his tweed sports-jacket with a turtleneck sweater underneath, and lent Brenda his fleece-lined overcoat, which, except for the slightly too-long sleeves, fit fairly well. She expressed surprise. 'It fits,' she said, turning in front of the mirror.

'I suppose . . . ' he paused for effect, 'I suppose that . . . what's his name . . . '

'Jack.' She smiled broadly.

'I suppose *Jack* is a mountain of a man.'

'Yes,' she said, though Jack was just a fraction over six feet. 'A veritable tower.' She indicated with her arms.

'A bull moose out of the Chicago suburbs. What luck!' And they both laughed.

We're laughing at Jack, Brenda thought, flicked by the injustice of it. Jack who was absent and innocent and who had done nothing to deserve ridicule – poor Jack, transformed into an oversized oaf. How could they do it to him? How could *she* do it?

They walked along gravely, arms linked, down the lit-up city streets, pacing themselves, peering into store windows at displays of perfume, jewellery, books, fresh fruit, bottles of wine, women's dresses, shoes, furniture.

They stopped at one window to look at an arrangement of living-room furniture that included an expensive checked sofa, a glass-topped end table with trim brass legs, a stone-ware lamp with a wide, pleated shade, and an imitation fire flaring in an imitation fireplace. 'Nice,' Barry said. 'Let's buy it.'

'Let's,' Brenda said. 'But can we afford it?'

'We'll buy it on time, dearest.'

'But we've never done that before.'

'It's time we joined the twentieth century then, don't you think?'

'In that case –' Brenda said.

At a dimly lit place called The Cheesecake Café, they sat at a table by the window and ordered cups of coffee with whipped cream and ground ginger. 'Lovely,' Brenda said, glancing around in the darkness at the clean, cool, marble tables and the iron chairs. The cafe was filled mostly with young couples with quiet, oval faces, at peace with the reflected gleam of tiny hurricane lamps. At the table next to theirs, two young men played chess, and Brenda could hear a fragment of their conversation, which was, 'It may seem cruel but – '

Barry leaned toward her and asked a question, but his words were drowned out by the sudden sound of a siren in the street outside.

'Pardon?' she said, and picked up her coffee cup. A fire engine came clanging by.

Barry mouthed something back which might have been anything. A second fire engine rushed past; Brenda saw the long, red gleam of its sides flash across the length of the café window.

'It must be a big fire,' she said into the suddenly clamorous air. People were pushing back chairs, getting up from their tables and crowding at the window. From outside on the sidewalk there came the sound of people yelling and running on the pavement. The cashier at the front of the café, a pretty young woman in a long skirt, stepped outside a minute, then came back in hugging her sides against the cold. 'It's the Franklin Court,' she announced in a clear, carrying voice that seemed both shaken and relieved.

Brenda gasped and reached for her coat.

'Let's go,' Barry said.

'Yes.' She was doing up the large buttons.

It was only three blocks, and they ran most of the way, dodging crowds of people as they went. The loose, heavy overcoat swished against Brenda's boots, dragging her down.

'Watch out for the ice,' Barry called.

'We're almost there. Isn't it around the next corner?'

'I think so. There's the furniture store we were looking in.'

'I don't smell any smoke, do you?'

'There it is.'

'Look at them all.'

'Good God.'

'I don't believe it.'

The sidewalk and street outside the Franklin was entirely filled with people.

But how orderly they look, Brenda thought, hundreds of people breathing out balloons of frosty air, speaking to each other in quiet tones, calmly stamping their cold feet on the pavement. A chain of police kept the area in front of the main door clear.

'Probably a false alarm,' someone told Brenda and Barry.

'Maybe even a fire drill, though you'd think – '

'Well, you never know. It could be a bomb scare. Large Irish population in Philadelphia.'

'They've got everyone out anyway, at least they think so. You got to give them credit.'

'Someone just having a good time, had one too many probably, got carried away.'

'Conventions – '

'I was sure I smelled smoke. Didn't you say you smelled smoke? You said – '

'We had to use the stairs for crissake. They wouldn't let us use the goddam elevators. Fifteen floors, all on foot – '

'The cables in elevators – '

'That's right. I read something about that in – '

'Could be arson. Like in Vegas.'

'Yeah, but where's the smoke? You see any flames shooting out? It's a false alarm, I'd put my money on it.'

'I just heard the cop over there say it's a wastebasket fire. One of the top floors.'

'Twenty-eighth floor, that's what I heard. Is that what you heard?'

'Did I ever tell you about the time I was at Cub camp and our tent caught fire?'

'You were a Cub Scout? Now I find that hard to picture.'

'One of the counsellors crawled in for a smoke and set the groundsheet on fire. We never squealed on him, though; we loved that guy. I saw him about a year ago. He's a circuit judge in upstate New York. Still a good guy. And I couldn't help noticing he still smokes Winstons.'

'Are you sure? Just a wastebasket?'

'Sort of an anticlimax. Why is it that every time something exciting happens, it turns out to be a wastebasket on fire. Metaphorically speaking.'

'Jesus, you mean they got us all out here for – ?'

'Just be thankful – '

'Is it out? I mean really out?'

'It must be. They're coming out now, the firemen. Look over there, behind that policeman.'

'Boy, they must be teed off, three trucks out and just because some dodo set fire to his wastebasket.'

'Getting all these people out – '

'Lucky it wasn't in the middle of the night. What a panic if we'd had to get out in the middle of the night.'

'Remember that fire on Long Island that time – '

'That was a real fire.'

'People jumping – '

'A wastebasket. Jesus Christ.'

'That's it, folks.'

'Hey, they're letting them back in up there.'

'Hurry up, I'm freezing.'

'Here, take this coat, why didn't you say so, for Pete's sake. You just got over that crummy cold – '

'I'm all right. You worry too much, that's your trouble.'

'It's my prerogative to worry.'

'Take it easy, folks, take it easy.'

'Will you look at that line-up for the elevators.'

'We'll never get in. We'll be here till midnight.'

'Want to walk up?'

'Fifteen floors. You got to be kidding.'

'Probably do you good – burn off a few – '

'No thanks. And I mean no thanks.'

'Wait'll the kids hear we walked up fifteen floors.'

'Do you want to walk up?' Brenda asked Barry.

'Twenty-four floors? We might as well; we're never going to get up any other way.'

They found the stairwell filled with people, climbing, puffing, leaning on the railing, moaning obscenities, calling encouragement. The cinderblock walls rang with noise. Brenda was reminded of certain spontaneous Elm Park parties she'd attended – all this gaiety, all this celebratory good-nature and exertion.

She and Barry rested on the eleventh floor, sitting on the far edge of the steps while people thronged past them. They rested again on the twentieth. 'I'm not going to be able to walk tomorrow,' Brenda said, and rubbed the back of her legs.

They leaned on each other, laughing. They were still laughing when they opened the door to Brenda's room and discovered a man and a woman standing by the window still in their coats, their hands joined. The man looked heavy, startled, but motioned broadly at them like a genial host. The woman smiled a wide welcome. She had a lively face, a red mouth, long untidy blonde hair. 'So,' she cried, 'we meet at last.'

Where have I seen this face? Brenda asked herself. But no, the smiling face was the face of a stranger. It was the coat that was familiar.

'How do you do,' the woman said, coming forward, her arm out. 'I'm Verna.'

Brenda for a minute couldn't think of anything to say except, 'I think that's my coat you're wearing.'

Chapter Twenty-Nine

STORTON McCORMICK IS A MAN WITH GOOD EASTERN MANNERS and a well-fitted suit that is so dark it's almost black. He speaks resonantly, like a radio announcer: 'Barry Ollershaw, I know that name, of course. You're from Canada, right? And Mrs. Bowman, so nice to meet you, sit down, both of you.'

Verna is all apologies. She takes Brenda aside and says, 'You must think I'm a thief, walking off with your coat like that. But there it was, hanging there in Stort's room, and we had had such a fabulous night, a colossal night, and in the morning Stort said to me, let's go out there and roll around in the snow. Not literally, of course. Well! Then, on Monday morning he got a call from his office – some kind of emergency – so he said, come to New York. So I said, why not? I've spent my whole life saying no to things. A Catholic girlhood, Baltimore, nuns. We took the train. Wonderful. More than wonderful. I can't believe I've known this man for only, what? Three days, well, four if you count today. We met on the elevator, can you imagine? Awfully corny, but – '

'I've got your blue ribbon,' Brenda tells her. 'You won first prize, did you know?'

Verna gives a shriek, twirls like a gypsy, then unzips her blue-and-red case and takes out a bottle of bourbon. 'I travel equipped for celebrations. I never want to miss out on another celebration, never. I've missed too many of those.'

They find four glasses. 'Here's to the quiltmakers of the world,' says Storton McCormick.

'Here's to the International Society of whatever-they're-called,' says Verna, clinking her glass with Brenda's.

'Here's to us,' says Brenda.

'To us,' Barry says, rising to his feet. 'To this night.'

For most of the night the two of them stayed awake talking in Barry's room. (It was decided after a single round of bourbon and water that Verna and Stort should remain where they were for the night.)

Should they share a bed? They discussed it, first lightly, then solemnly, then lightly again. They ordered a tray of sandwiches and coffee and got undressed.

'This ridiculous nightgown – ' Brenda said, and made a face.

'What about these?' Barry pulled at his pyjamas. Beige with brown piping. 'Christ!'

'I suppose that Verna must think we've been – '

'I'm sure she does.'

'The trouble is I can't disconnect,' Brenda said. 'I don't mean just marriage vows. I mean my whole life.'

Barry reached for another sandwich and said in a grave voice, 'You mean the philosophy of living for today isn't yours.'

'It's such a cliché. Someone goes away for a week, and what happens? It's so predictable. And I hate to think that just because a thing is possible, it has to be done.'

Barry smiling, asked if she was in the habit of resisting the possible.

'Not usually.' She had taken off her slippers and was lying flat on the bed. 'But when Verna said that about not wanting to miss any celebrations – '

'Yes?'

'When I heard her say that, that's when I realized I'd already decided – I don't know when, but a long time ago – that I *was* going to miss a few. That I was prepared to miss a few.'

'That sounds rather stoic,' Barry said after a minute. He too was stretched out on his back, but on the other bed. 'It also sounds a little resigned.'

'I'm glad you didn't say puritanical at least.'

'Not that. No, I wouldn't think that.'

'Of course it makes it easier that I got my period this morning.'

He was in a mood to talk. It was two o'clock; the room was in darkness; he was all candour. The fact was, he told Brenda, he wasn't much good as an adulterer. It didn't come easily; it would take time. At first there was a brief affair with a secretary in his office. Then with a divorced family friend. Then a woman who was quite a lot younger. He met her playing golf. He despises himself in the role of pursuer – the one who must telephone, make pleasing arrangements, bring tokens. He has been, in the last couple of years, through scenes of almost adolescent awkwardness, absurd fumblings. He is, he supposes, what is called today a lousy fuck. Probably he was married too long to one woman.

'I know,' Brenda said, not really knowing, but thinking of the privateness of sex.

Another thing, Barry went on, was discovering that there are just so many ways for human flesh to meet human flesh. And only so many degrees of loneliness that can be banished by an hour of ecstasy in a double bed.

Brenda decided, after all, to tell Barry about the year she stopped loving Jack, and about their trip to Brittany. He listened in silence, then said in a puzzled voice, 'I suppose it was one of those catalytic moments. Completely irrational, but difficult to deny.'

'Have you ever felt like that?' Brenda turned her head to see him. 'The world turned suddenly orderly and neat as a pin.'

'A transcendental moment? Yes, I think so, but not often.'

'I don't think it happens very often. At least not to two people at the same time.'

'No,' he agreed. 'It hardly every happens like that.'

They talked at length about Barry's wife, Ruth; would she recover? And what would happen to their marriage if she didn't? 'We've taken too many strips off each other,' he told Brenda. 'We're like a pair of cripples. But in an odd way we still depend on each other. That's the ultimate insanity, that we do.'

'You can't live with just that. It's not enough,' Brenda said.

But he surprised her by protesting, 'It's not that bad really. I've probably exaggerated. There are good days. We have breakfast together, and when it's clear we can see right down to the bay. It's just – '

'Just what?'

'Just that we were twenty-two when we were married. That's what we gave each other. Our whole lives. Bodies that were still young. You can't do that a second time.'

'No,' Brenda said, 'you can't.'

'Are you tired?' he asked after a long silence.

'Yes.' Then, 'Can you sleep?'

'I don't think so.' Another silence. 'I think I could if I could just hold you for a minute. Unless,' his tone was light, 'unless that would make you technically unfaithful.'

Such an easy thing to give, comfort. (It would have been an act of unfaithfulness to withhold comfort – that was what she would tell herself later.) She moved between the beds and slipped in beside him. His arms, encircling the copious pink flannel, felt sinewy and warm; there was something familiar about this heat, even something familiar about the odour of his body. His legs fit against hers, and the denser flesh of his penis stirred for a moment against her thigh. She felt herself grow luminous, transparent.

Sleep came to both of them almost at once, but Brenda, half-conscious, had a momentary vision of the colours and passions of the world, steep streets leading out of old cities, the cool orbits of planets.

They woke only once, when they moved apart in sleep and shifted into different positions. His lips brushed her ear, saying something that sounded like, 'I do love you.'

'I love you too,' Brenda murmured back, and from the spiralling shell of profound sleep, it seemed to her that what they were saying was at least partly true.

Chapter Thirty

L AST YEAR WHEN JACK AND BRENDA WENT TO SAN FRAN-cisco for the National Historical Society meeting, their plane circled over the bay area for several minutes in a holding pattern, then made a brief descent through sparkling air onto the baked runway. The landing was routine, smooth as glass after the first mild jolt, but for some reason the passengers broke into spontaneous applause the instant the wheels touched down.

Brenda looked sideways at Jack: why this applause? He made a gesture with his hand – a gesture that said, Who knows? Who can explain such things?

A single passenger perhaps, feeling euphoric after a good lunch, might have clapped his hands and started a chain reaction; the others would have joined in out of simple obedience and good nature. Why not? Weren't they thankful to be here in the white California daylight? The lipsticked stewardess, smiling in the aisle, seemed suddenly a gift from God, as worthy as the gift of providence, the gift of good health. Why not, in the burst of affection that binds fellow travellers at the end of a journey, give thanks for the solid earth?

In contrast, Brenda's landing at O'Hare on Thursday evening was brisk and without ceremony. The plane had not even reached a full stop when businessmen turned in their seats and began reaching down for their briefcases. The scent of leather and wet raincoats grew strong. Home. Safety. The seatbelts unbuckled. Brenda pulled on her coat. A slice of dark, industrial Chicago sky showed itself at the window, oily and dense and slashed by searchlights. Across the sheen of the runway, less than two hundred yards away, another jet was lifting off, and it seemed to Brenda that the twinkling taillights boasted of a more exotic destiny, Marrakesh, Bombay, God only knows where else.

She was home. She buttoned her coat and tied the belt. It would have to be sent to the cleaner's; besides the small stain on the collar there was a black smudge on the hem. Maybe Verna really had rolled in the snow.

Jack would be there to meet her. He would come alone, without the children, just as she always came alone to meet him after a short trip. This habit of theirs was like many of their habits, too firmly fixed to merit analysis or even thought. It must have begun out of a need to keep their reunions unclut-tered, to give them time on the drive home to find their footing again.

Jack would have prepared two or three amusing stories to tell her. 'First the good news,' he would say. Separation seemed to arouse in him an obligation to be once again the amusing and diverting stranger.

The strangeness would last all the way to Elm Park. The drive, in spite of the traffic, always seemed shorter than she thought it would be. As they neared home, the streets and the houses would grow increasingly familiar, until finally they were there, turning off Euclid onto Horace Mann, which led directly to Franklin Boulevard. They would pull up in front of their house and see lights burning in every window. Rob and Laurie were careless about turning off lights, and Jack, who was also careless, would nevertheless utter a soft moan and say, 'Lit up like a Christmas tree, for Christ sake.'

She imagined opening the front door: first the vestibule, then the waxed oak trim of the front hall and the paleness of refined light filtering from the old brass ceiling fixture. In the kitchen the floor would be sticky underfoot, but someone would have attempted to sweep it. She would come quickly to the familiar-ity of lingering supper odours and the circle of crumbs around the toaster.

Laurie's soft body would annihilate her with love, pouncing, squeezing, clinging. Rob would hang back, the sleeves of his sweater pushed up, scrupulously clean, a comb sticking out of his back pocket. He would eye her warily for the first hour, then relax.

The four of them would have some mint tea. The box of tea-bags on the shelf, and the mugs too, would declare themselves objects with an existence of their own, both novel and familiar. The mail would be spread on the table: bills mostly, maybe a letter from Patsy Kleinhart, who had never married – she was in Hawaii now, teaching school. There might be an invitation to a post-Christmas cocktail party or to the annual Alumni dance at DePaul, which they have never attended but always mean to.

Jack would finish his supply of diverting anecdotes and have a look at the newspaper. They might watch the news if they remembered. And then go up to bed. 'Well,' Jack would say, his arms around her, 'tell me all about it.'

They might lie awake for an hour or more talking. She would tell him about Verna of Virginia, who was coming to Chicago in April for a one-woman show at the Calico Gallery on Dearborn. She would tell him she has been asked to be one of the judges of the Novelty Quilts Division for next year's exhibition. Next year the meeting will be in Charleston, South Carolina; the hotel has already been booked; a woman she met from New Mexico has been elected to the executive. Jack will be interested in all these things – though Brenda knows what he really means when he says to her, 'Tell me all about it.' He is like his father, who, every Sunday morning when they arrive for breakfast, says, 'Well, kids, what's new?'

What's new, Grandpa Bowman asks, as though he is frantic for news, when all the while he wants to be told that there is no news, that no calamity has overtaken them in the seven days since he's seen them last. He wants to hear of the things which are continuing and already tested, and Jack, his son, is adept at knowing what can and what can't be told. His father does not want revelations; he does not want them to open every last cell in their bodies for him.

'I've missed you,' Brenda will say to Jack in the dark, knowing he needs to hear this and knowing also that it's true. 'I missed you terribly,' he will say, and then ask her if she's remembered to lock the bedroom door. Yes, she will say, readying her body for tenderness.

At this hour she occasionally feels the return of her younger self, the Brenda of old – serene, unruffled, uncritical, untouched by darkness or death or complex angers – a self that is curiously, childishly brave. The visitation is usually short in duration, but cordial. Brenda, older, less happy, but unconquerably sane, greets her old ally and merges with her briefly. Then, in the minutes before true sleep comes, she lets go, and drifts away on her own.

197

'Calcutta, you said? Bombay?'

'New Delhi, too, but that was just a bit of a holiday.'

'I see.'

'You in the same general field, then?'

'Not exactly. No. Not at all, in fact. I just phoned to offer my congratulations.'

'I'll have her ring you back.'

'Perhaps you could just convey my heartfelt –'

'Certainly, I'd be delighted to. Harriet will be pleased you thought of her.'

'If you could just tell her – '

'I'm afraid I missed your name.'

'Jack Bowman.'

'Wonderful, Jack. So thoughtful of you to call.'

'Not at all.' Not at all.'

Chapter Twenty-Nine

A T ONE MINUTE AFTER ELEVEN JACK PHONED ROCHESTER. The call went straight through. No cozy chats with Bell operators tonight; the world was back to normal.

'Go ahead,' the operator said.

'Harriet?' Was that his voice, that craven squeak?

'You wanted to speak to Harriet?' A man's voice, solid, educated, wonderfully baritone; Jack pictured a cask of a chest, plentiful hair.

'Yes. May I speak to Harriet please?' Ah, that was better.

'I'm afraid Harriet's out of town.'

'Out of town?'

'She won't be back for another three days, I'm afraid. She's out of the country actually. Is this long distance?'

'Yes. Chicago.'

'Perhaps' – the voice was polite, warm, solicitous, something British about it – 'perhaps if you left your number Harriet could ring you back when she gets in.'

'Three days, you said?'

'Yes. She's in Calcutta, but she's flying to Bombay tomorrow and directly home from there.'

'Calcutta?'

'May I tell her who called?' Yes, definitely British.

'A colleague of hers.' An old colleague – the word colleague came as an inspiration. Much better than old friend or fellow student or –

'I see. Well, Harriet dashed off to check a few sources and so on for her new book – '

'The book on Indian trade practices?'

'Yes.' A rising tone of wonderment. 'You know about the book, then?'

'Yes, well, I saw the announcement. In the *Historical Journal*.'

'Good lord, has it been announced already? Her publishers don't miss a trick.'

'Oh, I don't know.' Jack tried for a light tone. 'I'd like to say it was an act of charity.'

'Charity?'

'Or maybe I just want out.'

'Well, if that's what you want – '

'I think it is. I think – '

'Sleep on it.'

'That's the first advice you've ever given me, Bernie, you know that?'

'Really? Is it really?'

'Good night, Bernie.'

'Good night, old friend. See you – Friday I guess.'

'Right. See you then.'

Something always stopped him. Bernie might balk; he could be difficult; he had always been somewhat prickly, and just beneath his pale, neutral, abstract freckledness lay an unpredictable populism. *So you're too good for the old proletarian hangout,* Bernie might think (but never say). *So now that you and Brenda and the kids have entrenched yourselves out there in Elm Park, you're hankering for something a little more country-clubby, huh?* Bernie's moods of grouchy unreasonableness had simmered and sputtered along for years, beginning, Jack thought, about the time Bernie's wife Sue decided to go back to medical school. But lately these moods had become more frequent – Jack wasn't the only one who'd noticed. Bernie preened his pessimism now. Brenda thought he'd behaved erratically when she saw him late in the summer; something he'd said or done, she hadn't been able to put her finger on it, but something was wrong. There didn't seem to be any single cause, although it might be any of the half-dozen phantoms that flickered at the back of Bernie's life – his stalled career, his wife Sue, his retarded daughter at Charleston Hospital. (Jack, who had his own set of free-swimming phantoms – who didn't? – could understand that.)

Whatever the root of Bernie's malaise, it was beginning to erode the old Friday spirit; the lunches – and Jack found the fact painful to face – were losing their old intensity. Sometimes, after summing up a crucial point, he had had the sick, dizzy sensation that the same point had been covered back in '75 or '68 or even '59. In mid-phrase his mouth stopped moving, frozen solid and self-conscious, stuck on a multiple memory track, gone gummy with overuse. Or worse, he heard his voice plumping up with an over-ripened, artificial passion that might have been seemly at twenty-two, but that at forty-three lacked moderation and civility and the *au point* Johnsonian balance he vaguely aspired to. And hadn't the old analytical machinery been more cleanly classical, more firmly grasped and more fruitful in the past? The year he and Bernie had discussed entropy, they'd managed to carve it up, beautifully, without all this rhetoric and false claiming of territory; it had fallen open for them with an open-throated, almost Grecian grace, slowly, mathematically, like a flower; he had *loved* entropy. *Bernie* had loved entropy, leaping in with the razzle-dazzle of a gymnast, a magician, glittering as he sprang from point to point. Demo-

4

steamy eroticism? All you had to do was plunge your fork through the waiting, melting mozzarella and you were there, ah!

In 1958, Jack Bowman had eaten his first pizza at Roberto's, probably at this very table. Mushroom and green pepper. Bernie Koltz had been with him; it was the first pizza of their lives; neither of them could understand how this had happened. Jack was twenty-two years old, about to be married to Brenda Pulaski. The pizza – it was called *pizza pie* on the menu – arrived on a circle of pulpy cardboard, a glistening crimson pinwheel flecked with gold and green. Were they supposed to eat it with a fork? Neither knew. They had pondered the point, mock philosophically, until a comic courage seized them, and they had picked it up like a sandwich in young, decent, untrembling WASP fingers. The taste was a disappointment, catsup on piecrust, viscoid and undercooked, although neither of them remarked on it at the time.

In all probability, Jack thought, Bernie was fed up with Roberto's too. There was his ulcer to consider; these days Bernie automatically ordered the mildest dish on the menu and made at least a tentative effort to cut down on the wine. For some time Jack had wanted to announce, boldly, that they could both afford more than $6.25 for lunch these days; Bernie had tenure now (although Jack assumed, from Bernie's silence on the subject, that his promotion to full professor was not to be, not this year, anyway); Jack was slated to be Curator of Explorations at the Institute – it could happen any day now. They deserved better than these greasy menus and this lousy New York State wine, served in sticky glass carafes with bubbled sides; they should be kinder to themselves, move up a notch – nostalgia wasn't everything – and find a place where the tablecloths got washed and where the waiters looked less like hit men. There was food colouring, probably carcinogenic, in the spaghetti sauce – Jack could tell by the indelible pink swirls impregnated on the smooth moon surfaces of Roberto's lunch plates. On Fridays the place swarmed with wide-bottomed secretaries and sorrowing, introspective student lovers; it pained Jack to see how readily these lovers accepted the illuminated mural of the Po Valley on the back wall. It was time for a change, Jack had been on the point of saying to him. But he hadn't done it.

a glass wall so you can see the wall. The conclusion of an era which defines and invents the era.'

'I get the feeling you've rehearsed this. While you were shaving this morning, maybe.'

'Let me ask you this, Bernie. What do we remember about history? No, never mind *us* – what does the man on the street remember about the past?'

'I *am* a man on the street. You tell me.'

'We remember the treaties, but not the wars. Am I right? Admit it. We remember the beheadings, but not the rebellions. It's that final cataclysmic act that we instinctively select and store away. You might say, ' he paused, 'that the ends of all stories are contained in their beginnings.'

'It's already been said, I think. Didn't Eliot – ?'

'But the ending *is* the story. Not just the signature. Take the French Revolution – '

'We've taken that. A number of times.' Bernie sat back, groggy after his veal and noodles. 'We took the French Revolution last week. And the week before that. Remember that session you gave me about the French Revolution two weeks ago? About the great libertine infusion? Rammed into Europe's flabby old buttocks?'

'Not true.' Jack pushed his plate away, belching silently; a gas pain shot across his heart. After twenty years the food at Roberto's was worse, not better – it was a miracle they'd managed to stay in business – and the old neighbourhood around the Institute, with its knocked-apart streets and boarded-up shirt laundries and hustling porn shops, was shifting from the decent shade of decay that had prevailed during the sixties to something more menacing. These days violence threatened, even in the daytime; and disease, too – someone or other had told him at a party the weekend before that you could get hepatitis from eating off cracked plates, and God knows what else. Furthermore, Jack had grown to dread the starchy monotony of Italian food; everything about it now, its wet weak uniformity of texture and its casual, moist presentation – the sight and smell of it made his heart plunge and squeeze. Was there really a time, he asked himself – of course there had been – when Italian food, even the fake Chicago variety, had seemed a passport to worldliness? Worldliness, ha! When the mere words – cannelloni, gnocchi, lasagna – had brimmed with rich,

Chapter One

AT THE RESTAURANT JACK WANTED TO TELL BERNIE ABOUT Harriet Post, a girl he had once been in love with. He wanted to put his head down on the table and moan aloud with rage. Instead he placed his fork into a square of ravioli and said in a moderate tone, 'History consists of endings.'

Bernie was not really listening; he was removed today, empty-eyed and vague, pulling at a dry wedge of bread and looking out the window on to the street, where a cold rain was falling. For almost a year now the topic of their Friday lunches had been the defining of history; what was it? What was it for? It occurred to Jack that perhaps Bernie had had enough of history. Enough is enough, as Brenda, his wife, would say.

'History is eschatological,' Jack said. He stabbed into his small side salad of lettuce, onions, celery, and radishes. 'History is not the mere unrolling of a story. And it's not the story itself. It's the end of the story.'

'Uhuh.' Bernie's eyes turned again toward the curtainless square of window, made doubly opaque by the streaming rainwater and by the inner coating of cooking grease. 'And when,' he asked, chewing on a wad of bread, 'did you decide all this?'

'Yesterday. Last night. About midnight. It came to me, the final meaning of history. I've finally stumbled on what it's all about. Endings.'

'Endings?'

'Yes, endings.'

'A bolt out of the blue?' Bernie said.

'You might say that. Or you could call it an empirical thrust.'

Bernie smirked openly.

'Go ahead,' Jack said. 'Laugh if you want to. I'm serious for a change.'

'For a change.'

'History is no more than the human recognition of endings. History – now listen, Bernie – history is putting a thumbprint on

1

For Anne

Copyright © Carol Shields, 1980, 1982

All rights reserved under International and Pan-American Copyright Conventions. Published in 1994 by Vintage Books, a division of Random House of Canada Limited, Toronto.

Canadian Cataloguing in Publication Data

Shields, Carol, 1935–
Happenstance

ISBN 0-394-22359-4

I. Title.

PS8587.H66H36   1993   C813´.54   C93-093838-0
PR9199.3.85H36   1993

Happenstance, The Husband's Story was first published as *Happenstance* in Canada by McGraw-Hill Ryerson in 1980. *Happenstance, The Wife's Story* was first published as *A Fairly Conventional Woman* in Canada by Macmillan of Canada 1982. This volume first published in Great Britain by Fourth Estate Limited 1991.

Printed in the United States of America

3   5   7   9   10   8   6   4   2

HAPPENSTANCE

The Husband's Story

Carol Shields

Vintage Books
A Division of Random House of Canada
Toronto

HAPPENSTANCE

'There are other relationships,' he heard his voice ringing coolly, 'besides cause and effect.'

'My God, you're not going to be mystical and religious, are you, Jack?'

'Look. It's simple really. Here I've been grinding away at this Indian thing for years. And all the time she's been up to the same thing. Do you call that coincidence? Or do you call it historical destiny?'

'Destiny! Do you know something, Jack? That's a word I never thought I'd hear from you.'

' – and now the visible result. The ending. History.'

Bernie polished off his wine, licking the rim of his glass with the tip of his tongue. 'As a theory, isn't this a little on the surreal side? I mean, there are no real beginnings and endings. Mathematically speaking.'

'Maybe.' Jack eyed the drizzle of rain on the window.

'Anyway, it's lousy luck.'

'And if there's one thing I know it's that you don't pick a quarrel with history. You can't fight history.'

'Do you really believe that?' Bernie said, his head to one side and his hands spread in a lopsided Y. 'Or is that something you just this minute thought up?'

'I don't know. In a way I think I do believe it.'

'Well, do you know what I think?' Bernie said. 'I think your theory is a pile of horse shit.' But he spoke slowly, with compassion, bringing his fist down on the table so hard that the plates jumped.